GODS' Enemy

Derek E Pearson

Heaven's at war – and Earth's on the frontline

First published 2016
Published by GB Publishing.org

Cover Design © Mary Pargeter Design

CBP

GB Publishing.org
www.gbpublishing.co.uk

For Sue as always – and to Michael Worger-Ritchie who once made a joke and that gypsy thief, imagination, ran away with it. What follows is the result. Blame him.

Acknowledgement

Working with George, Christopher Ritchie, Bee and Mary Pargeter is like swimming naked in a lake of fresh cream, without ever leaving my keyboard.

The Satan series is a departure for me and couldn't exist without their trust.

Contents

Author's note

Caleb Sawyer is dead. I knew him well and I'm proud to have spoken with him for a number of months before he died. I respected him greatly. The stories he told me were shared over endless mugs of coffee while we sat at his big old kitchen table. The mugs were enamel, a working man's vessel. The sort taken on cattle drives. The table was wooden and scarred with age. He'd brought it with him from his house in the old town. It had deep sentimental value.

Often we spoke into the night and neither of us would've thought to prepare something to eat. I'd take him out for a meal and he'd push his food around on his plate like he was looking for answers on the white china.

Shortly after he died I received a letter from him. It had been forwarded by one of his executors and was the first such correspondence he had ever sent me. The letter was brief and written in a firm, neat hand. I shall quote just a few lines:

'My friend, do not mourn me. At last I am back in my wife's arms and we are safe together. I pity those of you still walking the front lines of God's war with evil. It is a real war, and if the Preacher falls, the Earth itself will fall with him. I pray for you all, but most of all I pray for him. I pray for you.

'The gates of Hell itself have been thrown wide open. Mankind's only hope is that he somehow finds the strength to close them once more.'

What follows is mostly Caleb's story. I tried to capture the spirit of the man and find his voice; but as you read these words and get taken up in a tale almost impossible to imagine, I must ask you to also imagine a strong old man sitting opposite you. His skin was almost unlined and he still had an enviable head of hair. He was handsome the way some older men can be, despite his slight wattle and long ear lobes. His voice was steady yet light and easy. When you looked into his tired, grey old eyes you saw honesty there; frankness, strength – and something more.

Thanks to my work as a journalist I had seen that look before; seen it in the faces of men who had marched to war and met with unthinkable horrors and faced terrible loss. It is the mark of an unplumbable terror so intense it reaches way beyond fear and out the other side. I believe Caleb's tale was genuine. Remember that as you read.

Not all of this will be Caleb's tale, you will hear other voices talking of things he didn't see and couldn't know. Some of what they tell you I know to be true, some I learned and the rest I deduced. I include it in the interests of telling the complete story of a man living and fighting in a town cursed with horror. He was not alone.

{1}

If it wasn't for the Preacher I'd be dead by now, I know that deep in my water. Of course he never was a real preacher, but I didn't know that back then. I couldn't even be completely sure he was entirely human. I saw him do things that'd make a sane man doubt his eyes. No, I saw him do things that'd make a madman weep for joy. But, anyway, he sure looked like a man and he acted like a man – most of the time.

If it hadn't been for him I'd be deader than that old camel skeleton out by Divided Rock. I used to walk out to it some days and wonder why it was there. I knew it was a camel because a Moorish professor from the travelling 'World of Wonders' show came with me one time and he looked at it then spat tobacco juice into its empty eye socket.

He told me, 'Camel from old Araby. Critter should be lying in the dunes by the old pyramids and roasting under that white Egyptian sun, not cooling its bones out here in the Lone Star state.'

I guess he knew his subject right enough. I wouldn't know a camel from a calliope without someone else's say so. Jeeze, sorry, my head's wandering again. Where was I? Oh yes.

The Preacher, yes, the Preacher. If it wasn't for him I'd be dead, and you know something? I sometimes wonder whether I might not have been better off that way. When I lost my new wife to influenza in 1870, the same year Texas re-joined the Union, I thought I'd lost everything of any real value, but I was wrong.

Some people believe things in this world can only have value when they've put a price on them. Well, Becky was worth more to me than a king's vault full of gold, and when she was gone to the Lord I sat all alone in our empty bedroom with my Colt in my hand. I thought all I needed to join her was put that barrel in my mouth and squeeze the trigger. That lead ball would have ended a whole ton of suffering right there, I can tell you.

But the Lord frowns on self-murder and I would likely have ended up somewhere hotter than Texas in mid-summer – and I knew for sure my beautiful Becky wouldn't be waiting for me there.

That day I put my gun back in its holster knowing I would never be a man to walk away from the grave, but also that I'd never deliberately lay me down in it. One day soon I hoped to join my Becky in Heaven and until then I guessed I'd have to listen to that traitorous organ beating in my chest where my heart used to be.

This was back before I knew Alice. She healed my wounded heart in a way I never expected nor hoped to find, not even in my prayers. A good woman brings succour when the Lord turns away.

Back then I believed my true heart was buried with Becky, and for a long while that old camel by Divided Rock was more alive than me; but enough of that. Becky was dead and gone and I missed her every live-long day. But I still had one thing of value to cling to, my righteous soul, and that is a gift beyond price.

I have a question for those palm-pinching, scrape penny misers who would try to put a price on sunrise. I ask them: how can you put a value on your immortal soul? You can't because you don't have one. Such men are soulless money-grubbers, puppet men, hollow bodies, empty vessels, and they shall not be given ears to hear the angels' trump come judgement day.

And now my old pump beats behind my ribs, counting out the mean hours remaining to me. Dust to dust, ashes to clay, we're rising to Heaven come judgement day – but only if the Preacher wins and Heaven survives.

But I get ahead of myself.

It's time to re-enter that place of lost shadows and listen to ghosts whisper while they nudge old memories back into the light. Everything I shall recount to you is true, especially the impossible, the strange and the plain unlikely. Some of it I saw myself and some parts I learned from others. You will soon see which is which.

You're making notes, I see. Okay. Good. Then let me set the stage for you. Before I moved to Shafter I'd been born and raised in the town of Mule's Ass. It's still down there in Southern Texas and even has a road now, a real blacktop road for automobiles. The stockyards and slaughterhouses still hum with the smell of bullshit and blood, much like the trenches over in Flanders where good Yankee boys are once more fighting for their lives. Fighting and dying.

I'm too old to fight now and I've no need to travel to foreign parts to die. I can manage that right here where I'm sitting with someone like you beside me, a friend, or rocking on my porch. And my neighbours will soon know if anything happens to me. They pop in to see if the old man's okay. They're good people. This is a good place to be old, or as good as anywhere.

Some think we old folk sit outside just to be sociable, but that ain't it at all. We sit in the open where we can be seen when the last day dawns so we won't die all alone and forgotten. I'll trust the local folk to be my pallbearers

2

come that welcome day when I shall awake to eternal glory – if the Preacher wins.

My folks named me Caleb, and I like it well enough. Caleb Sawyer. As I told you I grew up in the town of Mule's Ass, Presidio County, a town named after the last thing the founder was looking at before he threw down his pack and started building his future by the Sweet Alice River.

Some of the womenfolk never liked the name much and they tried to call the place 'Molasses' instead. And you know for a brief while it worked. They say changing names brings bad luck. Well, it sure did in Mule's Ass.

It was 1883 when the troubles began and I was a childless widower of more than ten years. It was a small town where folk wore more than one hat. I was the sheriff and the town's part-time barber/surgeon too. It had been eighteen years since the end of the Civil War and it was just after the first Great Depression. Railroads were spreading all across the south. Some called it the Golden Age. Well, from where I stood things soon looked dark enough to blot out the sun.

Up in the hills the Fulsome silver mine was beginning to show a real profit. There were other mines in Presidio County, but Fulsome was ours to fret over and it was my responsibility to keep things in order. Because of that mine we had a brand new Galveston, Harrisburg and San Antonio steam train stop in the town. It connected us to the mine and the company town of Shafter.

If and when trouble finally walked up Main Street the townsfolk figured it would likely be the result of Fulsome's miners getting drunk and horny, but they were peaceful, hard-working men as a rule. They'd even detoured a nook of the Sweet Alice and made a wash bed away from the flowing stream. That was thoughtful of them. It meant they didn't muddy our drinking water with spoil from sieving their ore. Even so, the God-fearing parishioners of Mule's Ass were wary of the miners.

I once heard someone say, 'As sure as eggs taste good and chickens lay them, I say where there's a mine there's men – and where there's men all together like that there's sure to be both carnal desires and unnatural acts.'

'*But I say to you that everyone who looks at a woman with carnal intent has already committed adultery with her in his heart,*' said old St Matthew and he sure put his words where his heart was. But me? I could never put a man in the cells for just thinking impure thoughts. I'd have ended up there myself often enough. Any man would.

Anyhow, we figured it was best not to put temptation in a man's way and we kept our womenfolk under canvas when the miners came into town with

3

their money come Friday. It's true that some of the town's younger women could turn a man's head simply walking down the boardwalk. Otherwise Mule's Ass was something of a carnal desert.

Was it evil to look at a pretty girl? I say no, not if you keep your thoughts and your hands to yourself. Even so, it was felt best for everyone that we kept those girls out of the way when the miners were in town.

There was one formidable creature who could walk freely on the town's streets or anywhere else she chose to roam. Grandma Teatree. Why she was called Grandma nobody knew – she was as childless as me – but I guess that old lady had notched up enough rings through her trunk to qualify as Grandma for the entire population of the whole Lone Star State if such a fancy took her. She was extraordinary.

You know the way a tree can be dead but doesn't know it yet? The trunk goes twisty and black and dry, and it thins down to near nothing like a skinny finger, big-knuckled and bent over fit to split. Then, come spring, a few scrawny leaves emerge from the bud – yellow, weak things that look embarrassed to come out of hiding and turn their faces up to the sun. That just about sums up the way Grandma Teatree looked, old and bent and dead. Thing was she never learned when to climb into her box and get herself properly buried.

Nothing I say could ever describe the sheer force of her personality. She was too ornery and stubborn to lie down and die the way Mother Nature and God so surely intended. If ever she went she would go on her own terms; and that would only be when she was good and ready.

Then came the day of the murdered raped man found face-down in a mound of fire ants and somebody – or *something* – opened the gates to allow Hell itself some play-time on Earth.

And that was when God's war got started.

{2}

It was the kind of thing a man would rather see on an empty stomach if he had to see it at all. The poor bastard was dead. Enough – why do that to him? I say some deaths are righteous and, perhaps, some even deserved. Some take a fellow to welcome rest away from life's hard labour, or free the suffering from pain. But others – others are just wrong. This man's death was way, way wrong. He was a mess.

He'd been found kneeling, his bare ass up in the air, with his pants pulled down around his ankles and his face and shoulders shoved into an angry nest. When he was discovered and moved, some of those ants proved real reluctant to abandon their dinner. They'd burrowed down into the red-raw flesh that'd once been the poor man's head and shoulders; and they were still in there, eating the evidence, when he was brought out of the sun and put to rest on a long butcher's bench in one of the slaughterhouse's coolest rooms.

The ants crackled while they ate. It was slight, but you could hear it well enough in that quiet room. I can hear it now, and though the day is warm I can feel that chill once more.

His body had gone stiff and then relaxed again, but that process had happened just a little too fast. Maybe the ants' poison helped speed things up, but it would have taken a smarter man than me to say for sure. Anyhow, we were grateful we hadn't needed to break anything to make him lie down flat on the table as we sometimes did – the big wooden mallet in the corner wouldn't be brought into play – but those ants had to come out of there before they ate him to the bone. Dead men become nature's own dining rooms unless living men do something about it first. That's a *fact*.

Baylee Baker was working by lamplight in that windowless room, patiently fishing those vicious little copper-coloured critters out of the man's face and dropping them into a big spirit bottle. He was being very careful and very thorough. The long tongs he used nipped at the struggling beasts and pulled them from their happy hunting ground. He seemed unperturbed by the terrible state of the man he was working on and ignored the suck-smack noise his tongs made when he pulled them from the flesh. He stood over his task like a fisherman in a stream, patiently waiting for a tug on his line.

I was expected over the street in the church hall where the Town Council was waiting for my report on the murder, but I was in no immediate rush. Grandma Teatree was on the Council and she had a way of talking to a grown man that made him feel like a raggedy-assed kid. I've seen tough men a good foot taller than her bowed down in shame and near to tears after one of her lectures. I wouldn't face her until I had something worthwhile to say.

I suppose the reasons she had become such an authority figure were simple enough. Anyone born and raised in Mule's Ass had grown up under that berry black gaze and learned to fear and respect the old tyrant from birth; and anyone coming in from outside soon learned their lesson. She had a way about her. Grandma was a pure force of nature. She was sharp as lightning and tough as mid-winter, and only a fool would mess with either of those.

No one in town was old enough to remember when she was young, not even me, and I was in my early thirties during that hot summer season. Tymon Lucas was sixty or more. He couldn't rightly remember his birth date and records were vague back then, but he swore she'd already been old as Methuselah when he was still on the tit. In his cups, which was frequent enough, he would tell anyone who would listen that 'Grandma walked through Hell's fires three times and burned all the dying out of herself; she's more like a stone tree than a natural born Christian soul.'

He told me, 'Grandma won't bend to anything. Not a storm, not a flood, not a twister – and never to any man's reason. She is who she is and likely always will be. Least 'til she finally bends that stiff old spine of hers before God Almighty hisself, if ever she does.'

Personally I think it was her eyes that did it. She would look full at you and you found you just had to listen. You had no choice. Her eyes, yes, her eyes. I see them now. They were black and cold and shiny as one of those deep, ancient rock pools you find at the back of a cave.

Her face was browner than one of those mummified babies they had in the World of Wonders. She wore time's shroud with pride the same way I wore my sheriff's badge. But she had way, way more authority than me.

I remember her skin was a puzzle of diamond shapes much as you'd see on the hide of a brown, water moccasin snake. It was as if every long year of her life had drawn a thin line into her flesh and now she was cross-hatched and etched by age. Her skin was shrunk back against her skull's bones so tight that it looked like just one more year, one more etched line, and she would shatter into fragments of polished clay. And it would be clay; all her flesh was dried up and gone.

There would be no blood from Grandma, not as there was seeping from the raped, dead man laid down before me. From her there would be just dry powder hissing into the air, powder fine as thought – black as deeds.

Her hair was fine and long and black and she wore it in a thick, tightly braided coil on top of her scrawny head. It looked wrong somehow. Like a hat of young hair thrown onto an old leather bag. She also had all her teeth, strong and brown to match her skin.

Tymon had neither hair nor teeth, but he was happy enough. Soup suited his toping lifestyle and he could grind a steak to paste with his tongue. It made my eyes water. Grandma wasn't like Tymon. No, she was purely and only herself. Her ancient eyes haunt me still.

Get me on the subject of Grandma Teatree and I'll circle her like a fly around spoiled milk. Or maybe I'm trying not to remember myself back in that cold room with the raped dead man and Baylee Brown with his long tongs and that big bottle of raw spirit half full of struggling fire ants.

The corpse stank, and it wasn't just because he'd been out in the sun a bit too long. I was glad he was face-up while Baylee worked. I had examined his rectum a little earlier and I had my strong suspicion that more than one Sodomite had taken advantage of his spread buttocks. He was a big man and it would have taken a lot to hold him down, but someone had. They took it in turns with him. Seed streaked his rectum and legs, mixed in with the blood. Shit was smeared on top of the other fluids. He had rope burns on his ankles, wrists and neck. The story they told was pretty clear. The way was still clear to bugger a bound man if enough hands held him down.

The man's neck was thick, bullish, powerful — and broken. I couldn't have managed it without a rope and a tree to hang him from. Some heavy people would probably have had to swing on his legs while he was hanging or he would have just swung there and choked for a half hour or so and that would have been cruel. What am I saying? As if the bastards who did this would have cared a split whisker about cruelty. More likely they got bored with the noose's dance and wanted to speed things up.

I looked closer at the man's throat while Baylee plied his silent trade with those long tongs. Pick, wriggle, drown, pick, wriggle, drown, pick, wriggle... Baylee was good at jobs that called for patient attention to detail. He was steady and reliable and he'd stick to any simple job until he was good and done. He'd never win an argument with any mule, but you could leave him alone and know the job would get finished. He was slow but he was *sure*.

I touched the dead man's neck, probing and kneading. Something stung me, hot and sharp, but I couldn't see anything. Probably one of those cursed ants. I almost put my hand to my mouth then snatched it away before touching my lips. Stupid! Who knew *what* was on the dead man's skin? It was best not to suck it and find out until I'd had a good wash.

'Adam's been lynched, hasn't he, Mister Cal?'

My hand hurt and I snapped at him. 'Baylee, have I ever called you Bay or Lee?'

'No, Mister Cal, not never.'

I nodded. 'Right, never. So, Baylee, would you do me a favour, please?'

'Sure, Mister Cal, for you. Just ask.'

'Thank you. Then from now on, please, call me Caleb. No need for the mister, okay?'

There was silence for a long, Lone Star minute while Baylee chewed this over. Then, 'Sure, Mister Cal, whatever you say.'

That reeking room was probably the coolest place in town that season, but it suddenly felt hot and oppressive. I turned away and within seconds I was the other side of the door and halfway down the corridor leading back out to the light of day. I wanted to get to the church hall where the Council sat waiting. Get my duty over and done.

It was a few moments before I realised I hadn't answered Baylee's question and that was plumb rude. Without simple good manners a man is rootless as a dry reed and my cheeks burned hot as my hand. I hurried back, pushed open the door and was instantly assailed by that alien stink from the man's body. *What is that smell?*

'Baylee,' I said quickly. 'Yes, you're right. He was lynched.'

'I figured so. Thanks, Mister Cal.'

Baylee returned to his task and I looked at the waxy, bloodstained body once more. It was clear the man had been raped first and then hanged. It was not uncommon for a hanged man's bowels to open at the point of death and his swathe of shit overlaid the seed. Bound, raped, hanged and then pressed face-down into a mound of fire ants. Why? Who was he?

And then I remembered something my ears had heard but ignored earlier.

'Baylee,' I said. 'Why did you call him Adam?'

{3}

Most towns get to vote for the people on their Council, but not the folk in Mule's Ass. We got a self-elected committee of four people with the greatest vested interest in the town's fortunes. Foster Teague owned the biggest beef ranch in the county with several thousand head of tough, scrawny longhorn and some fat English dairy cows he was trying to cross-breed. He was just as fat and soft as those cows. I wondered for a moment about his proprietary attitude towards those cows. I thought about the true meaning of *husbandry* – and then chided myself for being so mean-minded.

Mr S. Spindrift was the Preacher and he also printed the town's broadsheet, *The Presidio Star*. He had the bearing of a soldier and that kind of self-contained charisma you only ever see in the most capable of men. I'd never seen him handle a gun, and looking at him I prayed I'd never have to. His stillness was chilling, and despite his pleasant manner I considered him to be the most dangerous man I ever met. Still do.

Parrett Damsel-Childs – over and above winning every prize for the most stupid name ever written in a church register – was disturbing in a number of odd ways. He was the richest man in Mule's Ass and he owned the county bank with branches both there and in Shafter. Even so I just knew I never wanted to be left alone in a room with him. He never touched anything the way a normal man would. He'd stroke at everything with fussy, pampering fingers. He dipped at the world with intimate grace as if he was always touching its most secret parts. Watching him made me want to wash my eyes clean.

And then there was his tongue. It was long and antsy in his mouth, always moving about, licking and touching at everything as if he wanted to taste the room, to take possession of it. *Swallow it.*

He was a hollow man filled with a love of money. I imagined his veins were filled with rows of little black numbers. You could see them tumble past behind his eyes and drip down in counted rows into the empty vault of his steel-lined heart.

And then, of course, there was Grandma Teatree. She and Spindrift sat quietly while the voices of the rancher and the banker whined and oiled their way into every corner of the hall. I felt like it'd take a bucket of warm lye suds to wash the place down after they'd been talking.

They quieted when I arrived. I was glad for that little nugget of respect. No one invited me to sit so I stood with my hat in my hands while I told them what I knew for certain about the dead man, and also what I suspected.

All but Damsel-Childs paid close attention to me. He looked bored right up to the time I said the raped dead man was Adam Klosky, and that Baylee had recognised him from the fine tattoo of a mermaid leaping over his left nipple.

I kept to myself the fact that Baylee was always hungry for pictures of naked women, even girls with a fish's tail, and he'd pointed at the tattoo with a sloppy smile on his face.

'Look,' he'd said, 'she's got titties you can see. Adam used to show me when he was splitting logs. She's pretty.'

I explained to the Council how Klosky would take his shirt off on a hot day when he was splitting lumber and that on one such occasion Baylee had seen the tattoo. I'd seen Klosky around town without much never mind. He was a good-looking man in a thick-lipped, doe-eyed kind of way. Big and boyish and shy. I'd never heard an ill word said against him from any quarter.

Well, I heard some that day and they were all from the lively tongue of the banker. Humming and hawing he told us the boy was 'unnatural', a 'cow-eyed flirt' and a 'notorious tease'. I suppose Klosky had been a fine figure of a man, hard work will do that to a young body, but was he really a 'spur to sin' when stripped down and sweating at his job? I suppose it depended on who was watching. Everyone else in the hall was looking at Damsel-Childs with slightly raised eyebrows, waiting for him to finish his tirade, which he did with the words, 'Not that I, ah, would wish to, hm, speak ill of the dead.'

He tampered with his mouth for a moment. I swear he licked at his fingertips. I didn't think for one moment it was Klosky who was unnatural other than in that banker's most secret imaginings.

Grandma Teatree cut in. 'Adam Klosky was just a good-looking young fellow and he was no more a "spur to sin" than say Sheriff Sawyer here or Preacher Spindrift.'

I coloured at this but the Preacher remained impassive and quietly receptive.

Grandma continued, 'Men's lust is what killed that poor boy. Same as a tied lid on a kettle of stew will blow up in your face if it's left on the stove too long, a man's lust will be his undoing if it's fanned long and hot enough and finds no relief. To avoid a repeat of this terrible crime we need to untie the lid on that kettle of stew, relieve that lust before it boils over again; and there's only one way to do that.'

I was there that day and heard that dried-up old stick of a hag spout dreadful ideas out into the room, and I saw two out of three heads nodding in agreement. I didn't have a say in the matter but the Preacher sure did and he took hold of it with both hands and wrung that idea like a chicken's neck. It didn't help though.

While he was talking the banker and the rancher wheedled and weaselled around his words like ferrets snapping at a bull hound.

He was a man of God and he couldn't sit quietly while the Council voted on Grandma's motion, which, in a polished nutshell, was that the town should seek sponsors to open a brothel down by the stockyards. She even offered to be the madam; well, she said, her or Mrs Damsel-Childs, either of whom would be able to 'keep the rod straight'.

She said, 'The madam should take ten per cent. That leaves the rest to pay the girls and feed them − plus ensure any investors make a tidy profit. Those men digging up in the hills could prove to be the town's silver mine in more ways than one. Every man with blood in his veins and heat in his trousers could be a customer, and there's always repeat business from satisfied trade. Any girl with her mind set to it has been born with a gift that never stops giving until the well runs dry. And who knows, we might even drum up some domestic interest.'

The lines on her face darkened as if they'd just been etched much deeper and I realised she was smiling. A chill ran up my spine.

And that was when the Preacher had his say.

{4}

Teague and Damsel-Childs' eyes glittered like polished gemstones at the sound of a 'tidy profit'. I swear if there'd been a dotted line handy those men would've been reaching for their pens and their chequebooks faster than an angry rattler strike. But first they were required by custom to listen to Preacher Spindrift.

While he talked, Grandma Teatree's face looked as if someone was pressing it hard into a wire riddle, her wrinkles got so deep. If someone had sewn her eyes and lips shut with thick thread she'd have been the mirror spit for one of those pagan shrunken heads in the World of Wonders. It was uncanny.

Preacher Spindrift quickly got into his stride. He was talking about 'evil not earning its reward on Earth but on the day of reckoning'.

He said, 'In lust they have taken the life of an innocent boy. Shall you then reward these killers with the bodies and souls of Christian women in exchange for nothing more than a handful of silver? Are we come to such a poor pass that money means more to this town than murder?'

He spoke at length but in the end it was to no avail. He juggled with the concepts of morality, humanity and avoidance of sin, but one golden word had struck the balls from his hands and finally it rendered him mute. Profit. It was plain on Damsel-Childs' face and that of Foster Teague. Greed will always win with such people. What kind of fool, they ask, values a mountain of virtue in Heaven when there's a stack of dollar bills to be counted down here on Earth? A fighter knows when to leave the field and go somewhere quiet to lick his wounds.

I followed Preacher Spindrift when he finally stalked from the church hall, leaving the others to their unseemly plans. I pictured him as like a lion walking away from a pack of scavenger dogs snarling over scraps. Only one person had ended that Council meeting with any dignity and I had to hurry to keep pace with him.

'Preacher,' I said, 'please? Will you wait up?'

He slowed, looked at me, and sighed. His muscular face was tense for a second, and he seemed to be weighing me in some internal balance. I suppose the frosty creases that appeared either side of his thin-lipped mouth were as much of a smile as I could hope for under the circumstances.

He tilted his head and studied me. 'Shall I judge thee with the carrion crow who would feed on foolishness and frailty?'

'I'd rather be judged as a man with a question,' I replied.

He remained silent but everything about his pose invited me to continue. I angrily pointed across to the corrugated iron slaughter sheds next to the empty stockyards.

'Over there,' I said, 'Baylee is picking fire ants out of a murdered man's face.'

Preacher Spindrift nodded but said nothing.

'How,' I continued, 'how, in the name of all that's righteous, did the Town Council just move its focus from sodomy and murder to madams and cathouses?' I raised my voice. 'We don't even have a solid bar room with a proper barkeep and spittoons like they do over in Temperance and Watsonville, but now we're going to open a whore's den, a cathouse…'

'Please, Sheriff Sawyer, temper your speech,' said the Preacher. 'Mine ears are as windows open to God and he shall deem you a shabby scrap of a man should he hear you speaking so boldly. He is a stern Father.'

'And a forgiving one too, or so I'm told,' I said. 'Surely he will allow me some leeway in the face of such madness?'

If the Preacher was ever a soldier, as I suspected, he had surely been an officer. Authority rolled off him like mist from a mountain. Something happened as I stood there, angrily waiting for him to answer. My sense of perspective teetered off-balance for a moment and I had a sensation that something more massive than any single man stood before me. I staggered as if pulled forwards towards the edge of an abyss. My legs felt like jelly. If the Preacher hadn't caught me I would have fallen flat on my face. He took my shoulders in his big hands and held me firmly upright. He gazed directly into my eyes.

'Breathe out for me,' he said.

I had no choice but to obey. I emptied my lungs. As the air rasped out of me I smelt it again, that unearthly stench I had noticed around poor Adam Klosky. I shuddered and coughed and then spat away some thick, vile fluid that came up into my mouth. I retched.

I felt terrible, yet through my veil of misery I heard the Preacher's voice intoning words I didn't really understand. They sounded like commands and landed on my ears like hammer blows.

I distinctly heard him say something like 'Adonai non filii publius Suis,' and then, 'How shall I serve thee, Lord except as thine hand against the enemy? How shall I look upon thy face other than as a light upon the waters of the Earth? How shall I love thee other than as thy servant here amongst thy creation? I ask forgiveness and long for the day I shall have earned

13

redemption once more in thine eyes. Thy will be done on Earth as it is in Heaven. Amen.'

And he pressed his hand against my chest and I felt it burning through the fabric of my shirt. I swear on my wife's grave that what happened next was impossible – but it happened and it was real as taxes, or biscuits and gravy.

It seemed to me that he reached his hand right into my chest and I felt something moving around in there as if it was trying to escape. The pain was almost unendurable. Then I felt his fingers snap shut inside me and something powerful jolted at me from within.

The Preacher was almost singing now. 'Man was made as a mirror of thy spirit, Lord, not as a house for thine enemy. Thine enemy shall be cast out into the void. It shall be trampled under the feet of thy servants as the worm is trod into the furrows by the kine in the field. It is a low thing and despised by the mighty.'

He fished his fist back out of me, and I swear that whatever he got hold of in there just didn't want to release its grip on my gizzards. I felt my battered heart getting tugged loose from its moorings.

And then it was free and I saw something held tight in his grip. It was fat and streaked black and red, like a malignant skinned rat from my worst nightmares. I only saw it for a moment but I swear it looked straight back at me with an expression of pure malice and screamed at me with frustrated rage.

And then it was over and it was gone. And I was standing beside the Preacher and he was looking across towards the slaughter sheds with a resolute light in his grey eyes.

'And so it starts,' he said. 'So it starts.'

5

The Preacher asked me, 'Have you ever heard why this place is called Mule's Ass, Sheriff Sawyer?'

I was stunned: after everything that'd just taken place, his question seemed inappropriately ordinary somehow, but faced with his curious glance I responded. I told him about the founder and his mules, how he was driving a team of four and looking across from behind them when he saw the river and good land beyond and knew he had found home.

'Yes,' said the Preacher. 'Well, just like that mule's ass this town is full of shit.'

I must have registered my surprise at his language. 'Shut up your gob, Sheriff Sawyer. Open, it is a gateway for the Lord of Flies; closed, it is a rampart against evil.'

Sometimes I think the Preacher amused himself at my expense. He walked on and I followed. I had the idea that wherever he was going would surely be the safest place for me. That I would be repeatedly proved wrong was never the Preacher's fault.

Looking back across the many decades I can't think of a single time he specifically asked me to join him in what he did, but then he never warned me off neither. All I know is that, at that very moment, if the man had taken to the air and flown like an angel I would not have been at all surprised.

'Who are you, Preacher Spindrift?'

'Why do you ask?'

'Well, sir, I swear there's more to you than the black-suited man on a Sunday bringing sinners back to the field of glory.'

He eyed me with that enigmatic stare. 'You remember that bit in the *Bible* in which the Lord told his chosen people that he was a jealous God and what he would do if they bowed down to others, the whole "unto the third generation" passage?'

'Exodus,' I said. 'Why, yes.'

'Well, let's just say I should have read that passage a lot more carefully. Now, shall we see what's been happening to Baylee?'

We'd reached the shadowed lee of the slaughter sheds and the air seemed strangely chill. Rust leeched out of the corrugated sidings like stains of blood. It was silent as a chapel. He led me to the door I had exited so recently and even with the Preacher by my side I felt reluctant to enter. My skin crawled and I sensed something malevolent was close by. That stink was already thick in my nose and when the Preacher opened the door the reek was so bad I staggered backwards.

'Come, Sheriff Sawyer,' he said, with iron in his voice. 'This is just the scarecrow hung out to distract the fearful. Are you a carrion crow to be afraid of rags and mere illusions dancing in the wind?'

I was angry that he'd compared me to a carrion crow once more.

'Then what is it that hides behind the scarecrow, Preacher?'

'The enemy, God's enemy.'

I looked along the gloomy corridor with its single small window to where I could just make out the door leading to the cold room where Baylee was at work. At least I hoped he was.

'The Devil himself?' I breathed. 'The Devil, here in Mule's Ass?'

The Preacher snapped a withering glance in my direction and I once again felt as if I'd been brushed by something immense.

'What do you mean by "The Devil", Sheriff Sawyer? It is a vague title.'

'Beelzebub,' I stammered, 'the Lord of the Flies, ruler of Hell and King of Lies.'

'You learned that somewhere,' he said, 'but at least it rhymes. I think you mean Lucifer, most glorious archangel and now fallen from grace due to the sins of vanity and pride. Lucifer was the brightest vessel filled with the love of his creator, filled with love and worship for God. Then some of the other celestial beings began to talk about it as if it might be the equal of God, and they worshipped it, and it allowed them to do so. Foolish vanity. And Lucifer, the shining star, learned just how jealous its God could be.'

I knew I was only talking because my nerves were jangled loose and I was just trying to take my mind off that second door – which was getting closer with every step.

'Why do you call Lucifer an "it"?'

'You are full of questions, aren't you? What else should I call it? Do you think there are boy and girl angels getting married and giving birth to cherubim and seraphim? Lucifer was an angel created by the hand of God, touched by that divine hand…'

He paused. 'Lucifer was never the enemy of God. It was made to be God's creature and works for him still, trying to regain lost favour and to be allowed once more to bask in that ineffable light. What it has become is no longer the shining one and it has taken on a new name.'

We reached the door. 'So what is it called now?'

'It is now a he and must live as a man until redemption allows him back into the joyful throng. He is called Satan, and he has never been the enemy, as you are about to find out.'

And he pushed the door open.

6

The cold was intense. The mist of my breath coiled whitely around my mouth. That vile, alien stink had grown in force until it had become an almost physical presence; it clawed at my nostrils with vigorous energy. I tried breathing through my mouth but that just meant I could taste it as well as smell it. I felt the gorge rise in my throat.

And then the Preacher said, 'I think that's enough of that,' and it was as if someone had put a lid across an open charnel pit. The stink became little more than the background miasma it had been earlier, unpleasant enough but not overwhelming.

Baylee was working with his back to us. I couldn't see what he was doing but his hands were moving quickly, too quickly for someone carefully nipping at fire ants. It looked to me as if he was eating.

'Baylee,' I said, 'what are you doing?'

'Caleb,' he answered in a voice I didn't recognise, 'I've been waiting for you.'

And he turned to face us. And that was when I saw what he had become and he saw who was with me.

'Oh,' he said, in his new, cold, oily voice. 'It's you.'

I was frozen to the spot in horror but the Preacher was lively enough for both of us. He drew my Peacemaker cleanly from my holster and fired three times in the space of a single breath. I'd always thought he'd be good with a gun and, by God's grace, he was fast and accurate as a professional. How he knew where to aim was beyond me. His target was a mess.

Baylee had looked human enough from behind, but from the front I saw he'd become a black-eyed, blistered nightmare. I'd seen tentacles on an octopus before but nothing like those black tendrils writhing from his chest. And his face: it didn't look human. What had he spoken with? Where his mouth and nose had been was now a gaping maw and his eyes bulged huge and black from either side of his red-raw, peeled skull.

The Preacher's bullets smashed into his face, chest and gut and the man fell to the floor with a crunch of breaking glass. The sharp smell of raw spirit filled the air. Baylee's body quivered angrily and then was still.

I stepped forward to get a closer look but the Preacher held me back.

'Look,' he said.

Baylee had always been stocky, even corpulent, but now his belly was distended and thrust hugely from his opened shirt. I got the impression he was melting from some savage internal heat. His flesh was livid, splotched red and black, and it was blistered with angry boils. The boils seemed to be moving as if something was pressing at them from within. I saw coiled black worms pushing at the thin translucent skin.

'He's getting set to hatch,' said the Preacher, 'same as the man on the table.'

Klosky's flesh was crawling on his bones. It was a sick-making spectacle. Then both Baylee and Klosky split and sent a boiling mass of whipping tentacles spilling across the floor towards us.

Spindrift tore a box of big, red Lucifer matches from his pocket, struck one into a blinding flare and threw it at Baylee. There came a blue flash much brighter than I had imagined possible and a wave of intense heat. That was when the shrill, inhuman cries began, penetrating like drill bits into my brain. The sound was pure agony and terrifying. I stood quivering and paralysed with dread and confusion. I think I was screaming.

Rough hands pulled at me and I found myself thrust back through the door into the corridor. Spindrift slammed the door behind us and hissed, 'Run!' I didn't need telling twice. We began to sprint away from that nightmare place.

We didn't get far.

I guess I didn't hear the detonation that caught us, at least I can't remember it, but a hot fist picked us both up and threw us several feet towards the exit. I hit the wooden planking of the floor hard and the wind was knocked out of me. I was stunned for a moment and then I turned back and saw the cold room's door had been blasted open and almost torn from its hinges. Through the open doorway I saw ropes of oily flame cascading in thick columns from ceiling to floor, dripping and splashing like burning tar. The whole room had become an inferno and in the very heart of the fire something huge lashed about in rage and torment.

The Preacher got to his feet, thrust his hands out before him and mouthed words I couldn't hear. Since the force of the explosion hit me I'd been struck deaf and all the horror I was witnessing was made worse by seeing it in a world of utter silence. That was when a corona of sticky flames began to boil towards us down the walls, ceiling and floor of the corridor, licking and searching for us like a hungry animal let loose from its leash.

Something primal in me tore loose and I pulled out my gun and I fired through that evil door, the big Colt bucking silently in my hands. And then the sounds of the world fell back over me with a deafening shriek and I heard the Preacher howl: 'Clausum!'

The blackened cool room door slammed back into its frame as if a giant hand had pushed it home and glued it there. The sound and the fury instantly descended into shocked silence and I could hear my breathing loud in my ears, ragged and laboured.

The Preacher reached down and pulled me to my feet. He snarled. 'Sawyer, come on man.' And I followed him out into the street and found myself once more pressed under the mundane glare of hot, late afternoon sunshine. The whole terrible thing in the cool room had taken no more than a few minutes, yet my universe had just been turned upside down and I found myself looking around the town's familiar, rutted Main Street in a white daze.

Townsfolk walked the boardwalks and a man I recognised as Samuel Mead rode his wagon and pair away from us with sacks of supplies piled onto the flat bed behind him. They didn't know what had happened to Baylee and Klosky; they didn't know about the twisting nightmare burning in the cool room just a few feet away.

Fire, oh God, fire. 'Preacher, we have to tell people about that hellfire in there. This whole town could be burned to the ground. Look around you; just about everything here has been built from seasoned timber apart from the bank and my jail cells. It'll burn like dry tinder in a stove.'

He looked back the way we'd just come. I did the same. Overhead the sky looked hard, flat and blue. By then it should have been stained with smoke and alight with flame, but there was nothing.

I watched, fully expecting the cool room's corrugated iron roof to explode outwards and that coiling monster to boil out. Again, nothing.

I don't know whether it was due to shock or exhaustion, but all the strength ebbed out of me. My battered knees folded and I sat down hard on the baked earth. Spindrift stood beside me like a column of stone with just his head swivelling from the stockyards to the church hall and back again. It looked to me like he was waiting for something, or listening.

'Fire's contained,' he said after a few moments. 'Come on, Sheriff Sawyer. I need to pour me a man's drink even if you don't.'

I looked up at him, really *looked*. And something powerful and strange looked back. The word *adamantine* floated into my mind and stuck there.

'Stand up, Sheriff,' he said. And I did.

Creaking bruised and aching I stood up, then I drew my pistol from its holster, broke it and shucked the six spent cartridges into my palm. They were cool enough so I thrust them into my trouser pocket. Then I loaded the cylinder with fresh shells from the little sack tied at my waist. The gun stank bitterly of cordite for the first time in months. I hadn't needed to use it much and I kept it clean. I closed the cylinder, engaged the safety catch, and then holstered it.

'Yes,' I said, squinting into the sunlight. 'A drink sounds very good to me.'

7

From what I hazily recollect about what the Preacher told me that alcohol-fuelled night, the story went something like this: way back before Adam and Eve, a long time before the Garden, there was a place called Eden. He told me it was so far away that light from there would take hundreds of years to reach Texas. I must have looked at him queerly because he then told me that even the fastest ships built by Eden would also take many hundreds of years to get here, longer than the people of Eden could survive.

And their planet was dying.

'The people of Eden knew they couldn't escape,' he told me as I regarded him over my first glass of Belle of Nelson, a sour mash sipping whiskey so smooth I could easily drink it without a beer at its elbow. My eyes were continually drawn to the bottle's label where naked white girls were looking up at a colourful Moorish woman holding a pair of water pipes. I couldn't make the connection between the Oriental scene and my drink, and the naked women were a little too buxom for my taste, but I still found myself stealing glances at them. Baylee would have loved that label. Poor, poor Baylee. What the Devil had happened to him in that room?

I'm not a big drinker but I recognise good liquor when I taste it. That first glass just begged to be joined by its brother, and who was I to stand in the way of a family reunion?

Preacher was talking. 'The people of Eden couldn't escape but, they thought, thanks to ingenuity and careful planning, perhaps their seed could. It could be stored in special ships and sent out to new worlds where it could be planted and flourish. The Eden born might live once more. And the seed was to be cared for by specially designed servants that could endure the long, long voyage between the stars.'

He told me about the fleet of vast ships built to cross space, each sent to a planetary system where the people of Eden expected their servants to find native life something like their own. Our home was just one of the destinations chosen by the servants of Eden. All through the galaxy, systems containing planets much like Earth had been selected to receive the gift of Eden's seed.

'The ships have a communication system much like the telegraph,' he told me, 'and they have always been in touch with each other. Many other ships have also been successful in completing their missions. The Eden seed has been sown on worlds throughout our galaxy and it thrives. It thrives.'

My sour mash brothers turned out to be triplets. My head felt clear enough but my tongue was unruly in my mouth when I asked the Preacher, 'So... so those Eden creatures are here in town, are they? Is that what happened to Baylee and Klosky? Those Eden things got them?'

Preacher said nothing but he fetched a mirror from his bedroom and brought it to his dining table where we were drinking his whiskey by the light of an oil-lamp and eating good bread with fresh cheese and a sweet pickle I didn't recognise.

'Look in the mirror,' he said.

I did and a flushed, unsteady face looked back at me. It belched and I tasted pickle on my breath. 'S'cuse me.'

'Granted. Sheriff Sawyer, behold the face of Eden's seed as it is now on Earth.'

The face in the mirror squinted and its mouth opened. 'But... I don't get it, Preacher.'

'You have to fully understand what you're facing if you wish to help me, Sheriff Sawyer. You need to appreciate the very real dangers involved.' He shook his head. 'How can I best explain this? Yes, alright. Mankind was created in God's image. You understand that?'

The face in the mirror nodded and sipped at a full glass of quadruplet. The whiskey was helping me understand sure enough.

'Well, the ship from Eden has a name, they all do, and they are called General Organism Development Systems, or G-O-D-S... GODS.'

The face in the mirror was sly and wondering whether a quintuplet was going to be one family member too many. The fourth brother was still on the table but looking much diminished. I reached for the bottle and made a stab at topping my glass up, failed, and tried to put the bottle back down in mid-air. The Preacher caught it before it travelled an inch, recorked it, and then placed it out of my reach. I gazed at the naked ladies with drunken longing, and then realised what I had just been told.

'What?' I breathed hard. 'What are you saying? Are you telling me those ships are Gods? But... that's just madness.'

'Read your *Bible*, Sheriff Sawyer, and you will see GODS' work written in its verses. Eden's servants walked out into the world before men had evolved and they planted the stored seeds into the likeliest candidates. One genetic pathway led to mankind, *you*, and the other chose to escape the land and took to the sea. That creature you know as the dolphin. Bright enough but it has far too much fun to be taken seriously. Wonderful poetry though. The dolphin still has some kinship with mankind but as far as being a related

23

species goes I'm afraid you've been growing further apart over millions of years.'

'This is sheer tomfoolery, Preacher Spindrift. You're playing the jester with me and I'm surely a drunken tomfool to be listening to you at all. This is a tale for children and the simple-minded to dwell upon. I've seen two men turned to monsters and I saw it happen in this very town today. We burned them both, you burned them, and thanks to you we have said nothing to anyone about it since. What has any of that to do with dolphins and Eden and seeds planted before Eve ate her apple? Why are you twisting my nose so rudely? What does "effolfed" mean? What's a "genticknic pathway"? How would you know all this stuff, anyway?'

The whiskey had made me brave as a Dutchman. Later we would talk more calmly about the great ships from a distant star and the servants of Eden, and I would come to accept his story. But that night my brain had been soaked in smooth spirit and what little wits I had were scattered to all four alcoholic winds.

'Very well, Sheriff Sawyer.' The Preacher stood up.

My eyelids had become heavy and my fuddled head drooped, weighed down by the burden of the Bell of Nelson brothers' smooth seduction, but when he stood tall I felt the touch of that massively inhuman presence once more, and an icy touch of sobriety jolted me back into that room and cast away the lure of sleep.

I saw the Preacher hold his hands out straight from his shoulders and he stood a moment as if crucified with the palms of his hands facing flat down towards the floor. The air hummed around me and for a second there was the rush of an impossible wind. The Preacher seemed for a moment to be getting taller in front of my eyes and I blinked in confusion.

And then I realised what I was seeing and I dropped my empty glass to the Preacher's floor. It bounced unbroken on the polished wooden boards.

I saw him clear as I saw that glass and the bread on the board. I saw him, arms outstretched, hovering three impossible feet above the ground.

And then he smiled at me.

'GODS' servants were built to last, Sheriff Sawyer. They were built to last a long, long time.'

I think I fainted about then.

{8}

According to Preacher Spindrift, the enemy – the evil infection that took Baylee and Klosky – had been on Earth before the big ship arrived and before Eden's agents had started their work growing men from the 'genetic material' of dumb animals. He explained how the enemy had been a subtle brute that had once learned to be considerate of its prey.

Most of the time, he said, it was a quiet beast that would settle into its victims' bodies like a tapeworm. It would share its prey's food and take goodness from its blood without its victim even knowing what was happening. All the while the thing would be growing and putting its claws deeper into its victim's brain to direct its actions, waiting until it was time to breed. And then it would split and multiply at a furious rate. The victim would become a hatchery, just as I had seen in the cool room. It would reach out to more victims and more until it became big enough to dig down into the earth and create its nest. Klosky and Baylee were the mobile 'hatchling' stage.

The night before the Preacher had finally put me to bed in his room. I don't know where he spent the time until sunrise the following morning. I woke up with a sore drunkard's head and a mouth that tasted of sick and pickle. I hadn't vomited, which surprised me, but it had been a close call. I wrestled my way out from under the counterpane and sat on the bed for a while with my sorry head in my hands. As I say, I never was much of a drinker and when I did indulge it always took me hard.

When he heard me moving around, the Preacher came into the room, bade me the best of the day then brought me back into his living room where he served some strong coffee alongside a plateful of eggs and fried bacon with buttered bread on a tin plate at the side. I drank the coffee gratefully but eyed the food warily.

'Get something in your belly, Sheriff Sawyer,' he said. 'You'll feel much the better for it.'

He was right. Once I'd mopped up the yolks and bacon grease with a hunk of cornbread and fetched myself another cup of his good coffee, the Preacher asked me if I remembered much of our conversation the night before.

'Eden and the big ships,' I said. 'And your neat parlour trick of floating around the room three feet off the floor. That was a thing to see and no mistake.'

'Good, then there's no need to repeat myself. But I must also ask you not to repeat anything I tell you of this unless I say so. Agreed?'

I nodded.

That was when he started giving me a better idea of what we were dealing with. I knew what a tapeworm was, a horrible parasite that would eventually kill its host if it wasn't purged, but this hatchling creature sounded much worse. The food settled heavily in my stomach when I thought of those things pressing up through Baylee's belly. Then the Preacher continued, and his words stung me like that thing had stung me when I'd touched Klosky's neck.

'It is both an infection and a possession of the host,' he explained. 'Remember that creature I pulled from you yesterday? That was a motherlode ripe to burst. I caught it just in time. Once it accelerated and spread there would have been nothing I could do – both your body and your mind would have been completely contaminated.

'Sawyer, if that had happened to you the kindest thing would have been to shoot you down and burn you where you lay. I think of you as a friend but once that infection spreads – like it did with Baylee and Klosky – the man is lost to the beast.'

With a mounting sense of horror I pointed out that I must have been infected when I felt that sting while touching Klosky's corpse.

'From the time I felt the sting to the time you retrieved the beast from my chest... why, that was something less than two hours!'

I was skirting over the fact that the Preacher had rummaged around in my body like he was fetching something from a satchel. The previous twenty-four hours had been strange enough that my head already held more questions than could ever be answered in a man's lifetime. I didn't know what he'd done or how he'd done it but I was real grateful he'd been there to do what he did.

The Preacher chewed like he was tasting his words before spitting them out, and he studied my face closely before he answered.

'War has been declared,' he said.

'War?'

'A war of extinction.'

'Preacher, I tell you, my head's spinning fit to fly off my shoulders. Yesterday morning I woke up in Mule's Ass, but today I reckon I woke up on the moon. Are you telling me this infection thing has declared war on the *town*?'

'No, Sheriff Sawyer, I'm telling you this infection thing has declared open war on everything that GODS' servants on Earth have done for the last six million years. That's why it is moving faster than ever before.

'What would once have taken months or years is now happening in a matter of hours. The beast has never been recognised by human eyes. Any man of science who got that close to it was consumed and possessed before they could report their findings. And who would want to put their name to such an abomination? The beast has declared war on GODS' work and it has become GODS' enemy. If nothing else at least we have seen its actions in time to stop it here.'

My pulse was racing and it wasn't just because of the coffee.

'Six *million* years?'

'From the early days of the first upright ape to the rise of modern man – from the time we first sowed the Eden seeds to the current time of reaping. The enemy has waited until human communications became fast enough and our methods of travel swift enough that it could start somewhere small and then spread out, right across the globe. It wants every man, woman and child on this planet dead. It wants to devour and possess them.'

'But... why now? I don't understand why it waited so long.'

'Who can understand the mind of such a thing? But I believe it is because now you have steam trains and ocean liners, fast clippers and rapid transports. A world that was once huge has become small. The enemy is vile but highly intelligent. It has waited all this time until the tool-using ape provided the means by which it can quickly get to the four corners of the globe. Today it wants to eat Mule's Ass; tomorrow it will eat New York. Next week it will eat Beijing. It won't stop until the last man is blistered and burst, and then, and only then, it will know its work is done.'

'So, what do we do?'

'What do you think? We stop the monster here – even if it means we have to burn down the town and everybody in it; every man, woman and child. Once they become victims they become weapons against their brothers.'

'Shit.'

'Yes, Sheriff Sawyer. As you say, shit indeed.'

9

The first thing we had to do was find out who raped and killed Klosky. It must have been then that he had become infected with the enemy. We cleaned up using the Preacher's facilities and he strapped his own gun belt to his waist before we headed out to look at where the man's body had been found. I was pleased to see the Preacher's gun belt was plain and worn but in good order and loaded with ready-made forty-five calibre shells. His pistol looked as well maintained as my own. He settled the gun on his hip and drew it with a smooth, practiced action that spoke of long usage. He checked it was loaded then settled it back in its holster with a fluid gesture.

'Were you a soldier once?' We walked out onto Main Street where we were met by a sun a touch too bright for my booze-tendered sight. I tilted my hat a little forward to shade my eyes. Preacher did the same. I suppose the way his cheek muscles pulled his mouth into a thin line could have been construed as a smile.

'Did you often get beat in the school room?'

It was such an odd response that I had to replay it a few times in my head before answering him.

'Yes, I guess I did. Why?'

'You ask so many questions I do believe any teacher lady would quickly bring her whip to your behind and stand you facing the corner 'til close of class. Now let's start back in the cold room.'

'You want to go back in *there*?'

'And that's yet another question. Your behind must have been whipped raw.'

He chuckled at his own wit and I grinned at him. I made him wait a moment while I fetched my Winchester rifle from my office. I loaded it with fifteen rounds then levered one into the chamber.

'Good thinking,' he nodded when he saw the long gun. 'When you're hunting rabbits it's best to go loaded for bear – and we aren't hunting rabbits.'

'Pistols are fine when you're close enough to shake a man's hand, but if I must get involved in a gun fight I prefer some distance between him and me.'

'Amen to that.'

He shook my hand then. When he did so something seemed to pass between us. My spine straightened a little more and my head cleared somewhat.

We saddled our horses which were both lodged at Levin's stable, then led them on foot the short distance to the stockyards. We tied them to the rail and paused at the all too familiar door for just an instant before re-entering the corridor. A single small window set into the long right-hand wall cast enough light for us to see things clearly. The cool room door at the end looked a little scorched but was otherwise intact.

I thought of those wicked strings of fire and that writhing thing burning at their heart and I took a firmer grip on my rifle. Its cool weight gave me enough courage to follow the silent Preacher to our destination. Our footsteps seemed abnormally loud on the wooden boards.

We could see how the door surround was slightly blackened and there was a faint smell of charcoal. Preacher made a gesture like a catholic priest before an altar, and the door swung open easily.

The room was empty and practically undamaged. There was a smell like someone had recently struck a sulphur match and all the surfaces were covered in a fine grey powder, but otherwise there was no sign of the hellish conflagration we'd escaped just the day before, nor of the horrifically altered men's bodies.

'This is the work of the Devil,' I shuddered.

'I would be a great deal happier if that were true,' growled the man at my side. Then he led me back out to our horses. He gave no explanation and I asked for none, even though my head was ringing with questions.

From the stockyards we followed the trail that led past the end of Main Street and up into the hills at the west end of town. The cemetery we rode past after climbing an easy incline for a few hundred yards was one of the most crowded places in Mule's Ass and already sported its second perimeter fence.

'They put the graveyard here because of the view,' I told the Preacher.

'I'm sure the residents appreciate it.'

'I'm going to have a window put into my coffin so I can see it.'

'I shall clean your window and share some of eternity with you while I set awhile and converse, Sheriff Sawyer.'

Preacher had a way with words.

'I'd be obliged if you'd call me Caleb, Preacher Spindrift.'

'I would be proud to, Caleb. Proud to.'

'And what shall I call you?'

'Let me ponder that a while.'

Klosky had been found just over a mile from town at the bottom of a dry gulch. The fire ants were already busy at work rebuilding their mound. We

29

dismounted and hitched our horses to some shrubs a good distance away. A horse reacts badly to insect bites and fire ants deliver a mighty painful punch for their size. Some little soldier critters tried to warn us off as we approached, so we cautiously skirted them and eyed the scene from a distance. I've known men to swell up and die from enough ant bites and I was in no hurry to join them. My view of the town from the graveyard could hold a spell longer and those bastards' bites stung worse than acid.

The Preacher circled the mound carefully, looking intently at the dusty ground, and then cast a keen glance around him.

'Where's the tree?'

It was a good question and one I should have asked first. Klosky had been lynched sure enough. I had told Spindrift that much the night before when I was still lucid enough to make sense. So, where *was* the tree?

Everywhere we walked we were shadowed by a pink swarm of ants but we kept well clear of them.

Sweet Alice watered several hundred square miles of ranch and farmland down in the valley. Mule's Ass was fruitful and kind in her own way – she gave with an open hand to any man willing to work for her, but up there by the ant mound there was little of anything taller than sage brush, grasses and tumbleweed. There were some boulders and shrubs nearby, and the entrance to the ravine, but no trees. *Where was the tree?*

'Who found him?'

'A husband and wife out in their Sunday best wagon, a four-wheeler.'

'Two horses?'

'Sure.'

'How did they get to Klosky's body without getting bitten?'

'Husband was Kyle Vickery. He's the gang boss over at Teague's ranch. He can bring a running heifer down with a lasso from twenty paces. Pulling a dead man from an ant mound was a whistle in the breeze for old Kyle.'

'I know him.'

'A good man.'

'Handy with a lariat as you say.'

'They tied Klosky to the back of the wagon then high-tailed it into town.'

'A sorry thing for Mrs Vickery to see.'

'She's tough enough to wade naked through a cactus sea if she had to. Got bit though.'

'She *what*? Caleb, why didn't you tell me sooner? We must hurry. Do you know where we can find Mrs Vickery?'

He hustled me back towards our horses so quickly that Missy, my pinto, snickered with alarm and reared back. I calmed her, released the hitch and mounted up. Preacher was already in the saddle and sat impatiently, eager to be away.

'We may already be too late,' he said. 'Lead me to Mrs Vickery, Caleb. Ride as if the Devil himself was at your heels.'

I looked at his urgent face and saw the fierce light in his eye. I lashed Missy with the reins and she dashed away at a gallop.

The Devil rode at my heels.

10

The Vickerys had a stout, pretty little cottage by the cedar-wood break on the north side of the Teague spread. Teague liked to think he was cultured in the English manner and his stead had a quaint, round-shouldered look about it that belied the Texas heat.

Kyle was more of a long porch and rocker man but Bertha, his wife, liked the cottage. Whenever she had the time she would set to work in her flower garden wearing a wide-brimmed woven hat and a loose-fitting frock. That garden of hers drank a winter's worth of snow melt during the summer and the plants shrivelled up in the parching swelter regardless; but she loved it and Kyle loved her, and anyway he spent most of his day with Teague's longhorns.

They were both broad, sturdy folk as were their son and daughter, and they faced the world with open, honest faces. Kyle was the wall between the fat rancher and his hard, capable men. Teague's soft ways and affectations would probably have seen him gunned down by an exasperated gaucho if he hadn't had Kyle Vickery to translate his wishes to his ranch-hands and cattlemen.

Some of those cattlemen came running when the Preacher and I burst onto the scene at a full gallop and headed straight for the Vickery house without so much as a by-your-leave. There was a fancy black, two-wheeled rig hitched to a single mare outside the Vickery's cottage. I recognised it as belonging to Doctor Emerson from over in Shafter. Preacher swung quickly off his horse while I climbed out of my saddle. Teague's men noticed my rifle and Spindrift's pistol and were clearly alarmed by our armed state, but they were undecided as to how to react. The Preacher didn't give them time to mull things over.

'The doctor's in there with Mrs Vickery – who else?'

One of the men stepped forward. 'Comanchero Pete's helping Doc out, Preacher.'

'Where's Kyle?'

'Been a rumour of wolves or a pack of wild dogs scaring up the English calves over by the Longacre Ford. He took Lester Merry and Oliver Pickford with him to check things out.'

'When?'

'Yesterday afternoon. What's going on, Preacher?'

'Plague.'

The men took an almost instant step backwards away from us.

Preacher pointed at the cottage.

'Sheriff Sawyer and I are going in there now. If anyone but either of us two tries to come out, shoot them; but whatever you do, don't go near them. This plague is verily contagious and *always* fatal. Don't let them touch you. Don't let their blood touch you. Don't let any part of them touch you. Do you understand?'

'What kind of plague is it, Preacher? Choler or the Black Fever?'

'Nothing any of you want to catch, I promise you. Wait here and be watchful. When we come out we may be running. Have any of you got rifles?'

A few nodded. 'Then fetch them and form a perimeter guard at a safe distance.'

A powerful looking, bear-like man said, 'I got me a sawed-off twelve gauge, Preacher.'

'Forget it, Samuel. You don't want to get that close.'

'I won't. Sounds mighty infectious?'

'It is.'

Preacher Spindrift led the way to the front door of the cottage.

'Cover my back, Caleb.'

His speech might have scared Teague's men a little but it put the fear of God into me. I was shaking like a callow, pork-eating boy at his side. He put his hand on my shoulder.

'We have many advantages over the enemy, Caleb, but stay diligent and remain careful.'

He pushed the door open and I followed him inside.

The stink struck at me like a physical blow. I coughed at it and spat. There was a susurration in the hallway, a dark murmuring sound like a nest of bees deep in the trunk of a big tree. It was dark in the cottage and unnaturally cool. Beads of air sweat were running down the walls. I heard the creak of a floorboard from above our heads.

'All three of them are upstairs,' Preacher whispered. 'Quietly now.'

Carpeted stairs climbed up to a railed landing from which four varnished doors opened onto rooms or cupboards. I couldn't tell which. The cold intensified and I began to shiver from the chill instead of fear. Preacher lifted his chin and seemed to sniff the air. I did the same, but to me it seemed equally rank in every direction. He gestured towards the door at the end of the landing and moved forward in a slow, silent crouch.

We could see that the door opened inwards and he pushed at it, hard and fast. A brass bedstead gleamed by the light of an oil lamp and dark wooden furniture crowded the walls. It was a pleasant room, I suppose, and nothing like the Spartan rooms in my own home over the office.

Something large moved on the bed and reared up. Preacher fired once and pushed me backwards, threw something from inside his coat into the room and slammed the door shut. The panels of the door were instantly peppered with fine black needle points that beaded a thick amber fluid at the ends. Preacher snatched his hand away. From the bedroom came a rising, bubbling wail that grew into an inhuman shriek. I had seen the glass of the lamp shatter when the Preacher's ball hit it and its metal base bounce to the ground. Whatever it was that had been on that bed was sure to be burning fiercely.

'Why, Satan, you've brought a friend for us to collect − how kind.'

Preacher spun and fired twice in a smooth action, whipping his right hand across his pistol's hammer like a seasoned gunfighter. What had once been Kyle Vickery spilled to the floor and burst, releasing a mass of squirming, worm-like tendrils. Something in the room behind us exploded and the sturdy door shuddered in its frame.

'We have to get out of here, Caleb.'

Preacher glanced over the railing to the hallway below. It was probably a fall of some twelve feet. It looked further. Much further.

'Follow me.'

He vaulted the railing and caught at the banister with one hand as he fell. It slowed him, he hung for a second swaying, and then he fell the remaining few feet easily.

'Come on, Caleb!'

Whatever Kyle had become was sliming its way along the carpet towards me. *Shit,* I thought, *I'd rather break my neck than let that thing touch me.*

I leapt. Preacher caught me like a baby in both arms and lowered me to my feet. A blisteringly white billow of flame shattered the bedroom door and boiled along the landing, throwing up a twisting mass of crisping, thread-like limbs.

A great voice howled with pain and rage. 'SATAAAN!' And the walls shook.

The fire seemed to coil and whip around the upper floor of the cottage as if it was searching for something, then it poured like molten glass down the stairs towards us. We ran for the exit even as sticky ropes of flame dripped through the ceiling and fell around us. And then, at the very last moment as

34

we burst out into Mrs Vickery's flower garden, all of the windows of the upper floor shattered at once to hurl a blazing inferno of greasy yellow flame into the sky over our heads.

We threw ourselves under the doctor's wagon just as gobbets of a hissing *something* pattered into the dust around it. The horse was spooked, tore its reins from the post and bolted. Preacher threw an arm over me as the tall wheels rattled closely past our bodies and then clattered away, the buggy swaying like a drunk in a hurricane.

It was only then that we got to our feet and looked around to assay the situation, brushing dust from our clothes and collecting our guns from where we'd dropped them.

A fresh, belching burst of stinking flame drove us further away from the blazing building. The skin of my face felt seared.

'Well then, Preacher Spindrift and Sheriff Sawyer, would you care to explain just *what* the fuck has been going on here?'

The fat form of Foster Teague stood glowering at us, his fists pressed firmly at the rotund equator where his hips should have been.

'You men have some explaining to do,' spat Teague, his corpulent cheeks and ample chins floundering about on his boneless face. He was wet-lipped and blotched crimson with rage.

Preacher was reloading his pistol, ejecting the spent forty-five calibre shells from the cylinder then pressing the fresh cartridges home. He had fired three bullets before I'd even had a chance to aim. That man was fast, faster than anyone I ever saw. His cool demeanour seemed to rile Teague even more and the fat man pushed forward, thrusting his soft belly against the Preacher's hard frame. Preacher stood firm and it was Teague who bounced, staggering fatly back a few paces.

'You pushed me!' he sputtered. 'You fucking bullying ruffian, you pushed me! How dare you?' He flapped a hand in my direction. 'You, Sawyer, do your duty. Arrest this man at once. He has assaulted a fucking member of the town Council, burned down one of my buildings and committed God only knows what other crimes. Where are the good Mr and Mrs Vickery and Dr Emerson?'

He turned to the cluster of men at his back, many of whom cradled rifles in their arms.

'Well? Speak up somebody.'

'They're all dead in that unfortunate fire,' answered the Preacher. 'And we barely escaped with our lives as you just saw. But right now the Sheriff and I have a job to do over at Longacre Ford, so I'm afraid, Councillor Teague, we must be on our way. I'd be happy to pass the time of day with you when I have time to spare, but I fear we have much to do and little time to do it in before dark. Good day to you.'

We mounted up and made to ride away when a gunshot cracked loudly behind us. Preacher had his pistol cocked and pointed at the end of a long arm before I had even time to look round.

Teague was preparing to fire again. He had evidently torn a rifle from the hands of one of his men and taken a pot-shot at our retreating backs, like the cowardly creature he was. Samuel Meads put paid to his murderous plans by knocking him to the ground then slapping his hands away from the stout old Henry carbine.

'Sheriff, Preacher,' Samuel shouted at us, 'you've got your jobs to do, and from what I saw here just now I don't envy you none. We'll get Mr Teague here back to his house where he can regain his wind and curb his temper somewhat. It was right fortunate he was cussing so much he clean forgot to aim that old carbine of Willy Conroy's, or one of you would have a hole in you the size of a big man's fist. Good luck to you both, gentlemen.'

'He took it right outta muh hands, right outta muh hands without so much as a please or a thankee. Right sorry, gemmun,' whined a thin, bearded man who looked deeply offended. 'Please, don't blame the Henry for Mr Teague's actions. It ain't the carbine's fault is all.'

Preacher tipped his hat and I did likewise as we cantered away. My mind was buzzing with questions but two were foremost and I shouted them at my companion as we rode.

'Preacher, why are we going to the Ford? And why did that creature call you Satan?'

He reined in for a moment so we could talk in a more companionable manner.

'We've been told that Kyle went to the Ford with Lester Merry and Oliver Pickford. He came back on his own and you saw for yourself how he had been affected by the enemy. What happened to those two men he was with? We need to find that out before we continue our search for whoever killed and infected Klosky. Once we're done here I'll have to return up into the hills and seek out whatever tracks are still there to be found around that ant hill. Perhaps it would be too much to ask you to join me in this venture, Sheriff, but we're on the trail of a gang of cold killers and I guess you're as curious as me to see where it all leads.

'As for your other question... the answer is simple enough. The enemy called me Satan because that is how it knows me. I will explain more over a drink and some food later, but for now keep your eyes peeled. Who knows where, or indeed what, those men might be by now?'

It was several minutes later that an odd silhouette on the ridge above our trackway drew my eye and I blurted out, 'Look, there!' Imagine a potter had taken his wet models of men and horses and pressed them like living clay between his hands, moulding flesh to flesh until it was hard to see where men ended and horses began. Merry and Pickford had been friends once but the enemy had bonded them and their mounts closer than any Siamese twins.

The Preacher called Satan drew a large bore Winchester-Hotchkiss bolt-action rifle from his saddle holster and took a solid bead on the nightmare mash of man and beast when it started cantering urgently in our direction. He bade me to follow suit.

'Stop the bastard in its tracks, Caleb.'

37

Our shells tore into the chaotic mass of arms, legs and gape-mouthed heads until the monstrous creature finally stalled and rolled to one side, still squirming, stretching and yearning towards us. Horse legs, human arms and bug-eyed heads writhed in an insane stew that was still trying to regain its feet and kicking out in every direction.

'Stay right here and look after my horse,' shouted the Preacher. 'But keep your gun trained on that thing if you value your soul.'

He fetched something from his saddlebag and walked a good part of the distance between me and the raging beast. There came a faint pattering noise then, like fat rain on a dusty path, and the ground around his boots leapt and rippled. He took no notice but threw something underarm into the heart of the creature then drew his pistol, aimed and fired.

Every limb of the wretched monster closed around whatever he had thrown as if to protect it from his bullet, and then there was a fierce white flare that left a blinding red after-image which completely robbed me of my sight for a few seconds. My ears were still working though and I heard the whooshing crackle as the living stew of horses and men was completely immolated by purifying fire. Angry shrieks were rendered to bubbling sounds of agony.

My vision returned in time to see the Preacher settle back into his saddle and regard me with amused eyes.

'Ever had the feeling you'd have been better staying in bed this morning?'

The mound of mixed flesh roared and hissed as it burned. That dreadful midden stink intensified. It wasn't the smell of roasting meat you get when a man's body burns; I knew that well enough from the time Temple Peawhistle fell off the wagon so hard he rolled unconscious into his campfire and died there without ever waking up. I had to help the undertaker collect what was left of poor Temple's body and I swear I could still smell the mountain gin in the old rummy's roasted guts. It didn't help when Undertaker Crawlins made a joke about burnt offerings, but I guess his trade called for its own dark sense of humour.

The enemy stank like a burning wasps' nest stuffed with rotten fish and something else – something unearthly.

'No, Preacher, I don't. A man who stays abed when he's got a job like this to do is likely to have one of those bastard things come knocking at his bedpost. When I meet the next poor victim of this plague I'd rather be on my feet with a gun in my hand than hiding under the counterpane and trusting to God.'

He nodded in what I believed to be agreement. 'Come along, friend. If you wish to join me we've still got a job to do. And may I say I don't think I could have had a better man at my side during this terrible business.'

He thrust out his hand and I shook it right happily. Once more I felt that surge of confident energy. Then we turned our mounts back towards the hills and went looking for Klosky's murderers. It would prove to be a long and terrifying night.

{12}

And now we leave Caleb for a while and follow others who will prove essential to the telling of the story. Back in town events were unfolding that were to throw more fuel into the terrible fire.

Grandma Teatree had taken the bit firmly between her teeth once Teague and Damsel-Childs put their money on the table. She put a hustle in her bustle to get her plans into action, and her scrawny black shadow darkened many a door that day. That same afternoon she drew up and telegraphed an advertisement to the *County Courier* and placed a handwritten notice on the community message board in the window of Goody Marsh's Trading Post.

It was surprising to me how subtle Grandma could be with her phrasing. She was looking for scarlet women, whores who were prepared to sell their easy virtue for dollar bills. What she asked for was applications from 'Big hearted women who can bring comfort and easement for those uncomfortable natural energies that often arise in men of all ages. Experience preferred; many positions available. Bed and board provided. Only clean bodies need apply.' If she'd written 'bed and bawd', she couldn't have been clearer in her intentions.

She asked her prospects to contact 'Madam Teatree, care of Marsh's Trading Post, Mule's Ass, Presidio County, Southern Texas State.' *Madam Teatree*? She might just as well have asked them to contact 'The Cathouse by the Stockyards'!

The property she had her eye on was a thirty-year-old staging post which had recently lost out to the pell-mell expansion of the railroads. Rail was proving faster, safer and a lot cheaper than the old overland stagecoach. Though some determined bandits still made a play to rob the iron horses on the lonelier stretches of their journey, it was an unlucky traveller who ever lost their goods that way. By that time the plucky old Wells-Fargo postal stages largely depended on shorter distance travellers.

Grandma had hustled one of Damsel-Childs' clerks to that old building early on the same day that Preacher and Caleb were confronting the enemy on Teague's land. The town's bank with its big steel safe was deemed the safest place to hold keys and deeds and any legal paperwork on an empty property. Damsel-Childs had foreclosed on the staging post's previous owners so, effectively, he would be purchasing the property from himself. I have no idea of the amounts of money involved – but have little doubt that the buyer got a good deal from the seller during that transaction.

The staging post was a grey, rangy building of steep, expensively tiled roofs, weatherboards and shutters. The stables out back were still a going concern thanks to 'Heck' Levin's entrepreneurial ambitions, but Grandma felt certain that she and Heck could come to some arrangement regarding the discreet quartering of her customers' horses.

The post's shadowy interior was cobwebbed and dusty but promising. She and the clerk stepped directly through glazed double doors from the boardwalk onto a raised hexagonal platform that led down onto the main floor by two broad steps. Three squared columns marched down the centre of the long room and on the far wall was a wet bar complete with a brass foot rail and a big dirty mirror surrounded by shelves for bottles and fixtures for lamps.

The floor and all the fittings were covered by the grime of empty seasons and the scant light was filtered brown by filth on the window panes, but those long-forgotten craftsmen's hands had built well. The floor was sturdy and barely creaked as they walked deeper into the room, and a finger drawn through the dust of the bar top disclosed the healthy shine of old polished mahogany.

By the right side of the bar was an opening that led to a kitchen and wash-house plus a row of eight narrow rooms that ran the length of the building. Each had its own door and was furnished with a low and sturdy, rope-strung bed frame. Some of the rope had rotted but it would be easy enough to repair them. At the end of the corridor by the back door was a water closet.

They walked back into the bar and then ascended a flight of stairs which led up to an L-shaped landing lined with more doors. These opened to larger and better appointed bedrooms and Grandma hummed and muttered to herself.

'Rooms out back were for the stagemen and their roof passengers plus any poor traveller who just wanted a roof and a bed for the night and had precious few pennies in their poke. These were for the gentry who were better used to comfort and expected to find it wherever they set.'

She looked at the clerk with sparkling, midnight eyes.

'This will do. This will do very well. Tell your boss yes, we'll take it. But we'll have to polish it and furnish the place first. Leave me the key. I'll look around for a while. Off you go, hasty now or I'll set afire to your coattails.'

She listened to the boy's hasty feet pattering down the stairs then pounding across the floor below. Once she knew she was alone she walked along the landing and examined each of the rooms in turn. *Some warm suds, wax polish and elbow grease will soon set this place up,* she mused, knowing full

41

well that it wouldn't be her hands in the bucket. She liked hard work, harder the better. Women down on their knees scrubbing until their hands were ruined and raw; kept the little vixens busy and out of mischief. She could watch it all day.

The final door was the only one on the landing's west wall. Entering she found herself in a suite of rooms which included a bright, double-aspected drawing room, a water closet with a wooden comfort seat and porcelain honey bucket for night soil, plus a large, also double-aspect bedroom. These would be her rooms, she decided, when she was overseeing the place.

One of the windows in the drawing room's south wall sported a seat cubby. She swept it free of dust and watched fat spiders the size of her palm scuttle away into the shadows. She smiled to herself. No doubt there would be a lot of shrieking and panic when the cleaning women saw those. Silly pathetic creatures.

The late morning sun warmed the rippling glass in the frame and cast her face into a stark contrast of light and dark. Her eye in the sunlight gleamed with a rich, red hue. She closed her eyelids and allowed her senses to first dip into the corners of the room and then beyond. She allowed her mind to dive into the cool flowing waters of her river. Sitting still in the old staging post she felt the river's coolness enter her spirit, cleanse her, and make her whole. One day she would go home again. It would be on the day when she was finally too tired to accept men's foolishness and greed anymore, tired of all this dust and dirt and the cobwebs and the heat, tired of so much in the world. But not yet, no, not yet... she had a promise to keep.

In her mind's eye she had seen Preacher Spindrift and Sheriff Sawyer return to the stockyards and walk that corridor to the cool room. Sawyer needed his rifle to feel safe; Preacher didn't. Like her the Preacher had more senses than most – he could see much more than merely caught his eye. She had seen them ride up into the hills. She had taken particular notice of the Sheriff.

She opened her eyes and looked at her reflection in the rippled glass of the mirror and smiled at the beautiful young face gazing back, black-eyed, smooth-skinned and graceful. She continued watching while the shrinking illusion of age returned. It shrivelled her full lips and stretched the etched flesh tightly back against her bird-like bones. Peals of laughter rang out, clear as fresh water in the dust-choked rooms.

And now we return to Caleb's narrative.

Back near the ant mound we hitched our horses to the same tough little shrub. They nibbled at its stubby leaves, curling their long lips back away from its thorns. We had watered them at the river on our way there and I wiped flecks of foamy sweat from Missy's stiff coat. Those horses were tough, working animals but there was no reason to hurt them by making them go thirsty and we'd already run them hard. Missy was blowing a little but she enjoyed a good run. Preacher's big bay took everything in its stride.

We drank from our water canteens. Mine was a big, cloth-covered clay bottle. Some men used those Italian-style canteens made of wood, but I'd found if you stored them empty they tended to split and would leak when you filled them, and if you stored them full the water would soon begin to stink and turn foul. Preacher's canteen was big and round like two lids of a cooking pot pressed together and I could hear the water slosh around in there. He offered me a sip from it and I found the water to be cool, fresh and clean tasting as spring water. He was a man of many surprises.

Once he was satisfied our horses had been properly catered for, Preacher put his nose back to the ground around that ant mound. We could still see where the man had been thrust headfirst into it, but battalions of tiny workers had been busily at work repairing the damage ever since the Vickerys' unfortunate discovery and Klosky's removal the previous day. I saw ants following him around like an earth red shadow but he always remained firmly out of their reach.

'I'm not seeing any scuff marks,' said the Preacher, pointing at the dry earth. 'They didn't drag the man here. They carried him and then they posed him in that obscene kneeling position. That must mean he hadn't yet started to stiffen after death.'

His eyes scanned the surrounding scrub and he strode to a cluster of thorny brush a few yards away. I followed him and saw that his keen sight had spotted a few fluttering fibres caught there. He continued his narrative.

'Takes two to three hours for a body to go stiff on a warm day and then it can take anything up to eleven hours for it to wear off. You agree?'

'Guess so.'

He was squinting up the dry, rock-strewn gulch leading up to a crest of stunted trees. He began picking his way through the scrub until he stood at the base of the gulch and shaded his eyes with his left hand. I noticed how he always favoured his left hand. Again I followed him as he began to thread a cautious path up the narrow cleft in the rock face.

A running stream would have once cut this sharp groove into the landscape, but it was dry and gritty by the time we climbed it, and its many boulders might have provided plenty of cool shade for a sleeping rattler. Experience told us it was best not to accidently startle one of those critters. Three times that day we'd ridden past the last resting place for a few folk who had done just that in the past, and I truly believed the fine view across town really didn't make up for the lack of any future.

The Preacher was silent as we climbed. He was concentrating on his surroundings but also paying close attention to a cluster of squat trees above us. Their trunks had that whitish grey, petrified look that's often the case when its principal source of water has dried up or been diverted away from its roots.

'Look there, see?'

I squinted in the direction the Preacher was pointing.

'What am I looking for?'

'See how the clay has been kicked out there under that overhanging branch? I see the struggles of a big man trying to find purchase on the ravine wall, trying to relieve the pressure of the rope around his neck.'

Now he pointed it out I saw it too. I also saw the spray of shit the man had cut loose when he died.

'There's the rope, see?'

He was right. The overhanging branch had several tight coils of thick cord tied at its base. We had found both our murder scene and the weapon used. How long had the gentle lumberman struggled here at the end of the noose before he finally succumbed? Fate had dealt him a cruel blow.

'They stood right here and threw their weight on the poor man's legs. Look there. See how their heels scraped lines in the dry riverbed. Then they cut the rope and his bonds before carrying him down to where he was found by the poor Vickerys. It takes a sick mind to hang a man with his pants around his ankles, but what can you say about people who feed their victim face down to a bunch of fire ants like that?'

He asked me to step back a ways and he studied the marks in the hard soil more closely. 'Three men stood here – I can see distinctive differences in their heel marks. This man's boots are run down at the heel and look much worn. These look recently mended, proud nail heads. This one has a narrow Spanish look to it. I'd say two men in work boots and one in fancy cowhand boots.'

There was a pile of larger stones just a little way up the gulch from the site of the killing. A landslide had partially covered them and cut a notch out of the ravine wall. I walked around back of Preacher Spindrift and cast an eye over the stones.

'This is where they climbed down from up by the tree,' I said. 'There are four sets of footprints coming down but only one going up.'

I looked around me. 'There are a lot of questions to be answered here, Preacher. Why hang him here? Was it just to leave him in the ant mound? How did they get him here? He was a big man, maybe too big to carry too far, so where did they rape him?'

'We need to examine the spore up there among the trees to see if we can find some of your answers, Caleb. I think I've learned everything I can from down here.'

That was when my horse started screaming. At first I didn't know what the terrible shriek could be; it almost sounded like a terrified woman. The Preacher didn't waste any time looking around. He straight away looked back down the gulch and started to run with me at his heels.

Missy was rearing and kicking out at something I couldn't see. As we got closer I saw her ears were flat back and her eyes rolling white in their sockets. Her lips looked bloody and swollen. Her hide looked wrong. It seemed to be rippling strangely. And then she went quiet and stood quivering. All around her was an earth-coloured shadow.

The Preacher grabbed at my shoulder and pulled me back when I thought to reach out to comfort her.

'No, Caleb, stand away. We've lost her.'

He reached inside his long coat and pulled out a glass ball.

'Cover your eyes,' he said, and threw the ball hard onto the swarming shadows between Missy's legs. She watched what he was doing with a strangely mocking stare, her eyes now bulging and a gleaming black. She bared her teeth and had just made as if to step towards us when the column of blazing white fire poured up into her belly.

She died, but not like any of God's creatures in a sane world.

She screamed again, long and loud, but this time with a harsh, bubbling wailing sound that died to a whimper while her body crumbled into a burning mound. It was as if she had been made from thousands of tiny pieces that were all falling away from her as she died; hundreds and thousands of them, all melting and burning and flowing down and around her, spilling out onto the rusty ground.

The rust was a mass of terracotta-coloured fire ants and the wall of flame swept along them as if they were purest whale oil. The stench was one of pickled acid and the fire's acrid smoke watered my blinded eyes and choked me.

My saddle sat in the middle of a circle of flame. It was all that remained of one of the gentlest and most loyal creatures I had ever known.

'Caleb, stand away.'

The Preacher had run over to his own horse, which had remained quiet and untouched during Missy's ruin. He fetched some things from his saddle bags which he stuffed into his coat's inner pockets, and then hurried back to my side.

'I should have thought of this earlier,' he said. 'If Klosky had been infected before he was thrust into that mound he would have infected the nest of ants while they were attacking him. On the other hand it might have been the ants themselves that infected Klosky. Either way,' he pulled another crystal globe from a pocket, 'these evil little beasties have to be dealt with before we do anything else.'

He tossed the globe at the mound and drew his pistol in the same smooth action, fanned the hammer back and fired before the globe had quite landed.

I knew to look away that time but even so was shocked by how the immediate landscape was thrown into deep relief by a stark solar glare. There was an explosive whoosh and the ground underfoot trembled and jerked like a sprung wooden dance-floor during a full-blooded waltz.

When the soil fell away from under our feet like a scaffold's trap-door falling open, we both dropped like helpless sacks of grain down a chute and the world became black as pitch.

{14}

I came round unhurt and safe, cradled in the Preacher's arms. He'd apparently grabbed at me and cushioned my fall with his strong body. As soon as we hit the bottom he'd clasped me in his arms and run for it, carrying me boldly away from the giant conical mass of the ant mound. What we'd seen of it above ground was little more than the very tip.

I'd read about what happens when a volcano erupts. I reckon what happened to that mound must've been something like that. The strength of the blast woke me from my daze and over the Preacher's shoulder I saw a solid wall of white fire boiling towards us.

'Preacher,' I cried.

He looked around and then dropped to one knee. He opened his coat and held it around my shoulders. A wave of intense heat sucked all the air from my lungs. Preacher opened his mouth wide and planted it firmly over my mouth and nose. When I gasped I sucked in sweet air from the man's throat. I had my eyes closed and I didn't struggle – I knew whatever he was doing, the Preacher was protecting me from harm. I relaxed and breathed and waited until he told me what to do next.

'You okay, Caleb?'

His voice stirred my dreams. I couldn't believe it – I had fallen asleep in his arms. I lurched into a sitting position and tried to shake loose the dumb stupor from my senses.

'Don't worry, Caleb. Shock likely took you away from your wits for a breath or two. You're back now. It's been a few hours but you're dandy.'

With a start I blurted, 'The fire!'

'Yessir. Those ants won't be biting any more horses, I can promise you that much.'

I felt too calm. I should have been twitching like a frog on a hot metal shovel but instead I felt just fine. Even the hangover that'd been biting at the back of my eyes all day had ebbed away to sit like a distant horizon of black storm clouds on an otherwise sunny day.

'Where are we?'

A pallid light was filtering in from somewhere, but it didn't seem to be making much difference to the view. Black and grey dust had softened the outlines of everything around us. My eyes began to water as they strained in an effort to make sense of what I was seeing.

'I reckon we found our way into some old mine workings.'

Preacher did something with his left hand and a cone of white light shone out. Everything else around us was plunged into inky darkness.

'There's tool marks on the walls here and that tunnel over there looks like it's held up with props of timber.'

He indicated his findings with his beam of light the way my school teacher used to point things out on her chalkboard with her cane – when she wasn't using it on my behind to 'learn me a good lesson'.

Preacher looked around him. 'Reckon there's no point in trying to go back the way we came. While you were sleeping I took the opportunity to have a look-see back there and the walls of the cave-in are almost entirely vertical. We can't go up and the tunnel's a dead end.

'We'll have to find another way out of here and my bone of direction tells me to walk down that man-shaped path with the props. What do you say, Caleb? You ready to walk a few miles deep under a hill until we smell fresh air?'

I heaved myself to my feet, in the process throwing off a shower of fine dust. My mouth felt clogged and tasted bitter with an aftertaste of lime and vinegar. I took off my hat and beat at my clothes until I was surrounded by a grey haze of silky powder.

'I'd give my teeth for a drink of water.'

'Already got my own teeth, but you're welcome.'

The Preacher handed me a cylinder that was cold to the touch and showed me how to unscrew the top. That thing was as neatly engineered as a Swiss watch and the water was cool and compelling to the tongue. I could've drunk a lakeful but I tried not to be greedy and restricted myself to a few welcome mouthfuls. I screwed the top back on and handed the cylinder back to the Preacher who made it vanish into the depths of his coat. He bent down and picked up my rifle which he pressed into my grasp.

'Safety's on, Caleb.'

He led the way by the beam of his miraculous light. I didn't know what time it was but I was feeling hungry and those few sips of water had barely touched the dryness gripping at my throat.

'Preacher, how long do you think before we get ourselves out of here?'

'Caleb, my friend, just like you I am a stranger in a strange land. I have not walked these roads before and hope never to again.'

'You don't know?'

'I don't.'

In a way it was a relief. My companion had taken on an almost supernatural glow over the past forty-eight hours and a lot of what he had done, including that breathing trick in the fire, floating around his living room and the magical light he held in his hand, smacked of witchcraft.

Now, I swear on a hill of *Bibles*, I didn't hold with devilry then and I sure don't hold with it now, but if the Preacher was a bad man then I am one of the world's biggest fools for judging a sinner a saint. He was fast with a gun and had pockets full of tricky gee-gaws but what I'd never seen the like of before, but if it came to a fight I'd still rather have him at my side than any other man I'd ever met – and that despite everything I'd learned since I first clapped eyes on God's enemy.

I slid off the safety of my Winchester and made sure my pistol was smooth in its holster. If a man has to draw his gun, he doesn't want it snagging in his vest. I've seen men wearing their holsters so high on their waist that the grip of their gun sits up by their elbow. I hope they never have to use it in anger. By the time they've dragged their hands up that high, any opponent with a lower set weapon will have plugged two shells into their belly.

A man's gun is like any other appendage: use it right and it'll be your friend, but use it wrong and it may just kill you. Preacher wore his belt gun low, just like me, but he favoured his left side.

The tunnel ceiling began to close in and we had to crouch at the waist to keep moving forward. I still had that strange lightness in my mind. I felt like I could cope with anything fate threw at us. My belly was tight with anticipation.

That was when the Preacher turned to me and put his finger to his lips. There was a fierce warning light in his eye.

15

We leave Caleb and the Preacher and return to town. While they were crawling around like dust mites under that hill, Grandma Teatree was taking tea with the banker.

Parrett Damsel-Childs tasted the air around her with his quick, sharp tongue and played with the fluting of his delicate, bone-china cup. Grandma wondered why the man's eyes never pointed in the same direction as his nose. Watching him made her hair itch and she was happy to stay a full table's width away from him.

'How, hm, soon before, hm, we can open the, ah, Palace of Pleasure?'

'Is that what we're calling it?'

'Hm, sorry?'

'The Palace of Pleasure; is that what we're calling it?'

'Hm, ah, well, why not? Have you an, ah, alternative?'

'It's your money, Banker Childs, you name it as you see fit. But those men who we hope will undertake to provide us with their custom are working men. Pussy Parlour might be better. Call a spade a spade.'

The banker looked appalled and gazed askance at Grandma while twisting his mouth around the word as if he would prefer to spit it across the room.

'Hm, no,' he sputtered eventually. 'I will not associate my, ah, name, my reputation, nor my, hm, money with any hint of, hm, the word pussy. Ah, best think, hm, again.'

'Whatever we're going to call it, your ladies are in there right now chasing out the hairy little eight-legged lodgers and screaming like Irish banshees while they do so. I'm told the repairmen are also at work and the kitchen is getting overhauled. The bar should be stocked in about two days and all the rooms will be ready by then.

'We've got red leather divans being delivered tomorrow so the girls have somewhere to sit and look pretty while the men drink and make their assignations. You've promised me bar staff, cooks and a handyman to deal with trouble. If we have the girls we can open by this coming Saturday, if not Friday evening.'

'So, hm, soon? It seems incredible.'

'Goody Marsh at the trading post has told me she's already had a few telegraphs in response to my notice in the *Courier* and the first prospects will be here on the noon train tomorrow. In Texas we do not let the grass grow under our idle feet. Speaking of idle, where's the Sheriff and our reluctant councillor, Spindrift? Has there been any news from them about the murder of that poor boy? A public hanging will be sure to bring customers from far and wide.'

The banker's shoulders quivered while he fluttered his eyes and made an odd snorting sound. Grandma eventually realised that he was laughing with pleasure at the thought.

'Perfect,' he giggled, 'to, ah, hm, speed the return on, ah, our, hm, hm, investment, a man shall dangle from a rope. To break a murderer's neck in a noose seems so apt when we want to quickly, hm, hm, break even.'

His eyes glinted at the thought of money sliding back into his coffers; or was it the vision of the scaffold's polka being danced in the last few moments of a man condemned? Grandma wondered why his speech had suddenly become much less hesitant at the thought.

The door to the room slammed open and the gross figure of Foster Teague poured into the lamplight like a sack of angry butter.

'That God-bothering ass smear of a Preacher needs his reins tightening! I should strap on a pair of Mexican spurs and ride his murdering hide to the hangman's scaffold. And I may just do that.'

'Teague, hm, ah.' The banker gave a warning nod towards Grandma, who was so small the rancher had missed her in the shadows.

'Mizz Teatree, please forgive me. An angry tongue is a thing of shame, I know that. I 'pologise to you fully and without reservation, ma'am.'

'You seem annoyed with the good Preacher Spindrift, Foster. What has he done to set you so at odds with yourself? A man should never let another man get him so riled he forgets himself in front of a lady.'

'Your pardon, Mizz Teatree, but I am sore burned at him. That looned mountebank killed my foreman and his wife, plus the doctor and one of my Mexican hands, and then he burned down their cottage. A cottage, may I say, which was on my land and which I own, and in fact was built to my own particular design. And then he pushed me around in front of my steer wranglers as if I was nothing more than a common little ragamuffin on a spoil heap.'

He pouted with indignation and puffed his purpling, ample cheeks in fury. 'If it was not for my natural poise I might have lost a degree of respect in the eyes of my men. Why, can you believe it? I had to let a good man go because he questioned my authority after seeing the Preacher manhandle me. He manhandled *me*! Then one of my own men pushed me to the ground and *slapped* me? I couldn't keep him on after that, now could I?'

'Which, ah, man did you, hm, have to let go?'

51

'Meads, Samuel Meads. I just saw him. He's over having a beer at Goody's bar in the trading post.'

The banker called to one of his clerks and sent him to fetch Samuel for an interview – if the man was still looking for a position at present.

'We, hm, need a, ha, handyman who, ah, can handle himself.'

'You're giving Meads a job after I turned him away for violence against my own person? What kind of topsy-turvy justice is that?'

'No,' said Grandma. 'If I understand Parrett correctly, we are all offering him a job, including you, Foster. But only if he fits the bill.'

They waited in silence for a few minutes. The only sound was the precise ticking of an extremely ornate ormolu clock on the mantelshelf of the room's elegant fireplace.

Damsel-Childs broke the silence. 'Foster, hm, I'm curious. Why have you not, ah, reported Spindrift's wrongdoing to, hm, Sheriff Sawyer?'

The gross balloon of a man sat down in a chair that creaked painfully under his weight.

'He was there. He was fully complicit in the Preacher's actions. I should've shot both of them while I had the chance.'

'That would have been plain murder, Mr Teague. I could not allow you to make such a play behind a good man's back.'

The square shape of Samuel Meads filled the door frame. He brought with him a faint reek of the bar room.

The rancher blustered and wheezed but said nothing more. He remained collapsed fatly in his chair and waved a flaccid hand at the doorway as if to dismiss his former employee.

Grandma's face creased tightly. 'You are a man who is aware of the rights and wrongs of the law, Samuel Meads?'

'I know enough to not stand by and allow one man to shoot another in the back if I can help it. I will not stand party to a murder or a lynching. Mr Teague was not in his right mind when he took up Willy Conroy's old Henry carbine and took a bead on the Preacher. He had not been fully apprised of the facts of the day and acted on pure instinct. That act could have seen him strung up at the end of a rope. I figure I got let go for saving both his life, and the life of an innocent man. But so be it, such is the hand I've been dealt and now I must play the cards as I see fit.'

He looked around the room as if uncomfortable in such company.

'Fact is,' he said, 'I do believe something unnatural and ungodly has come to the town of Mule's Ass and the Preacher Spindrift and Sheriff Sawyer are out there trying to lay the wicked thing to rest. What I see is abomination coming, and right now I believe a wise man might be better served in looking for employment elsewhere.'

'Please, take a seat, Mr Meads,' said Grandma. 'If you might reconsider that last statement, we may have a proposition for you.'

'Mights and maybes never buttered no greens. So, begging your pardon, Mizz Teatree, but what is it you're asking me, in simple terms?'

'True, Mr Meads, well said. I apologise. May I put it another way? Would you like a job?'

16

Caleb and the Preacher's tale continues.

I could hear it coming from some way ahead of us. It sounded mostly like a waterfall landing on gravel or someone frying a big pan of bacon. Just the thought of food was enough to set a burn of hunger twisting in my belly. It surprised me at first – I thought that after all we'd been through, food would turn my stomach – but I guess a man's mortal body must be fed and we had already endured a great deal that day.

Preacher was almost bent double and had angled his light downwards so it wouldn't give us away too soon. Something told me that his light was largely there for my benefit. Without it my world would have been darker than it was for Captain Ahab in the belly of his whale. Or Jonah.

And then, just as I was thinking of Jonah, he dowsed his light and the tunnel became darker than a moonless midnight. My eyes ached just trying to make out something, anything, in that sable nothingness. I think I must've whimpered like a scared child. I froze.

'Wait, Caleb,' his voice hissed by my ear, 'wait just a few moments longer.'

I was finding it difficult to breathe. The darkness was pressing down on me like a physical force. I was clutched in a great paw and it was squeezing the jelly from my bones. That crackling noise no longer sounded like a big pan of welcome bacon – it sounded more like a giant cat stalking towards me across a forest of dry ribs and splintering them to dust.

And then the miracle happened.

Like the promise of a pale dawn I began to make out shapes around me. The silhouette of the Preacher with his pistol still trained on our way ahead, pit beams and props pressed into the tunnel wall, rats pouring around our feet and back the way we'd come.

Rats. The sound I'd heard was the skittering claws of a torrent of rodents, fighting and clambering over each other to escape whatever was behind them. They were terrified, and whatever put the fear into them was surely sitting in wait for us some way ahead. Or it was set in our direction and would arrive soon. I began to feel sick.

The Preacher started to wade through the living tide of rodents. They were climbing the walls around us in their desperation to get away from whatever had spooked them. The floor and walls of the tunnel were alive with a grey flowing mass of long-tailed muscle and fur.

'Snakes,' said the Preacher.

He was right. Sinuous serpents slithered along with the panicked critters. I wondered for a moment if they were wiser than me. They were running away from something terrible and the Preacher and I were still picking our way towards... what?

That was when bats began to flutter, rustle and peep their way around our ears. *What next*? I wondered. *Racoons? Camels?* We were like two fish trying to fight our way up a melt-filled stream. I wouldn't have been surprised if we'd been suddenly clawed into the teeth of a hungry grizzly, the way I'd once seen salmon caught up in the highlands.

The sound crescendoed until I could have screamed and no one would've heard me. That volume of noise would've swallowed a gunshot. It was impossible to withstand and I was set to fall backwards and be swept away in a fierce torrent of screeching life.

A firm hand took me by the arm and pulled me on through the cascade of cave vermin and we fought our way through until, as suddenly as it had started, it ended, with nothing but the last whispering trickle of spiders big as my hand scuttling away.

The creatures sounded and echoed behind us for a while and then all was silent apart from a metallic drip of water somewhere, regular as a metronome.

'Are you as curious about this as I am, Caleb?'

I wanted to sound brave the way he did, cool and collected. I failed.

'I guess so, Preacher. But what could cause something like that?'

'I think we're going to find out very soon.'

I made sure my safety was off and almost instantly nearly slid onto my ass. The tunnel floor was slick with a thick layer of everything you'd expect when a million terrified rats have just stampeded your way. The stench of it was terrible.

'Easy does it, Caleb.'

We were still walking without lights along a tunnel drilled deep into a hillside. It was impossible to understand how I could see anything in such pitch darkness, but I was grateful for my ghost sight and had decided not to question providence in case it stopped working. The memory of that total darkness chilled me more than the flood of creatures ever could. I prayed then that I should be allowed to die peacefully in my sleep before I ever became old and blind.

What are you thinking about? I reprimanded myself. *You're more likely to die down here without ever seeing the sun again than live long enough to lose your sight to old age. Don't be so foolish.*

I can't explain why but that thought raised my spirits somewhat and I slithered more confidently through that river of rat shit, hastening to keep up with the Preacher's receding back.

Suddenly my feet went from under me and I was bowled over, slamming into the tunnel wall. I cracked my head against the stone and in a sudden shower of sparks was robbed of my ghost sight once more. Yet in the last of the pallid ghost light I'd seen the Preacher staggering to his knees. In a fierce burst of agony and desperation I managed to cling on to my rifle, thinking with whatever was left of my scattered wits that if I dropped it onto that cesspit of a floor I might never find it again, and would I really want to search that hard in such a noxious place? I supposed not.

The tunnel quivered and bucked like a bull steer at a rodeo. Something ominous creaked around me but I decided I'd rather die where I stood than stagger through this nightmare of moving rock, rat filth and blind darkness.

At last the final ripple of fluid movement trembled the stone under my feet and then the world became still once more. I remained frozen in place, too terrified to take my first blind step into the unknown darkness; the utter, utter blackness. I lost all hope. And then, slowly, stripping away the blackness dark veil by stubborn veil, the welcome grey ghost light returned to my eyes and I began to breathe again. Then the first thing I made out was the Preacher, sprawled in a heap and unmoving. He was just a few yards from where I stood. My heart stopped beating. Without his calm wisdom to guide me I prepared to die in that dreadful place. I splashed to his side, any sense of renewed hope draining down out of my ruined boots. Was he dead? Quietly I began to pray to anything that was listening. *Please,* I begged, *don't leave me alone in the dark.*

I reached down to make sure my pistol was still holstered. Its cold hardness brought me little comfort. The Preacher lay still and silent at my feet.

{17}

Back in town events are gathering pace.

Meads accompanied Grandma Teatree over to the staging post so he could examine his new place of work. They stopped at her old rooms first to pick up a few things for her new suite. It was for the best that Meads was a strong man and the distance relatively short. Grandma had been collecting house goods for a long, long while and she intended to take all of them with her. They walked together in comfortable silence until they got to the busy brothel-to-be which was a blaze of light. The sun had gone down a few hours before and the day was getting late, but Damsel-Childs' people were still busy at their work. Enough lamps had been lit to illuminate every dark corner of the place in case some eight-legged incumbents had escaped the earlier purge by scything brooms.

Meads stood for a moment on the hexagon and gazed at the unabated activity in the bar room. A layer of dust floated at eye level and eddied around anyone who walked through it like smoke. Every trace of cobwebs had been cleaned away and the great mirror polished until it was a gleaming slab of light.

Grandma looked at the display of industry with a satisfied smile. The divans would go around the pillars the next day and barrels of beer would be laid then tapped and spiled ready for their twenty-four-hour settle before the grand opening.

Crockery, glasses, food supplies, ashtrays and brass spittoons would be delivered by first thing Friday morning. Her estimations for a weekend grand opening had begun to look conservative. If the girls she timetabled to see the following day fit her ideal image for a decent prostitute, well, she may even be able to bring her opening day forward by twenty-four hours and open her doors Friday evening – and for most of her clients that would be pay day.

'Mizz Teatree, sorry to break your train of thought, but where do you want me to settle your tack?'

'Of course, Samuel, sorry... I was making my plans for the next few days. Those things must be getting heavy. Follow me.'

She led him up the stairs and along the L-shaped landing to her door. She wondered at how she had already begun to feel fiercely proprietary about the place.

She had given instructions that her rooms should be cleaned first and the women had scrubbed and polished at the woodwork until it looked like the inside of an expensive jewellery box.

Fresh bedding had been laid and decent furniture placed in the salon. Even the water closet had been scoured and anyone so inclined could have eaten a meal from its china honey bucket.

While Meads emptied his aching arms onto her table, Grandma glided on silent feet back out onto the landing and addressed the beavering crowd of mop wranglers, scrubbing brush handlers and idiot stick pushers.

'Ladies, thank you. Your work today has been exemplary. That's enough for one day. I shall tell banker Damsel-Childs how pleased I am with your work. Please, go home to your families and your dinners. Well done, you have earned your time of rest. Good night and once again, thank you.'

There was a muttered chorus from the floor and the women carefully stashed their cleaning things in the kitchen. Grandma heard one of the older women mothering and fussing at her colleagues and approved of the way the besom sent some of the younger girls out back to ensure there were no stragglers still hard at work.

In a matter of minutes the last of them had scurried out and Grandma was left alone. She surveyed her silent kingdom with great satisfaction.

'Mizz Teatree?'

She jumped. She had forgotten Samuel Meads.

'Mr Meads, bless you. I was wrapped up in my thoughts.'

'Sorry if I spooked you. I'm all done here. Would you mind if I left and settled myself somewhere for the night?'

'Why of course, Mr Meads. By the way, where do you plan to sleep tonight? I forgot you'd lost your home with your former position.'

'I'll be fine, Grandm... Mizz Teatree. I've got my bedroll and a slicker if the weather turns ornery on me. I'll put myself safely out of the way and grab some shuteye before the morning.'

'You'll do no such thing, Samuel Meads. Come with me.'

She hustled to the next room along and pushed the door open. The room was clean and spare and it had a bed with a straw mattress. A wardrobe was built into one of the walls. An etching of a Wells Fargo stage racing through a cloud of dust and drawn by a team of eight galloping horses was framed on another wall.

'This will be your room, Samuel. Go and fetch your gear and settle in. We'll sort the rest of your fixings tomorrow. Have you eaten?'

Meads looked around the room with mounting pleasure.

'Sure is better than the bunkhouse, ma'am. This is just fine. No, I haven't eaten since lunchtime but that ain't no never mind. I've been hungry before and I guess I will be again.' He paused. 'Never had my own room before. This is just grand. My, my, yes, this is just dandy.'

'Glad you like it, Samuel Meads, but I will not have you going to bed hungry. When you've settled your tack come join me in my salon. I told the ladies to furnish me with a cold dinner because I planned to move into my quarters tonight. We shall share pot luck before retiring.'

'That's right Christian of you, ma'am, but I can't rob you of your meal.'

'I shall be grateful for your company. Now, get a move on, man. It's already late and we'll be starting early.'

Meads grinned and strode out of his room whistling happily. Grandma followed him as far as the bar room then diverted away to hunt for victuals in the kitchen. She eventually found what she was looking for in a zinc-lined cold room set back away from the heat of a big stove range and baking oven.

Back in her salon she set the table, placed two chairs and then went to fetch a few lamps. One she set by the bed in Meads' room and the other she hung from a convenient hook over her table. By the time Meads returned she was busying herself turning off all the lamps on the ground floor and making sure everywhere was locked and secure.

'I could have done all that, Mizz Teatree. You needn't have bothered yourself with such things.'

The face she turned on him was one of such fury that the bearlike man took a step backwards.

With a voice like a hammer on metal she said, 'We're getting on just fine, Samuel Meads, but if you make the mistake of thinking of me as a useless old woman or a failing body that needs picking up after, well, we shall have to rethink the entire nature of our relationship. I do not need to be looked after by you or any other man. We've wasted enough time on this and I see you are laden with your tack. Go settle your room and then join me in my suite. Shake a leg, man.'

Minutes later he stuck his head around her door and rapped his knuckles on one of its panels.

'Samuel, come in. Have you washed up yet?'

He examined his hands. 'I guess not, ma'am.'

'In there is some water in a jug and a bowl. There's good white soap in a dish and a towel on the rail. Get yourself clean and then join me.'

He looked longingly at the food on the table for a moment and she heard his stomach grumble like a starving bear, but he meekly walked into the water closet and she soon heard him splashing around.

Cold pie, crusty white bread, cheese, ham and apples were mounded under the lamplight alongside a pat of fresh butter and pots of pickle and mustard. The still damp Meads waited until Grandma had said grace and filled her own plate before he addressed his own needs.

He's a polite boy, she thought, watching while the big square man fought his natural inclination to fill his mouth until his cheeks were bulging.

'Samuel, I find food so much more satisfying when I chew it, don't you?'

He swallowed a mouthful of pie and said, 'Guess so, ma'am.'

She poured them both a cup of light beer from a cold jug and raised hers to him.

'To the future, Samuel Meads.'

He put his knife down long enough to take up his drink.

'The future, Mizz Teatree.'

And that was when the floor began to shake as if it was trying to tip them both out of their chairs and the lamp started to swing wildly on its hook.

{18}

In the darkness Caleb feared the worst.

I'd barely reached the Preacher's inert body when he stirred then leapt to his feet. I'd never seen a man move quite like it. He seemed to jump from sprawled and broken on the ground to upright and ready for action without any middle ground. He came up like a jack rabbit in a lightning storm come Easter.

'Caleb? You're bleeding.'

'I am?'

'This is not the perfect environment for an open wound, my friend. Come... sit here on this rock for a moment.'

I sat like an obedient schoolboy with my rifle pressed across my knees. Preacher reached into his long coat again and pulled out what looked like a silver box and a pouch of some fine material. Thanks to that unearthly pale light I could see what he was doing well enough, but everything I saw was drained of colour. That pouch could've been red, blue or green and it'd have made no difference to the way I saw it that night.

Preacher took a bottle from his pouch and sprayed something onto his hands, and then he did the same to me.

'Now,' he said, 'rub them together. Like this. That's it, good. Now, please, shut your eyes.'

I did as I was bid. Something tart and cold washed over my forehead and I felt a sharp sting followed by a brief tugging sensation against my skin. A fine streak of heat warmed the flesh directly over my right eyebrow and I felt Preacher's fingers rubbing away a layer of gritty, salt-like stuff.

'We both need a bath,' he said, 'but that should keep us going until we find fresh water. How do you feel, Caleb? You can open your eyes now.'

I hesitated, afraid the ghost light had deserted me, and then looked up. The Preacher's strong face looked back at me from just a few inches away, concern stamped into every feature clear as daylight.'

'I'm fine, Preacher Spindrift, I am, thank you; but what about you? You were out cold for a while there. Are you really okay?'

'Caleb, I'm one tough nut to crack. Takes more than an earthquake to bring down a Spindrift, I can promise you that. You ready to find a way out of this?'

I got gingerly to my feet. I would've liked to stretch some kinks out of my back but the low ceiling kept me slightly crouched over. The parts of me that didn't already feel bruised were threatening to cramp.

'Let's get going.'

We didn't talk much. I felt as if the weight of the entire world was pressing down on my shoulders, and I needed to concentrate hard to avoid slamming my head against knuckles of stone jutting down from the ceiling, or sliding onto my knees in the filthy, slick mess we were wading through.

The Preacher muscled his sure-footed way through those tunnels like he was born to it. I'm sure he could've left me behind any time he felt like it, but he stuck by my side until we finally smelled a current of delicious fresh air coming from somewhere ahead.

Thankfully I was still feeling strong enough to climb up the tumbled slope of rock and scree we finally reached after another uneventful hour or so of crouching our way through those haunted tunnels. Preacher surmised that we must've been climbing upwards for a while and, without knowing it, got close enough to the surface for a roof collapse during the 'quake to open us a path to freedom. I didn't care which way it had happened, I just wanted to get out in the open and near caused a landslide in my mad scramble up that slope to clean air and freedom.

I dread to think what civilised company would've made of us had it met us gratefully climbing up out of a dark hole in the ground and into the fresh, sweet air that night. They might've taken us for devil-damned dead men clawing their way up out of their righteous graves. I suppose we should rightfully have *been* dead after our series of calamities. I certainly looked battered and dirty enough to be a revenant.

I stretched my aching back like a long cat and looked upwards; all thoughts of murderers and the nightmare creatures we'd met and killed were washed away under that vast bowl of night sky.

I'd never seen so many stars. Anyone who has ridden the range at night has to know their way around the heavens. The Lord put pointers up there that act like a guide and a compass in the darkness; and the stars tell tales older than Methuselah, if you know how to read them.

I wrenched myself away from that black Hades of stone and stink and stood tall under millions upon millions of stars. I saw clouds of sparkling colour and streamers of light burn in glory. I almost wept for joy.

Beside me the Preacher was praying in words I didn't recognise except the last one, 'Amen', and my heart was right there behind every sound he made.

Amen, and thank you, Lord.

'Your vision will be back to normal soon, Caleb. For now enjoy seeing your creator's work through the eyes of an angel, and those of an archangel too!'

I wanted to breathe under that impossible sky, run in that fresh light and bathe in Holy Spirit. But first I needed to wash rat shit from my hair.

'Where are we, do you think?'

The Preacher looked around. I swear for a moment I saw the universe reflected in his eyes. I wondered at how awesome he looked and his skin shone like precious metal. Then the scales of glory fell away from my sight and the familiar man spoke to me once more with merely earthly lips.

'The mine's over there where that orange light glows. Sweet Alice flows down there and the caved-in ants' mound is some four or five miles away in that direction. That puts the town over yonder. We have a ways to walk before we see any trails, but I suggest that whatever we do, we do it away from here. Any more of that tunnel roof collapsing will drop us straight back down into those mine workings we've been so very pleased to escape.'

'Let's get away from here. I'm right behind you, Preacher.'

He paused a moment and looked up into the heavens. 'Come, let us take our path like silent thieves in the night, our stolen treasure scattered across the dome of heaven.'

'Say, what?'

'Have we not stolen the gift of the heavens by escaping from the dark earth? And do we not walk as the Gods themselves once walked upon the land?'

I said nothing to that. What could I say? But I guess my face spoke volumes.

He looked at me and laughed; a light and easy sound.

'Don't worry, Caleb. I guess you had to be there to make sense of that one. That story was told long ago and I'm still paying the price for my crime.'

He slapped me across the shoulder and the bitter, acrid tang of tunnel dust filled my nostrils.

'I may never wear these clothes again,' I said.

'We'll freshen up soon enough when we're back in town.'

Then he hissed, 'Caleb, quiet. Get down.'

Mule's Ass had also suffered the effects of the earthquake.

As soon as the floor stopped swaying like a small boat in a big swell, Grandma leapt to her feet and raced faster than a whipped Arab into Mead's room. Startled by her spry turn of speed, he chased after her and found her bent over by the side of his bed, which was still cluttered with the tack he'd fetched a scant hour earlier. The thick smell of coal oil came up to their noses.

'Thank God for that.'

'What?'

'I put a lit lamp in your room, Samuel. See – it tipped over but the flame has gone out. We were lucky there.'

She made a little gesture with her right hand and touched her shrivelled lips to her swollen knuckles.

'No, ma'am, it wasn't providence. I tamped the lamp down. I didn't see why we should waste good coal oil on an empty room, and anyhow, I see well enough in the dark.'

'You are a blessing, Samuel Meads, a blessing. And now I suppose we should go out into the town and see how we may be good, thoughtful neighbours for any souls who need us. Damn, I'm tired, but getting shaken about like a rat in a barrel has waked me up. Samuel?'

'Let's go out there and do some good, Mizz Teatree.'

When they carried their lamp down to floor level they saw that the big mirror had fallen and smashed behind the bar.

'That's seven years of powerful bad luck right there.'

'I disagree, Samuel. Our customers will have something much better to look at than to admire their own mule faces in a glass. A besom and a shovel will clear away any bad luck in but a few minutes.'

Out on Main Street dazed townspeople stood talking in groups. Grandma and Meads moved among them, taking an elbow here and placing a reassuring hand on a shoulder there. Levine asked for help to rescue some ponies that had become trapped when part of one of his stable roofs collapsed and a number of men joined him, grateful to find something useful to do.

The shock had been hard and brief but also relatively harmless, or so it seemed at first. Goody Marsh was tending Sung Li, her cook, who had been scalded on the arm when a big pot of chicken stock nearly fell off the range and he rushed to rescue it. He had tough cook's hands, which were unharmed, but a splash of hot liquid had blistered his forearm and caught one of his cheeks.

He often worked through the night to make his signature gravy, which went just as well with biscuits as it did with many other things on Goody's famous menu: steak and potatoes, stewed mutton, pork with Polk salad leaves or twice-cooked chicken with beans and bacon were among the most popular.

The poor man sat looking disconsolate with his arm bathed in a bowl of ice cold river water and an ice pack at his face, but he was still able to nod and reassure people that his precious stock had been saved and gravy was still on the menu.

Goody told him it was a result of his skills in the kitchen that people came to the trading post with their mouths watering 'fit to drooling like hogs at the trough'.

'But none of them,' she advised, 'want to find out what *you* taste like boiled up like stew meat. Next time that pot starts to fall, get out of its way. We can always make more gravy, cook man, but we can't replace you!'

Some horses had hurt themselves while lashing out in fear, but only one needed real attention to draw a long splinter from its hindquarters. The splinter came out cleanly but the horse needed a stitch or two to stem the flow of blood, an operation performed with immense delicacy by Heck Levine himself and overseen by a nervous audience.

There had been one fatality. Willy 'Aces' Cotton had won a fistful of cash at the poker table in front of a number of witnesses. He had won the money fair and square but was worried some 'misbegotten sly boots' would try to take their share during the night.

He fell asleep with the money under his pillow and his gun cocked and loaded on his chest. When the quake tumbled him from his bunk he must've landed wrong because he managed to shoot himself under his jaw with a .44 ball at point-blank range. The second person to find him the next morning, the owner of the boarding house where he was a guest and late for breakfast, was horrified to see his corpse on the floor with most of the top of his head missing and his cot a mess of blood, brains and bone.

Her shriek brought other guests running and they all took one long look at the dead man before ushering the poor woman out of the room. Two of them had lost a tidy sum to Aces the previous evening and they made a careful sweep of his room in the hope of getting some of it back. There was nothing to be found. Whoever had discovered Aces' misfortune first was considerably the richer for it. Exactly who it might be was never discovered.

Heck Levine claimed Mule's Ass had 'ridden the earthquake like a gaucho at a ranchero's rodeo' and his neighbours agreed. Some plaster around the windows in the bank would need repair and a few tiles had come off the jailhouse roof. Other than these the other, wooden buildings seemed untouched. Some of the townsfolk proudly celebrated their town's toughness by falling to their knees in thanks and a hasty service was called in the church hall by the school mistress, Annie Davey. Others took to their cups and let off steam by drunkenly riding their ponies around the stockyards and loosing shots from their hand guns into the air until their chambers were empty. Luckily they were also too drunk to reload them.

The questions were legion. Why had the town suffered an earthquake for the first time in recorded history? What was Samuel Meads doing walking out with Grandma Teatree? Where was Sheriff Sawyer? He should have been right there pouring oil on the drunken troubled waters by the stockyard. And it wasn't just his lawman's badge that was missed. Some men hadn't seen a straight razor for two days and it was considered a real boon that no one except Sung Li had been badly hurt because Sawyer was the closest thing they had to a saw-bones. The nearest real doctor was way over in Shafter and he charged by the hour including travel. News of Dr Emerson's demise at Vickery's place had still to become general knowledge.

The few townsfolk who suffered cuts and abrasions were treated by Heck Levine and none were the worst for it. Some even tried the green stuff he administered to his injured horse as a sedative before threading his needle. For some time afterwards he made a lucrative income from selling bottles of his 'horse remedy' to those same people. I never did learn what was in it – but I never tried it either.

And, the people asked, where was Preacher Spindrift in this hour of need? Annie Davey was pretty enough to stand before the congregation and offer up words, but you need more than cow eyes, auburn hair and a slim waist when it comes to thanking the Lord properly for his bounty. You need fire and brimstone and the Preacher brought both to the altar.

Others wanted to know what had happened to Baylee Baker. He did all the little jobs that others preferred to leave alone, and without him the town was taking on a distinctly unpleasant aroma. Night soil was beginning to fill unattended honey buckets to the brim and piles of horse dung had begun turning Main Street into a stinking and slippery morass. Baylee was a simpleton but he was also an iron-backed grafter, and without him Mule's Ass was becoming too true to its name.

The strange stench that had pervaded the town ever since the quake was laid at Baylee's door – and some of that was justified – but that alien stink was about much more than just horses' dung.

It would later prove to be a precursor to a nightmare.

{20}

Caleb and the Preacher had far more pressing concerns than horse dung and gravy.

I heard men's voices coming closer. They were speaking quietly but sounded angry and were talking over each other in a rapid, oily growl. Preacher pressed me down flat to the ground and lay next to me with his hand gun stretched out before his face.

The mysterious ghost light that illuminated the mine's tunnels for me was still working, but even by squinting I couldn't make out what I was looking at other than it was a mass of moving shadows.

Then one line of speech rang out clear as crystal and suddenly I could hear the whole sorry gang damning themselves from their own filthy mouths.

'Took forever to break that lumber boy's neck; someone could have stumbled on us while we worked.'

'If'n we'd known then what we know now we could've let him be and welcomed him to the Host.'

'He was squealin' like a pig at slaughterin' time. Choking him at least shut 'im the fuck up.'

'He was a real good fuck too. Lucky you boys loosened up his ass a mite for me. For a big man he was so tight, I'm surprised he could shit through that little girl's butt hole.'

'No longer our concern is it, flesh of the Sha-aneer?'

'Sssss, we have a whole world to fuck now.'

'These are golden days for the Host, sure enough. Now, where d'ya think that noise came from…'

They continued in this fashion as they stumbled past us, ignorant that every word they uttered was heard by the ear of the law. They were crowded together so tight they were tripping over each other's feet. Then they paused.

'That shite pile, Satan, is here. I can smell it. That ancient soul stinks of Eden.'

The men stumbled around in a closely packed group and I became very aware of an all-too-familiar stench. The Preacher sprang to his feet and shone his bright light directly at the murdering curs. What snarled back at him would have made a coyote throw a fit.

Once it had been three men – and in a way I guess it still was – but it was three men mashed together into a boiling ball of pus and kicking worms. The thing issued a high-pitched wailing howl and tried to run at us but the

Preacher emptied his Peacemaker into the mess and it dropped in a writhing heap, parts of it lashing the ground like a whip.

I had my rifle butt to my shoulder and blew some chunks out of the dreadful creature but the Preacher put his hand out to stay me.

'Wait... not yet.'

He already had one of his crystal globes to hand and he lobbed it underhand at the beast. It landed intact.

'Now,' he said.

I shattered it with a single shot and I could see the black and red flesh of the monster trying to stretch as far away as possible from the spray of glass and thick fluid.

The flare of white flame blinded me and I threw up an arm to shield my dazzled eyes from its glare. A spray of fire enveloped the twisting mass and its shrieking howl got louder and higher until only bats could've heard the sounds of its agony. I don't remember much heat coming off the inferno, but I reckon that pyre would've been plainly visible for miles around if anyone had been looking to see it.

I sat down feeling weary and sick. We had come full circle and destroyed the men who had murdered Klosky, but who knew what nightmare had taken them in its sway? The Preacher sat beside me and we watched together as the fleshy furnace burned brighter, brighter, brighter – and then was done. The abomination had been rendered to a fine, clean ash.

'I think that's enough for now, Caleb. Our job's done for now.'

Preacher climbed stiffly to his feet and reached down to help me stand. Every knock and scrape I'd suffered for two days twanged in my sinews like a Jew's harp played by a tone deaf fool, and I groaned softly. Spindrift strode through the ashes left by the beast's cremation but I had a more delicate sensibility and walked carefully around the drifting mound of fine grey powder.

'Satan? Once again they called you Satan. Why?'

He continued walking without missing a step but I saw his shoulders stiffen. In the grey light of pre-dawn I saw he was carefully reloading his pistol from the cartridges at his belt. The shells for my rifle had been left in a sack in one of poor Missy's saddle bags and had burned with her. I mourned for my fine horse, her strong back and legs. She would not be carrying me again. It was going to be a long walk back to town.

Preacher found a hog trail down the hill and the going got much easier. I was able to walk by his side instead of dogging him Indian fashion. When he realised I was at his left shoulder he stopped abruptly and allowed me to gain a few paces on him. He then re-joined me, only now he was walking at my left side.

'Never let a man crowd your shooting arm, Caleb, not even a good friend. I'm a southpaw and you're right-handed. Walking this way, we're both free to fire if we need to.'

He was right, but I'd never thought it through like that before. I nodded and said nothing.

'Satan,' he said, quietly. 'It's my name, the one and only, the original. Anyone else with the name is worth less than a plugged nickel. The enemy knows me. It's known me for a great number of years, almost longer than I care to remember, and I've been waiting for it to make its move. The time has come.'

'Preacher,' I said, 'so what? Satan or Caleb, what does it matter? It's just a name, after all. I can see by looking at you that you aren't some horned beast from Hell. Why, you wear a collar and a cross and you shoot a straight pistol. You walk tall and you fight the good fight. I don't know just what it is we're fighting, by the way, but I would be dead and gone or turned into a thing of nightmares if it wasn't for you. You're aces with me.'

'Thank you, Caleb. I'm happy to think of you as a friend too. We've seen much this last night and I fear the game is still far from over. But look, we have time to rest for a spell and I have a story to tell that just might prove too thick a piece of gristle for a Christian man to swallow.'

After giving me a pauper's taste of the tale he would speak no more on the subject while we picked our way down that dry gulch. The sun rose and shone directly into our eyes and I had lost my hat in the night's confusions, so I was squinting so hard my eyes were almost closed tight against its glare. I guess that was why I nearly fell back down the hole where the ant mound had been and the Preacher had to haul me to safety.

The place where Missy had burned was still grey and scorched, but it was cool and cleaner smelling now. There was nothing left of her or my saddle and bags. I marvelled aloud at how hot that fire must've burned.

I felt a deep fatigue grip me and I resigned myself to the long walk back to town. I hoped the Preacher wouldn't mind if we took a few minutes to rest up in the cemetery where there were some weather-beaten benches where we could set up and enjoy the view for a while. I admit I was feeling mighty sorry for myself; my spirits had sunk to a really low ebb.

That was when I heard a low nickering noise and I looked up to see the Preacher rubbing the nose of his bay horse. That animal was one of the proudest examples of horseflesh I had ever seen and they looked real pleased to see each other once again. The pure loyalty of a brute beast can shame lesser men.

The Preacher mounted her then called me over to join him. I said no at first, that I would be right pleased to walk, but he insisted and I gratefully climbed up behind him.

I think I must have dozed for the whole time we were riding, because the next thing I remember was the face of Grandma Teatree pressed up close against mine.

{21}

New members of the cast had taken their first steps onto the town's stage.

The first girls to answer Grandma's invitation sent a ripple of interest through the town when they stepped down from a coach of the GH&SA Texas and Pacific midday flyer. They had an exotic quality about them that the townswomen instantly distrusted and men folk reacted to like they were human catnip.

There were five of them and they fluttered around the railroad stop in a chirruping flock. Meads watched them from one side, careful not to approach until he was absolutely certain he was getting the right signals. He didn't want to ask an innocent woman if she had just arrived for her interview with the madam of a cathouse.

'Ladies, excuse me,' he eventually called. 'Are any of you here to see Madam Teatree?'

They were. He bade them follow him down Main Street and found himself explaining to one large creature that the house was close by and they wouldn't require a carriage for such a short distance – and then to another that, yes, refreshments would be served at the house.

The women walked in a dense cloud of sweet scent but he was also keenly aware of something earthier. He noticed some of them wore clothes that would need repair before long, and that none of them carried much baggage. He had little personal experience of women of their profession and his curiosity was piqued. He wondered if there would be much call for clothing in their immediate future. Before reaching the house he had decided to set his mind to rest and reasoned he would learn everything he needed to know soon enough.

Other than the paint, perfume and fancies with which they were adorned the women carried themselves with a thrusting gait he had never seen in a woman before – or a man for that matter, except perhaps some of the more flamboyant Mexican gauchos.

The tarts strutted through the town and gazed around the place with a predatory, proprietary air. *Wherever we walk,* they seemed to be saying with every sinuous step, *it's ours. We own it, cock, stock and baggage.* Meads liked women as much as any man, but these women were much too aggressive for his more conservative tastes.

Damsel-Childs' people were still bustling around the old staging post when he led his little flock of whores into the bar room. The remains of the shattered mirror had been cleared away but the ornate gilt frame had been rehung in its old place. He found himself looking at the section of wall surrounded by the frame as if it held some special interest for him.

The place was coming together despite the quake the night before. Red leather divans had been positioned around the long room's pillars and the station behind the gleaming mahogany bar looked properly stocked and ready for business. It looked welcoming enough as a bar, but he wondered how it would appear with the new arrivals draped all over it.

Grandma Teatree called down from the landing outside her suite of rooms.

'Samuel, bring the ladies up here. They must be parched after their journey and we would be poor hosts if we didn't remedy that forthwith.'

Grandma's salon had been furnished with a motley collection of chairs, but in the first instance the women just wanted to dump their gear and pour themselves pints of beer or lemonade from jugs on the table. The large woman asked Meads if there was any gin to hand 'for a thirsty workin' girl', but it was Grandma who answered her question.

'What's your name, girl?'

The whore looked down at Grandma with frank curiosity.

'You be her, Madam Teatree?'

'I am she, yes, and you?'

'I'm known as Long Lizzie.'

Grandma nodded. 'Lizzie, remember something will you? This is my house. This house has not been opened to be a place where you girls can get drunk and stupid in the middle of the day, but as a place where paying customers can take their ease and enjoy a little female grace – at a price. This is a good clean house, a house that will reward you for your services. In return I expect you ladies to be professional and make our clients feel so welcome they will come back and ask for you by name. Do you understand me, Long Lizzie?'

The big woman shrugged; an action that set a lot of her anatomy into dangerous motion. Meads had to drag his gaze away. Grandma's black eyes glittered with a hard brilliance.

She said, 'I will accept one such shrug from you, Long Lizzie, just the one and no more. You do not know me yet, and I shall make allowance for your ignorance. So, once more, do you understand me, Lizzie?'

This last was said with a menacing purr.

'Yes, Madam Teatree, I sure do!'

'Thank you, Lizzie. I appreciate it when such a simple lesson is so quickly learned.' Her ebon glare swept the room. 'I trust all of you ladies are in agreement with Long Lizzie here?'

The force of her character was so strong that Meads nearly joined the women's chorus of 'Yes, Madam Teatree.'

'Excellent. Then I am sure we shall get along just fine. Now then, shall we get to our business? Samuel, will you please shut the door?'

Meads did as he was bid. He had no idea what Grandma intended but he also didn't want a Long Lizzie style talking to in front of a group of whores.

'Thank you, Samuel. Now, ladies, I would be grateful if you were to give me your names.' When all the women began to respond at once, Grandma held up her hands.

'One at a time, please!' She pointed at a wriggling brunette. 'You, my dear.'

Mary Gold, Pony Black, Red Jane and Lauren Maplesweet joined the roster begun by Long Lizzie, and their names were duly entered into a small leather-bound book next to that day's date. Grandma tucked the book and her silver pencil into a pocket at the front of her skirts.

She creased her prune-like face into a mask of cross-hatched lines.

'Very good. Excellent. So then, ladies, I would like you to remove your clothes.'

There was a sudden flutter of consternation among the women, some of whom glanced coyly at Meads and then back at the diminutive tyrant. Napoleon himself could have learned lessons from Grandma Teatree when she was under a full head of steam. Her iron will would never bend to that of another.

'Let us not be foolish,' said Grandma, reaching out a shrivelled yet surprisingly strong hand to grab at his sleeve when Meads made as if to leave the room.

'I believe you, ladies…' She paused for a moment when she said the word as if trying it on for size. 'Ladies? Yes, why not? I believe you, ladies, have been buck naked in front of men before, and Mr Meads is a professional gentleman. You need have no modesty before him.

'In fact,' she warmed to her little tirade, 'if I am not around at any time you will treat Samuel Meads as if he was me. Am I clear, ladies?'

There was another chorus of yelped yesses.

'Good. Well then, ladies, why don't we all make the actions fit the words and get naked as nature intended?'

For a few dreadful moments, Meads had a very real fear that Grandma was also planning to disrobe, and he was extremely grateful when it became evident she had no such intention. He had a rich imagination though, and a fearfully dry and wrinkled image leapt to his appalled mind with cobwebbed vigour. He dragged his attention back to reality and saw Grandma regarding him with puckish archness.

The tarts stripped down to their gartered stockings and their painted faces stood out in stark contrast to their raw-boned, pale carcases. In next to no time he was confronted by what seemed a butcher's gallery of silk-covered legs and beribboned raw flesh – and in the centre of it stood Grandma Teatree. With a sense of creeping nausea he realised the wizened old madam was sniffing with deep concentration at the exposed bodies of her new charges.

22

Another, distinctly individual, man enters the story.

For what seemed a detested age, Emmanuel Maria Fernandez sat mournfully on his stool of comfort above his deeply dug cess pit. He had a fierce hatred of all bodily functions, and the filthy effluent his body insisted on creating on a daily basis, no matter how little he consumed, depressed him intensely. He considered his bowels as traitors to the purity of his soul. He wished he could disown them completely and live like a flower by absorbing sunlight and rainwater. He had nearly achieved his goal. Thanks to his almost non-existent diet, Emmanuel had rendered himself down to a ragged leaf of a man, an exhausted reed trembling in the slightest breeze. His breath smelled oddly chemical, like pear drops.

His ribs shelved down to a hollowed belly and his hip bones stood out as sharply as his ridged eye sockets, out from which sunken bowls gazed black, smudged orbs of a rich brown. He refused to look in a mirror because his eyes reminded him of everything he hated.

The stink, my God, the stink... it was worse that day than ever before. He would have to throw some ashes down there again.

Someone had once told him that brewer's yeast did something to combat the foul smell. He'd buy some from the trading post when he next visited town. A sudden up-draft made him retch. He'd go into town the next day. It had become a priority.

His body had finished its despised functions and he wiped himself and then washed himself scrupulously with white soap and water that had been warm when he first entered the narrow outhouse but now was merely tepid. He buckled his pants back around his waist and sighed. He would have to punch yet another hole in the leather and the slack already almost circled his shrunken frame twice.

That was when he noticed the little red and black bug on the door frame. He hated bugs too. This one had a wormy look to it. He didn't recognise it and wondered how it had found its way into his outhouse. He supposed it was one of those vile things that floated under a canopy of silk until it could embed itself in some poor dumb brute's hide. *Bastard little beasts!*

The stench from the cess hole strengthened suddenly and with furious malice he rammed his thumb down to crush the squirming creature. He felt it press against his skin – and then it was gone. He looked at his thumb... nothing. He squinted at the door frame expecting to find clear ichor and the creature itself smeared flat. Nothing there either. He washed his hands with soap and water again then emptied the wash bowl into the cesspit.

Before opening the outhouse door he looked out through the crescent moon shape cut into its wooden panelling. He'd been told bears were sometimes attracted to such places and he didn't want to meet one empty-handed. He supposed he could crown it with his wash bowl and wondered why he hadn't brought his Smith and Wesson out with him.

He'd dug this latest cess pit a good distance from his house so he wouldn't be able to smell it when he wasn't using it, but it also meant he had a greater distance to cover both on the way there and on his way back. He'd seen bears in the distance; he didn't intend to get close enough to dance with one.

He walked the long yards to his house in cautious spirals until he reached his back door and unlatched it, and then he quickly scampered to the drawer where he kept his gun. He drew it out and brandished it wildly in the air. The effect was reduced somewhat when his pants dropped to his bony ankles and almost tripped him up. *Time to sort out that belt again.* He hauled the corduroy puddle back up to his waist, thrust the heavy pistol into his pocket and went down into his kitchen where he kept his awl, cinching his pants tightly to his navel with both hands.

He found his awl and sat in his bentwood chair. He drew his belt tight, marked the spot where it would hold his pleated trousers firmly around his shrunk hips, and then set to boring a new hole.

His thumb stung while he worked and he looked at it with dulled curiosity at first and then mounting horror. In the centre of the ball of his thumb was a swelling blister, and clearly visible under the liquid-filled swelling something alive coiled and lashed around. Emmanuel whimpered in shock.

In frantic desperation to deal with such a dreadful invasion of his body he rushed over to his stove and thrust the tip of his awl into the flames. He held it there until the skin of his hand began to feel roasted and the hairs on his forearm crisped to a light ash.

Once the sharp point of his awl was white-hot he thrust it into the ball of his thumb. The reaction was instantaneous. From fingertips to elbow his left arm bloomed with an incredible white light and his kitchen filled with a smell like boiling vinegar. He dropped the awl and it scorched a black line on his wooden floor. Emmanuel held his arm away from his body with a dull moan. The pain hadn't reached his brain yet – it was too swamped with his terror.

Unattended, his trousers fell to his ankles once more and he had to shuffle like a shackled felon to his long-handled water pump by the big butler's sink in the corner of the kitchen. The brilliant flare that had once been his hand and forearm was weakening. The vinegar smell became one of roasting meat. With the wild strength of despair, he pumped cold water into the sink and thrust the stump of his arm into the icy stream. The heat of its flame had cooked and cauterised the stump. Even the bone had burned away to a fine ash and left behind a shiny, domed, tar-like cap just above where his elbow used to be.

Shocking waves of pain began to pulse from his vanished fingertips, and Emmanuel's moans grew into desperate howls of agony. He scattered dishes by the sink until he found a big enough bowl to fill with water in which he could bathe the blackened stump. The cold water soothed the pain a little. At last he was able to hitch up his pants with his remaining hand and, with considerable difficulty, press the tongue of his belt buckle into the new hole he'd just made.

Carrying the bowl in his right hand and sloshing water all around him, he lurched back up the stairs to his bedroom. His body was becoming twisted and tortured in mounting waves of almost unendurable torment and he was uncontrollably quivering in shock. He gritted his teeth and pulled himself together, cursing at himself for a weakling and a fool.

Neither was true. Emmanuel was an imaginative and sensitive man, but he was also a dogged survivor. Whatever had invaded his flesh had been burned away in cleansing flame. He had not expected the filthy infection to be quite so deep-rooted but it was now gone. That was the result he had wanted when he stabbed at it with his white hot awl. Half an arm was a great price to pay, but it was better than to allow the disgusting vermin full access to his starving body.

On the cabinet by his bed was a green fluted corked bottle of what he thought of as his 'sleep tincture'. His wolf-hungry belly often tormented his dreams at night, and Emmanuel had found a few drops of his tincture in a small glass of sipping whiskey would allow him a deep and dreamless repose. It was paregoric.

He opened the bottle with his teeth, spat out the cork and threw down a mouthful of the bitter, brown, anise-flavoured stuff. The relief was almost instant. He sat on his bed and breathed deeply. The bowl of water almost fell from his knees and he snatched at it. A wave of lassitude swept over him as the opiate took a firmer hold and he almost surrendered to sleep, but his will to live was stronger.

He shoved his pistol into his belt and his recorked bottle of paregoric into his pants pocket. With a weaving stride he made his way outside to work out how he was going to saddle his sturdy little pony using just one hand.

23

Caleb woke in a state of bemused confusion.

Grandma Teatree gazed closely at me in mute examination, and then turned to face the Preacher. I looked at him too. It had been a long two days and I hadn't slept much. I was barely awake and floated in a kind of watery dream state, but I remembered everything he'd told me. He said he was the original, the gold-plated, the one-and-only Satan. What was I supposed to do with that revelation?

He also wore a collar and a cross and, Goddamn it, I liked him. He had saved my life without once ever asking for thanks, but he'd also done things I couldn't explain, or even quite believe, when they were pulled out of my memory under the cold light of day.

He had dragged that skinned rat thing from my chest and made it vanish, caught me when I jumped at the Vickery's place like I was a baby, and given me air to breathe while also protecting me in the burning white heart of a fire storm. The number of strange things he'd done would've given any sane man pause to wonder, but I just accepted them because he was my friend. He was the Preacher, even when his actions made my head spin. He didn't like to be pestered with too many questions, but if ever a man gave rise to questions it was Preacher Satan Spindrift.

A sharp voice barked out, 'Are you trying to get this boy killed?' Grandma waved an angry arm at me like a tiny black fury. Her glossy black hair was loose and hung down her back. In my dream state I wondered at its youthful gleam and I wondered what she'd looked like when she was young. I wondered whether she'd turned men's heads or their stomachs. Something about her confidence told me it was probably the former. Under that time-ravaged hide her younger self walked in beauty. I smiled to myself and wished I had a magic glass so I could see her the way she once was.

'You're alright, Preacher, you can walk away from those nightmares without a scratch, but poor Sawyer here will get his neck broke or worse if you aren't more careful.'

'He's a very good man to have at your side in a tight spot,' said the Preacher. 'He won't lose his head when the wrong cards are dealt, and he won't turn his back on a fight no matter what gets thrown at him. He has a good, strong heart, and I know I can trust him. Hush now. He's awake.'

I made out I hadn't been listening. I was certainly groggy enough to be convincing on that score. I realised I was back in the Preacher's bed and made to sit up and that thrust my body into a whole world of pain. I groaned.

Grandma came over and spoke softly to me. 'You've run a very hard race, Sheriff Sawyer, and your body is taking full payment for carrying you that long, long distance. How do you feel?'

'Fine,' I groaned, 'but I wouldn't want to wrestle a bear for the next few hours. I'm thirsty as hell and hungry as a hog, but I mostly feel fine thanks, Mizz Teatree.'

The Preacher leaned across with a moisture-beaded clay pitcher and a tall glass.

'Drink this, Caleb.'

I ignored the glass, held the pitcher in both of my shaking hands and took a long draught from the cool, fresh-tasting liquid. It was delicious and I felt it flow down my parched throat to bloom like an ice flower in my chest. I gobbled another mouthful and then another until the pitcher was empty and then I breathed out a long, satisfied sigh.

Whatever that good brew was it wasn't alcohol, but it buoyed my spirits just fine. The pain ebbed out of me and I felt my head poised high on my shoulders once more. I felt strong and my head was clear as dew. *Bring me that bear,* I thought. *I'm ready as I'll ever be.*

I climbed out of bed and stretched like an athlete before I suddenly realised I was buck naked in front of the old crone and looked around for something to cover my shame. It was too late to jump back in bed so I stood stock still with my arms folded across my chest and waited for the screams to start. They didn't. Grandma made no pretence about being shocked or looking elsewhere. In fact the game old pirate just grinned like a happy prune and looked me over like I was a stud horse at an auction. Then she slapped a hand to her forehead.

'That reminds me,' she said. 'I've got the first girls turning up in about an hour. I'd better go get things ready. Good to see you looking so... fit and well again, Sheriff. Let me know if you need anything. Be seeing you too, Preacher.'

And with a last, long appraising glance at me she was gone.

'That was embarrassing,' I said.

'Old girl takes her pleasures where she may,' offered the Preacher.

'Well, yes. I suppose so. Anyhow, I'd better get back to my office and see what's been happening. Have you my clothes handy, Preacher?'

'I'm afraid they aren't fit to wear, Caleb. I've taken them over to the Happy Time wash house and laundry. Mrs Chang promises to do the best she can to make them presentable. She didn't look happy and let her daughter handle most of it. Told me to come back in a few days, or maybe a week. But I've put out some of mine that should be okay until you get over to your own wardrobe. I'm a little taller than you but we're close to the same build. Please, bring them back when you join me for dinner this evening. I have a story I promised to share with you and it'd be best listened to with some food in your belly.'

And so it was that I wore Preacher's black while I covered the short distance across Main Street to my office and the quarters above. I was pleased to find it open and looking tidy. One of Damsel-Childs' people must have been over to look after it. I swear I expected to see that man voted in as a Senator one day, or maybe even rising to the heights of the Presidential office itself. I could imagine that strange man licking his way through the White House like a hungry lizard, though I wouldn't want him to suffer the fate of Mr Lincoln in Ford's Theatre eighteen years before or President Garfield in '81.

Upstairs in my rooms I peeled myself out of the Preacher's sable rig and climbed into one of my own outfits more suited to my working day. I was surprised at the quality of the Preacher's duds. There was a fine richness to the fabric and the stitching was so precise his apparel seemed almost seamless. That reminded me of the robe of Jesus which was also made of whole cloth. I chided myself for a blaspheming fool, but I folded his clothes with particular care and left them out of the sun so they wouldn't bleach unevenly.

And then I went back down to my office. I had a lot to deal with. I'd need to see Heck Levine about finding a replacement for Missy plus a new saddle, tack and holsters. I hoped we could come to some arrangements over good, second-hand equipment and terms for payment. I then set about cleaning my guns of dust and rat droppings and waxing my belt back to a decent shine.

I was loading my rifle and checking the smoothness of its lever action when a one-armed skeleton reeled through the door and collapsed into my red swivel barber chair. Something told me he hadn't come for a shave.

{24}

'I felt like a man trying to mend a busted water-pipe with a poker,' explained Emmanuel Fernandez to the Preacher and me. As soon as he had begun talking back in my office I knew the Preacher had to get involved and I asked the reed-thin man if he could walk just a few more yards to share his story with an expert.

He didn't question my dash upstairs to fetch a bundle of clothes, nor why I carefully buckled on my gun belt to cross the street in the middle of a quiet day. His eyes had something of a vacant glaze to them and his head wobbled heavily on his scrawny neck. His knees buckled slightly when he stood up and he looked around my office like a baby bird searching for its mother.

As soon as we reached his home the Preacher ushered us in. He sat Fernandez down and studied him keenly, looking deep into his eyes and gently examining the man's stump. He then asked me what medication the man was on. I admitted I didn't know, which was when Fernandez fetched out a carelessly corked green glass bottle with a carefully written label.

'Stickney and Poor's Opii.i,' said the Preacher. 'Very well, that's good! I can work with that.'

He left the room for a minute or two and while he was absent I watched confusion bloom across the starveling's bony features. Something dreadful had happened to the poor man and at last he had the time for shock to take a good hold. He began to shiver and his lower lip quivered. He was on the brink of tears. He gazed at his burned stump of an arm and held it up to show me.

'Look,' he said. 'Oh, look.'

It near broke my heart to watch him and I was grateful when the Preacher bustled back in with a blanket, which he handed me, and a tray containing a needle filled with amber fluid, a cup of something that looked like water but smelled of lavender, and a long flat box of shining metal. He told me to wrap the man in the blanket but to leave his ruined arm free. He gave the cup to Fernandez and bade him drink, waited until he had done so, and then injected his stump with the amber fluid.

I watched the burned man's eyes come back into focus. He looked at us with clear intelligence and then back at his black-capped stump of an arm. That was when he made his observation about trying to mend a water pipe with a poker.

'It can't work, of course. It doesn't matter what you do,' he said. 'That hole in the pipe keeps getting bigger. That was how I felt today; things got out of my control and just kept on getting worse.'

And he told us the whole story from the time he was sitting in his outhouse right the way through to his frustration while trying to saddle his pony one-handed for the first time in his life. He held up his stump and explained how he kept trying to use the left hand he no longer had and had become increasingly angry about its loss.

'Anger was my salvation,' he said. 'I would not surrender to my circumstances.'

I stared at the fleshless creature and wondered at the single-minded determination that'd kept him alive when pressed into such an awful, tight corner. I do not know if I could have survived such a series of misfortunes. His courage must have been almost bottomless. You wouldn't think so to look at him; I've seen brush turkeys with more meat on them. Hell, I've helped put healthier looking people in a box.

Despite everything that happened afterwards, Fernandez was the only person who took the enemy on in a head-on fight, and beat it. He walked away bloody but unbowed, and gave us invaluable information into the bargain. There should be a memorial to the man.

He watched with cat-like curiosity while the Preacher probed the tar black cap on his stump with a fine, crook-backed needle he'd taken from his box. Fernandez never winced once and his hollow eyes drank in every one of my friend's gentle ministrations. Even when the Preacher deliberately drew blood to see if the rest of the arm was still vital, his expression remained one of trusting resolve.

'Mr Fernandez,' said the Preacher eventually. 'I think it best to remove this black cap and clean your stump properly. We need to make you sleep for a little while. Are you agreeable to this?'

'I am, and much obliged to you for your kindness, sir.'

'You are welcome. Caleb, please help Mr Fernandez to the table and make him as comfortable as possible.'

Without a grumble that big-hearted, slender fellow lay himself down on the hard wood and patiently waited for whatever was to happen next. I must admit it was beyond me. I would have loaded him with morphine, put a leather strap between his jaws and gone at him with a boiled meat saw, and then probably stitched my own fingers to his stump in my rush to close him up.

The sophistication of the Preacher's equipment made me wonder if he'd got it from back East, somewhere fancy like New York or Boston. I'd heard tell of miraculous things happening to medicine back there, and that some panjandrum from someplace had said 'science was become a cathedral without walls, we have no more to learn from it, for all is known'. I say hogwash and hokum to that kind of hoorah horseshit. We don't know everything. Why, we barely scratch the surface. But I believed the Preacher understood more than most and that is still my view.

Talking quietly all the time, the Preacher lay a large white cup, rim down, over Fernandez' mouth and nose then told him to take deep breaths and to count with him. He got to eleven when Fernandez' eyes fluttered and closed. Preacher opened one of those eyes and took a good hard stare, mumbled something, let it fall closed again and nodded to himself.

'Caleb,' he said, 'while I get ready will you please bring me a large bowl filled with water you will find boiling on the stove in my kitchen.'

He told me where I would find a bowl and some clean white towels. I busied myself for a few minutes. When I came back with everything he requested, my fingers scorching a little on the hot enamel of the bowl, I found him with his shirtsleeves rolled back to his elbows. He was tying the strings of a crisp linen apron around his lean belly.

He took the bowl from me as if it was cold and balanced it on a stool beside him. He then placed a number of glittering instruments into the water: probes and knives and something that looked like a small, steel crowbar. He emptied some clear liquid into the water from a frosted bottle, washed his hands and forearms in the same liquid and then handed the bottle to me. He evidently wanted me to wash my hands too. A pungent, clean, chemical smell filled the room. It caught at the back of my throat.

'Caleb, I will need the help of your good strong hands while I work. Our friend on the table is asleep but he may react powerfully when I start cutting. Will you hold his left arm still for me until I'm done?'

I told him I was right pleased to help. He had me roll my sleeves back and tie on my own apron, which meant I had to wash with that liquid again. I remember thinking if he did too much more of this kind of thing he was going to need a much bigger bottle than the one he had.

Preacher used some tongs to pull a pair of long scissors from the bowl and he used them to cut away the injured man's shirt, exposing what was left of his upper arm, shoulder and breast. He tutted at how the skin was pulled taut and followed the precise shape of the bones underneath. Fernandez could've been used as the model in an anatomy lesson.

85

'Whatever else happens, Caleb, this man will have a good meal with us before he leaves.'

'Amen to that.'

'How did he manage to do all he did when he was so wasted? He is an extraordinary specimen of the species.'

I didn't waste breath on a reply. He wasn't asking me, after all; he was telling me. I pondered his use of the word 'species'.

He took one of the white towels and dunked it in the bowl of water. I saw him fully immerse his hand and felt sure that the water must have cooled some in the few minutes since I brought it from the kitchen. But the cloud of steam coming off it made it look plenty hot enough to me. He wrung the towel and then dosed it liberally from the frosted bottle. With gentle strokes he cleansed his patient's body, lifting the stump to wash every inch of exposed flesh. For some reason the image of the Lord's feet being washed by the Magdalene sprang into my mind.

I realised he was wiping away a fine layer of grey dust. The clean meat of the arm looked a little like boiled ham and I wondered at the agony Fernandez had suffered.

'Very well, Caleb,' said the Preacher. 'Time for you to get hold of that arm firmly and get ready for whatever we need do next. If you will be so good as to oblige me, thank you.'

{25}

While Emmanuel Fernandez held all of the Preacher and Caleb's attention the business of The Palace continued.

It was the neat little half-breed named Pony Black who had drawn the attention of Grandma's keen nose. The other whores were told to dress, but Mizz Black was led into the bedroom by Grandma and the door closed firmly behind the pair of them with a loud click.

Meads instantly became the centre of attention. The cat had gone off with its victim and the mice decided to play with the only toy in the room. They had previously seemed reluctant to shed their clothes, but now they appeared equally reluctant to put them back on. They grouped in the centre of the salon where sunlight played intimately across their bodies, and they made a great show of touching each other, stroking, tweaking and commenting on everything on show, all the time looking in his direction.

If Meads had suffered any great curiosity about the naked female form he would certainly have found most of his questions answered that day, including a few most men would have preferred not to ask.

He was not of the Quaker persuasion or a devout Presbyterian, and he had taken great pleasure with the opposite sex on as many occasions as fortune allowed an unmarried man who spent most of his adult life with cattle, but this marshalling of naked women like shop-bought goods confused him, as did their apparent enjoyment of it.

He was also agonised by the fact they were getting to him in the most direct fashion, and that he was suffering a painful awakening in his manhood for the first time in several months. When Grandma was in the room the whores were somehow diminished, but without her they blossomed around him in all their predatory glory.

He wondered if they had to bend over quite so much; and always with their hindquarters aimed directly at him as if positioned by a cannon master. Long Lizzie's body was well used and sagged a little but the other girls were firm enough and Mary Gold was really quite pretty – if you ignored the bruises on her elbows and the bright colours smeared across her china-white face.

He was finding it hard to know where to put his eyes and felt his standing predicament below the waist must be obvious to such experienced teases. After all, these women had made their living from first exciting the interest of men and then quenching it. Lust mocks both the weak man and the strong alike when temptation wears a come-hither smile – and opens its legs wide enough.

'That's enough, ladies.' Grandma's voice fell across the room like a clapper striking a bell, hard. Meads felt his body relax once more. The boss was back in the room and the centre of gravity was back where it belonged.

Pony Black strutted back into the salon and dressed as if she was alone there. The other whores asked her questions but she had become both deaf and blind to them. Once decent she checked through her meagre tack, bowed to Grandma, and then departed the room, the building and, as soon as the afternoon flyer to Shafter hauled itself to the Mule's Ass boarding platform, the town.

Grandma addressed the women Meads had come to think of as her 'pussy posse', a description he never shared with her.

'Poor Miss Black brought a little more with her than just her luggage. She could not stay. I have paid her for her time and her travel back to Shafter. This is a clean house. It will start clean and remain clean.' She tapped her nose. 'We will not allow unclean clients into our rooms; and we shall not entertain the pox in our box, understood?'

After a short bark of shocked laughter, the four remaining whores nodded their agreement.

Grandma continued, 'While you are with me you will not behave like cat-girls, doxies, whores, Westminster geese or prostitutes. You will always believe yourselves as good as the stiffest-backed matron on the boardwalk. You are ladies of pure pleasure, and your work is as essential as that of any nurse. You are here to provide a valuable service, and to get properly paid for that service. So remember, before you open your legs, open your palms – unless you would rather we institute a door charge?'

The ladies of pleasure didn't like the sound of a door charge. It would mean anyone who spent their evenings lying around doing nothing rather than hard at work on their backs would get the same wages, and that, they all agreed, wouldn't be fair.

Meads showed them out and down to their rooms behind the bar. The rope-slung beds were now topped with clean straw mattresses, linen, pillows and blankets. Each room boasted a wooden stool, a dresser and a tallboy. On one wall was a mirror and on the other a framed French engraving, each depicting a different scene of men and women taking pleasure in each other's company.

Each room was almost identical but the women took their time over choosing their new homes.

Long Lizzie gave Meads a slow once-over. 'You ever want to dip your candle in the corporation wax,' she said, 'I'll be right in here.' And in a cloud of scented white soap and rosewater she was gone.

Meads hastened away to the bar room where he sat on one of the divans and leaned back against its padded pillar.

'We need another four.'

He looked up to where the tiny black figure of Grandma was leaning against the railing and gazing down, straight at him.

'Samuel, while we settle the first of our working girls into the "Palace", could you track over to Goody Marsh and see if we've had any more replies to our notice? I'd be very much obliged.'

He lifted his hat and was on his way out onto Main Street a matter of moments later. She might be small but Grandma Teatree had the authority of a County Judge. The only person Meads could imagine standing up to her was Preacher Spindrift, and possibly Sheriff Sawyer, if he had a good tailwind. He pondered that while he walked down the boardwalk towards Goody's trading post.

He noticed that the road had been cleared of horse spatter since the earthquake and wondered if Baylee had found his way back from wherever he had got to. That was when he spotted a cart piled high with manure and two squaw women in sober dresses emptying buckets into it. They weren't Comanche, he thought – too short.

He asked Goody while he downed a light beer at her bar and wondered if he had time to eat something. The aromas coming from the kitchen had set his belly to rumbling.

'They wouldn't thank you for calling them squaws,' she chided. 'They're hard working mothers of the Kickapoo tribe and they can trace their family back further than you, Samuel Meads.'

'I meant nothing by it, Goody!'

'Just remember is all. You planning to feed that starving wolf you got shacked up there in your belly, boy?'

He asked if anyone else had answered Grandma's notice and was introduced to three women eating fatty pork belly and beans at a table in the darkest corner of the post. He joined them and ordered a plate of steak and potatoes with gravy. By the time his food arrived one of his new companions had rolled herself a cigarette from a pouch of "Old Gold" tobacco and passed the makings around. He held his hand up to say no when it was offered to him.

Mary Peach looked like she had taken a wrong turn on her way to a church social – she looked too homey for the oldest profession – while Mary Kelly, known as "Kitten", looked born to her trade.

Meads thought it was probably Kitten Kelly who had condemned the trio to the darkest corner of the room. Her ready smile was eclipsed by a plunging décolletage that revealed a very fine bosom to any who chose to look. She leaned forward when she spoke, and she really liked to talk. Every time she did, Meads found it almost impossible to avert his rapt gaze from her pregnantly rounded and smooth fleshed breasts.

The last was the cigarette smoker, Ellie Willis. She could have been beautiful if someone or something hadn't smashed out three of her teeth on the left side of her upper set. You could only see it when she smiled, but her loss became very noticeable when she did. She took advantage of the gap to thrust her smoke in there without unclenching her teeth, and she could blow perfect smoke rings through it. It was quite an art.

None of them had paid for their meals so Meads got everything put on the staging post tick and signed the docket. He then led his three graces away to meet Grandma Teatree and the other ladies of pleasure.

{26}

Caleb took a firm grip and admired the Preacher's skill with a knife.
The medical profession lost a natural surgeon when the Preacher followed his calling into the mother church. He had me hold Fernandez' injured arm while also gripping a tourniquet tight, and then he dipped his fingers into that bowl of steaming water and took out a long-bladed metal knife that looked spitefully sharp.

He studied the stump for a long few moments, angled his blade carefully, and then used long, fluid strokes to flense away that odd, black cap. We were both relieved to see a healthy seepage of blood from the exposed meat.

Preacher had me release the tourniquet a little and blood spurted down the table. I tightened it again. There was so little of Fernandez to begin with I doubted he could afford to lose too much. Humming to himself, Preacher cut back the muscle tissue and sawed then cleaned the bone. He worked swiftly and expertly until he'd made two decent flaps of skin which he sewed carefully over the end of the stump. When he finished, the skin was flat with a slight ridge where his small stitches tacked across a newly smooth dome. He snipped away the end of his thread and examined his handiwork. The operation had taken all of fifty-five minutes according to the clock on the mantle and I had no reason to doubt its honesty.

He bade me release the tourniquet slowly while he held a clean towel against his neat sutures.

I said, 'I haven't ever seen work like that before. Fernandez will thank you for the rest of his natural life.'

'Let's both pray it'll be a long and happy one.'

'Well, if it ain't it sure won't be thanks to any of the work you did here today. That stitching would grace the finest London-made kid gloves. A thing of beauty.'

'I'm sure Mr Fernandez would rather he'd not required my ministrations, Caleb, no matter how beautiful the work. He woke up this morning with two arms and he will retire tonight with but one. He's a tough-hearted soul, but that loss will be a bitter pill to swallow when the opium wears off and reality bites hard once more. Poor fellow, a soldier sorely wounded when he didn't even know he was on the battlefield.'

Preacher put layers of fine linen dipped in a carbolic acid solution over the scar to promote healing and protect it from chafing, and then bound the wounded wing with a length of wide cotton dressing which he tore and tied closed with a small knot.

'Not too tight or the sutures will fail, not so loose that the dressing falls off. Let's put our patient to bed, Caleb, and then I think we will have earned that drink.'

Once the man was safely asleep in the Preacher's bed, and the table had been cleared and washed clean of blood, the Preacher busily polished his instruments and put them away in their box. I poured two glasses of whiskey and once more fell to wondering what naked women and water pipes had to do with the smoothest demon drink I'd ever tasted.

Preacher followed my gaze to the label and smiled ruefully.

'Most men look at naked women and think of pleasure, Caleb; the makers know that and play on it. Forbidden fruit and huriyah make wonderful mind mates when we're in our cups, but you wouldn't know that.' He smiled. 'You're perhaps a little *too* pure-minded sometimes.'

I frowned at him, wondering if he could somehow read my mind. As if answering me he said, 'I'm no mind-reader, my friend, but I saw you looking from your glass to the label and back. It was evident to me where your thoughts had taken you. Let me get our food and then I have that story to share with you.'

He made a rapid assay into his bedroom to check on the patient and then disappeared into the kitchen. He came out with two steaming bowls of spicy meat and vegetables and two spoons, fetched a platter of bread and then joined me at the table.

Rather than once again drink myself clean through the drunkard's curtain and out the other side, I thanked him for a pot of light beer to meter my intake of whiskey. Then I set-to with my spoon. I really wanted to hear the Preacher's tale but I was hungry. That stew was the first solid food I'd put behind my ribs for near two days and I was almost sick from hunger.

Preacher spooned meat into his mouth with a precise delicacy while I tore hunks of bread and mopped up the juices. I piled one mouthful on top of another until my mouth was so stuffed I couldn't chew, and I started to gag on the rich food. He kept his gaze averted until I'd swallowed a solid chunk of something painful. I slowed down after that but it was difficult. The food was delicious.

'I told you about the GODS craft that once crossed space with their cargo of Eden seed,' he began.

I grunted and nodded, chewing like a ravenous cur. Something hot in the stew's spice was making me sweat, but it was a good sweat.

'The great ship that seeded Earth is still out there beyond the orbit of the red planet, Mars. It's hidden among space mountains of rock and iron that fly up there like gigantic birds. The ship is black on the outside, stained by dust and time, but inside its skin is a taste of Eden, the home planet.'

His eyes looked wistful and distant. 'It is a beautiful place, Caleb. To be barred from there once you had fallen in love with it would be a terrible punishment. Terrible.' His eyes seemed to widen and fixed upon mine. 'The creatures who live there call it Heaven. It is a blessed place.

'I've been banned from Heaven, Caleb. The last of Eden protected by the GODS was my home for hundreds of years, longer, and then we reached your system. We gardeners came to Earth in pods. We fell into the seas. The pods dissolved into salts of precious metals and we swam to the lands. There were hundreds of us, all what you would call "male" I suppose. We had organs like men. It was how we had been designed to plant the Eden seed into the ripest species. We were taller than any primate on the planet – remember your *Bible*, Caleb? Genesis six, verse four? "There were giants in the earth in those days; and also after that, when the sons of God came in unto the daughters of men, and they bear children to them." Remember?'

'That was you? You and your people?'

'Yes. But instead of coming into "daughters of men" we seeded the most advanced apes we could find.'

'You had carnal relations with monkeys?'

'Not monkeys, no. Strictly speaking, Caleb, I had carnal relations with your great, several generations removed, grandmother.'

I had finished eating, which was handy because my mouth swung open, loose-jawed and ready to catch flies.

'Don't look so shocked, my friend. It was hard work and we were designed for it. We didn't see those ancient creatures as apes. We saw them as... well, you, the end result. We imagined later generations of Edenkind walking here on Earth and building a new Eden. We saw the future, and we had been asked to remain on Earth until the seed was well-rooted. Once that happened we'd been promised we would be taken up once more unto our reward in Heaven. We would be allowed to go home.'

The way he explained this last damn near brought tears to my eyes. He spoke as if his heart was breaking. Whether I believed him didn't really matter; I could tell he was living his story. He was back seeing those far off days, remembering. And then a question fell into my head like it'd been thrown there, hard, and the words fell unbidden from my lips.

'Wait, Preacher, help me understand this. Are you telling me you brought Heaven here with you in a big ship, and that we learned the word of God from you Eden people? Are you telling me there is no immortal soul? Are you saying Heaven is just some place out there somewhere, where rocks fly like birds? Are you telling me that? Is *that* what you're telling me? Surely this is blasphemy!'

I was crimson with anger and embarrassment. Listen to what I was asking him. I was as loon-headed as he was. But right there, right then, I did believe him. He was not as other men.

'No, Caleb, no, that's not what I am telling you. You have an immortal soul, my friend, all of the Eden-born have. In fact, here on Earth, *only* the Eden born have such a thing. And that is the terrible crime the enemy inflicts on mankind when it possesses you. It both devours the flesh and consumes the soul. Your species is the tastiest tid-bit on Earth and the enemy has an insatiable appetite.

'Klosky, Baylee, the Vickerys, all the men and women we have seen infected and destroyed have gone completely. They are wiped away, become nothing more than bitter, soulless dust. Why do you think we must fight the enemy and destroy it utterly, man? That beast is at war with redemption. It's at war with the resurrection and the life – it's at war with Heaven itself!'

That night when I returned to my rooms over the office I fell almost instantly into a deep, dreamless sleep. I had left the Preacher to tend Fernandez alone. I needed to sleep, to think. He'd told me things that'd turn a March hare's fur white, and everyone knows they're mad as a drunken Indian. Before closing my eyes, I looked out on the star-bright sky and wondered at all the other people out there – people making plans, living their lives and going about their day. I also wondered how many were looking back at me and from how far away. I thought of Heaven.

The next morning I missed breakfast and settled for a few cups of coffee, a wash and a clean shave. At that time it was the fashion for men to wear a moustache and often a beard, but I found facial hair annoying. It itched. And anyway, I had a lucrative business shaving faces and cutting men's hair; my good, clean shave was worth more than a notice in the paid-for pages. Or at least so I believed.

I stropped the fine, straight blade of my American Knife Co razor and set-to at the lather around my cheeks and jaws. In the wrong hands a sharpened straight razor could prove a deadly weapon, but I'm certain a blunted one has shed more blood. I kept my blades keen as mustard.

While I was rinsing my face, be-whiskered men filed in and sat waiting on every free flat surface, which began me a busy morning and earned me several dollars-worth of silver nickels. Some of them asked for a jigger of cologne to sweeten their hides which earned me a few more cents but also made my office stink like a tart's parlour.

When the shaving was done I locked up and I went to see Heck Levine about a new horse and tack. He was nearly as upset about Missy as me. That man loved horse flesh and he knew his trade well. Many horse people are good with their brothers and sisters too; I had often noticed the truth of it.

We sat chewing the fat awhile, the subject matter no different to the one in my barber's chair – whores, tarts and easy virtue. The brothel was bigger news than the earthquake and was having an even greater impact on the menfolk. I began to realise why my razor had proved so popular that morning and nearly laughed out loud.

Heck and I shook hands over a pretty grey mare he described as 'young and strong but sweet tempered as an old hound'. She was called Pearl, which suited her colour very well. He had her saddled up and bridled with barely worn second-hand tack from his store. He didn't ask if I wanted new.

Missy's feed and stabling was already paid for until the end of the month so I had a new horse and Pearl had a new home in Missy's old stall.

I climbed into the saddle and took Pearl out for a 'getting to know you' jaunt. I didn't want to head west towards the mine or south towards Teague's place. North would mean fording the river. I headed east after crossing the rails and generally followed the Sweet Alice. The sun was high and hot, casting a short shadow. I didn't expect to meet anyone on the trail at that time of day – most sensible folk would be sitting down to their midday meal, but I carried my loaded pistol in my belt holster and kept a wary eye on my surroundings.

I preferred to be alone whenever I could and took great pleasure in silence. I had ridden with men who filled the air with idle chatter and some had even blustered away to their mounts as if they also spoke American. I say that is a waste of air and a strain on the horses' patience. After a while the poor mount's eyes are rolling in its head and it starts champing at the bit while the yapping fool in the saddle regales it with nonsense. Silence is better.

The river opens out at a bend where animals come down to drink. Trees dip down towards the water and there are rushes and shrubs on the bank. It is a regular oasis on the flat, dusty stretch of hog trail I was following and I dismounted to let Pearl grab a drink while I cut the dust with a mouthful from my bottle. That was when I heard the splashing a little way upstream.

I tied Pearl where she could reach the water and nibble at fresh leaves and I crept along the bank to see what critter was comporting itself in the sluggish current. I wondered if it was a beaver or a river otter. I loved watching them at play and moved quiet as thought so as not to alarm it.

I reached a place behind a dense bush from which I saw ripples arcing away from an iron-flat stretch of river. I ducked down so I could watch from cover. Seconds later I spotted a shadow rising a few yards from the bank and then a smooth creamy back crested the surface before rolling over and then diving back down into the weedy depths. My mistake was made very clear to me at that moment. It wasn't a beaver or an otter taking its pleasure. It was a naked woman.

She looked young and lithe and she clove to the river like a fish. I can swim well and I had taken a dip on that very spot in an equal state of nature on more than one occasion, but this woman was clearly in her natural element. I watched entranced and almost breathless as she danced through the gentle waters and at one point spun up into the air then scissored back down into the olive flow with barely a ripple.

If it was not for her fine, shapely legs I would've thought her a mermaid, but I can state for the record there was nothing of the fish about her person. Watching her made me feel large, brutish and clumsy. She was beautiful and had the rounded curves of a grown woman, but she was small as a girl and hairless apart from her long black hair that spread like a cloak in the waters around her. My heart pounded in my ribs and I was afraid to be thought a spying Tom, but I couldn't tear my eyes from her.

Finally, she climbed from the river and disappeared into a clump of trees. I hurried back to my horse, untied her and mounted up. I hoped that if I met my watery beauty just riding along the trail she'd think I had just arrived and we could strike up a conversation without her knowing what I'd seen. How much I'd seen. We could talk and I hoped not to trip over my stupid tongue in the process.

I rode back a short distance and waited until I believed the woman had been given enough time to dress and might be making her way from the trees towards her destination. I didn't recognise her from town or any of the homesteads around Mule's Ass, but she may have been visiting family, or − and this thought stopped Pearl in her tracks as I hauled on her reins − she might be one of the whores newly arrived. Taking herself for a curiosity walk she had found herself a good place to swim on a hot day. It had to be true. My heart sank.

And then a slight form dressed all in black walked out of the trees. She was coiling her thick, damp and silky black tresses into a pile on top of her head. My Lord, it was Grandma Teatree.

{28}

The gaze she cast up at me was flat, black and feral. I stared at her, looked over at the copse of trees and then back at her. I was being asked to swallow too many impossible things in too short a time. I really needed to think hard about my diet.

'Get down off that horse, Sheriff Sawyer.'

Her voice held more menace than her eyes, and her eyes were plenty menacing. I hauled myself out of the saddle and stood like an oversized schoolboy before her. I had a loaded six-gun in my belt, over-topped her by a good eighteen inches and out-weighed her by at least one hundred pounds – so why did I feel outnumbered and surrounded?

I thought back to a stocky little man who had been a regular attraction in the Travelling World of Wonders. He was a Chinee fellow like Sung Li in Goody's kitchen and the Changs in the Happy House laundry, but this man, who called himself General Sun, was no more a cook than I am a laundry maid.

Sun stood like a rock in the centre of a wooden circle while the black fellow known as the Baron – he ran the show and always wore a top hat and an ancient frock-coat – invited onlookers to strike at the little Chinee with anything they could bring to bear except bullets.

That black man's voice sounded like it came from the deepest cave on Earth. It came from way, way down. That voice carried the man like a dog a bone. It filled him and when he released it, it rang out and you just had to listen. Then he'd smile and when you saw his big white teeth in that lean ebony face you wondered what he'd ever seen to make him smile like that. Whatever it was it wasn't funny. There was no humour in it, no warmth. He looked hungry.

He charged folks ten cents to attack the General. I knew it was a poor investment and always held on to my pocket change, but some others felt they had the grit for the job and they went at the little man with everything from old army cutlasses and sabres to walking sticks and shovels. He egged three men to come at him at once and they were all carrying heavy cudgels.

The Baron took a nickel from everyone who wanted to watch and pressed his thumb against the back of their hands once he had the money. When he took his thumb away there was a little blue eagle printed onto their skin. That would be your pass to enter his Tent of Wonders after the General had finished his display. It never took long.

It looked easy while he was doing it and nobody got hurt much except perhaps their pride, which took a real pasting, but the little General shrugged off knives and staves and shovels and sticks with the same fluid motions you get from a talented dancer on stage. It was elegant to watch. He never punched anyone, but the more effort someone put into a strike the harder they fell. He never stepped out of his wooden circle but his attackers flew every which way. No one got through his defence and some of those that tried I knew to be hard-nosed trouble just looking for the right place to happen. Afterwards you could tell from their baffled expressions they didn't have the first inkling about what the Chinee man had done, or how he had managed it. He'd never even break a sweat.

They were outmatched by what the Baron described as a 'Martial Art', and standing before me like a black twig in widow's weeds, Grandma Teatree reminded me of General Sun. She had that same quality of compressed energy and swiftness allied with a kind of natural balance.

I looked again at the copse of trees and then bowed my confused face to hers.

'How long have you been here, Sheriff Sawyer?'

She waited a few moments without taking her black gaze from mine, and then her open palm lashed out and struck my cheek so hard I nearly staggered into Pearl. It was after that stinging blow had rung my senses like a church bell that Grandma's shoulders slumped a little and she bowed as if to study the ground at her feet.

'Oh well,' she muttered, 'if it had to be anyone I suppose it was best it was you.' At that she tilted her wizened face back up towards mine and softly said, 'Come here to me.'

I bent my back and held my face closer to hers, half expecting another stinging slap. Instead she pressed her lips against mine and kissed me, long and hard. Have you ever kissed a crone? Until that moment I certainly hadn't and the experience was completely unexpected. Instead of dry, withered flesh and sour breath I was feeling soft, full lips and sweetness. Her tongue darted into my mouth and explored it. I had closed my eyes in horror but at that I opened them in shock and recoiled.

The girl from the river regarded me with impish glee, and I swallowed a cool, juicy tincture I'd found upon my tongue. She blurred a little then settled in my sight and there was no more in her of Grandma Teatree.

'Am I so repulsive?'

I was very confused. 'Which is real?' I asked. 'Is this some black-handed kind of witchery?'

'I have only ever kissed one man before, Caleb, and he's been dead these past two hundred years or more. What you see before you is the whole truth, and from this moment you will only ever see me as I truly appear. You only see through the old illusion now because I trust you. Fail me and you will break my heart − do that and I will break your neck.'

'Two hundred years? What are you telling me?'

'I like your horse, she's nice, but tie her up and walk with me awhile.'

I tethered Pearl where she could nibble and sip as before. I studied the girl as I walked back to her side. Grandma's weeds couldn't disguise her youthful, slender curves or her lithe athlete's body. She was breath-taking.

'Are you an elf?'

'No, don't be silly.' She chuckled at the thought. 'Caleb, forget make-believe and fog-me-stories, this is real-life.'

She took my hand and pressed it to her warm and, oh, so solid cheek. Her corneas were so large her big, slightly slanted eyes looked almost black under full, handsome brows and masses of shining black curls. Her face was an angel's with full lips above a narrow chin and a delicate nose between curving, dimpled cheeks. The inhuman beauty of her shone and blinded me to everything else. I kissed her again, kissed until I was forced to come up for air, and I held her against me until I could feel every inch of her pressed to my body, and I found myself getting hard for her then.

'Not that,' she said, 'not yet.' But she didn't pull away. Instead she held her flushed face to my shoulder and laughed with an earthy amusement.

'Very well,' I said into her hair, her perfumed hair. 'You're not a witch or an elf, but you're so much more than any woman I've ever known. What shall I call you?'

'Call me Alice,' she said, 'for this, this is *my* river.' And she told me a story while we stood clasped in each other's arms and Pearl happily munched at glossy leaves by a placid artery of clean water called Sweet Alice.

{29}

When the silver mine manager, Prester Montague, called his men to the table for their week's money and to put their mark next to their names in the cash ledger, he later told me he had a pretty sound idea where some of it was going to end up. He didn't approve of whoring, but The Palace was opening its doors to customers later that afternoon and a man had the right to spend his money any way he saw fit. There were no choirboys at the Fulsome workings.

Each of the family men placed some of their cash into envelopes already hand-written with the name and address of their wives or oldest child and boasting a brown, George Washington, two-cent stamp. Prester bagged those sealed envelopes into canvas sacks and personally delivered them under armed guard to the Mule's Ass rail boarding office.

The rail depot at the silver mine was solely dedicated to marshalling the precious metal and belonged to the County Assay Office in Shafter, not the Postmaster-General in Washington. As a result, Prester and four of his men had to make their weekly journey down into town with itchy trigger fingers, rifles at the ready and cricks in their necks from constantly studying the terrain. Some people would rather steal a dollar than earn one, a fact as true back then as it is today. Such men have black hearts and no respect for another man's hard work or property. Those envelopes would have made a fine prize, and it was best to ride the Mule's Ass road with caution.

Prester could have had the cash converted to postal orders for safety in transit, but his men liked to keep the amount of money they sent home under their hats. The system worked and he didn't fight it. It gave him an excuse to visit town once a week and shoot the breeze while sharing a beer or two with some old boys in the trading post.

He watched Marlow Fisher load the sacks into the safe at the back of the rail office and took his receipt. They would be loaded into a secure postal sorting carriage on the next Shafter-bound train, and the clerks in that coach were so fast each envelope would be bundled with any others destined for the same post office before the flyer had reached the next town on its route.

He released his guards for the rest of the day and crossed Main Street to my office and barber shop, but all he found in there was a Mexican asleep in the red leather tilting chair who jolted awake as he entered, bolted upright and stood sheepishly turning his big wheel of a hat in his hands.

He asked if he might have a shave.

Prester said nothing. He turned on his heel and made his way out of the office and headed up the boardwalk towards the trading post. He had wanted to talk to me about three of his men who had gone missing during the last week. They had disappeared before the quake so he didn't think they were still down the mine somewhere under one of the caved-in tunnels. He had some men clearing those just in case and they had found nothing so far.

He was lost in a brown muse that had nothing to do with the bright day, but when he looked up he instantly recognised me riding in on a grey horse. He was evidently surprised to see I was sharing my mount with the old Teatree woman. He remembered having to deal with her and another two members of the town council over some mine business, and the memory was not a pleasant one. She reminded him of a scrawny, black little bantam hen that would peck a man just to draw blood.

Prester stepped down onto the road and walked across to meet the odd couple. He removed his hat. 'Mizz Teatree, Sheriff, good to see you both on such a fine day. You're looking mighty well, Mizz Teatree.'

'Good day to you, Mister Montague. I'm sure you haven't just come over to flatter an old woman who knows a chicken-shit lie when she hears one. You want Sheriff Sawyer and you find yourself with me into the bargain – and I'm no bargain.'

Prester protested feebly and Grandma flicked his words away like irritating flies.

She held out her arms. 'Do something useful and help me down.'

Careful where he put his hands, the mine manager assisted the crone off the horse and onto the hard, rutted earth of the street.

'Thank you, sir. Most gallant.' She looked up at me and her expression softened. 'Think about what I told you, Caleb. We shall discuss the matter at greater length and in finer detail when time allows. For now I have things I must attend, and every minute lost is a leaden burden to me.'

And she scuttled off towards the brothel with frequent glances over her shoulder. I watched her go. The woman I was seeing was young and vital and it was hard for me not to grin like a Tomfool on a spring holiday from his senses.

'She's a remarkable creature,' said Prester Montague.

'One of a kind,' I replied.

He squinted up at me, his mouth screwed up under his moustache. 'I believe she has a kind spot for you, Sheriff Sawyer.'

'She's known me since I was no more than a wrinkle in my mother's belly. She looks out for the town-born folk. But she will also bring down the wrath of an angel of vengeance on you if you play the smart card with her. Most everyone has felt it at least once.'

'Yes, at least once. Sheriff, may I speak with you?'

'Right pleased, Mr Montague. Will you walk with me while I stable Pearl here? Or shall I tether her and we can go straight to my office?'

'There's a Mexican in your office who wants a shave.'

'Then he can wait.'

I dismounted and we walked together and talked all the way to Levine's, where I gave a boy a few cents to settle Pearl in her stall. I drew my rifle from its holster and slung the big water bottle over my shoulder. He told me about the missing men and the details of his day. We went around the back way to Goody's and fetched our light beers to the darkest table in the room; the very one Meads had shared with three whores the day before.

I thanked Montague for the beer and it was mighty welcome. In no time at all we had started our second glass and after that we slowed down. The demon in sour mash does not reside in light beer, just a full bladder and a belly of gas later in the day.

Montague invited me to call him Prester and I insisted he call me Caleb. We were getting on so well I wondered if we should call on the Preacher to publish the Banns and announce a date for the wedding. That was when the very man himself walked into Goody's place, shadowed by the pale, one-armed wraith that was Emmanuel Fernandez. I called them both over to join us. Fernandez sat with a grateful sigh and cradled his stump. Preacher fetched four beers.

He sipped thoughtfully while Prester and I explained about the missing men. Prester said they were no loss to the mine because they'd proved to be trouble-makers who had bullied some of the younger men and worse.

'I've no concrete evidence against them,' he said, 'but I believe they were unnatural creatures with sick appetites and desires. They went everywhere together and would touch the boys and laugh at them. They would loiter by the butts in the mornings when the men washed and laugh again. Some of the boys were going to take the law into their own hands and there was even talk of a lynching, but I wouldn't allow such a thing. I was going to let them go at the end of this week, but they disappeared on Monday afternoon and not a scrap of any of them's been seen since.'

'Prester,' said the Preacher, 'something tells me those boys are no longer your problem. You would've heard something about them before now if they were still around. My guess is they got out while they still could. A man knows when he isn't wanted.

'But why don't the Sheriff and I ride up to your mine with you right now and see what we can find? I bet the clues are there if you have eyes to see.'

And his eyes glinted in the shadows.

30

Over in The Palace the story took a darker turn.

Long Lizzie liked soap and water. She always tried to keep a scented bar of white soap and a basin of clean water in her room wherever she was holed up, and she would refresh the water from the pump every time she washed. It was this fastidious habit that finally killed her.

Damsel-Childs' Kickapoo Indians had done a sterling job of cleaning up the town. The cess stench that had haunted the place since Baylee disappeared had been erased along with human night soil and horse dung, but to Lizzie's sensitive nose there was another, alien stink in The Palace and it seemed to her to be getting stronger.

She became convinced that people would believe the smell was coming from her, from her most intimate parts, and she had become even more fixated with cleanliness than usual. She had worked so hard at her washing that the part of her body most closely associated with her trade had been rubbed red-raw, but she didn't worry about that. Long experience had taught her that by the time a man got that close he had precious little in the way of wits about him and would care nothing for her tender condition. If he noticed anything afterwards she could put it down to having been pummelled by such a bull-fist of a man. *Even the least of them likes to hear how mighty they are in the saddle,* she thought. *Bless them all.*

If cleanliness truly was next to Godliness the whore, Long Lizzie, was fit to be canonised by mid-afternoon on that Friday in the heart of a Texas summer. And she had yet to even see a client.

She was washing once more in her room when the carpenters mounted the big fascia with its fancy scrollwork to the front of the building. In a fine hand-painted facsimile of gold lettering it was emblazoned with the words, 'The Palace', the final name agreed between the banker and Grandma Teatree. Once the hammering around that fascia was done the brothel's doors would be open for business.

A number of freshly shaved and gussied-up men loitered out in the street and they were giving the erection of that fascia more attention than almost any other building work in the town's history, since the roof had been raised on the church hall. The hammering ceased. Inside The Palace, Meads walked down the back corridor and rapped on each of seven door surrounds.

'Show time, ladies, show time!' he called out. 'Time to take the customers.'

Lizzie was distracted for a moment and that was all it took. She missed the tiny, red and black wormlike creature coiled on the towel she used to mop herself dry between her thighs. It was gone when she drew the towel away. Sore as she was, she didn't notice the sudden slight sting burning inside her. She joined the other women as they trooped out into the bar room.

'Any woman can drape herself around a tie post wearing nothing but a possibles bag and still look like an angel, but those girls are lovelier than sunrise in the desert.'

Maker Doyle and Wiggins Bull were the first men to stand at the bar and survey the bounty afforded by The Palace. They'd fixed the fascia in place and received payment, and then Grandma Teatree had invited them to take a drink to 'wet the sawdust'. She was confident she would see some of that money back in her hand before sundown.

Maker repeated himself, 'Lovelier than sunrise in the desert.'

Wiggins giggled uncomfortably. Unlike Maker he was both unmarried and unversed in the ways of women-kind. The older man talked constantly about the fairer sex. He extolled his 'better half', the 'smell of a sweet cunny' and the joys of 'taking a handful of warm lovin' on a cold night'.

Wiggins had seen his boss's wife. She reminded him of his mother and smelled the same way, of sweat and cooking. She in no way resembled the exotic birds of paradise sitting in their underwear on red leather couches around the pillars down the centre of the bar. Nobody he had ever seen before did, not even in his dreams.

Slanting sunlight bathed the girls with a forensic glow and Wiggins was sure he could see through their scanties to the naked flesh underneath. He swallowed hard and felt the money turning hot in his pocket.

More men came into the bar and all of them skirted around the girls to belly up to the counter and order a tall beer. Once served, they too leaned back against the counter and surveyed the merchandise. Wiggins couldn't take his eyes from a smiling blonde woman with an ample bosom. She seemed on the point of laughter. He thought she looked nice.

Maker was astonished when Wiggins put down his pot of beer and marched like a sleepwalker to the blonde's side. He held out his hand as if asking her to dance and she rose daintily to her feet, took his hand and then led the young man away.

A Mexican in a sombrero strode into the long room. He ignored the counter, choosing instead to strut along the pillars with his hand on his hip and examine each girl in turn. He was the only man in the room whose face was dirty with a two-day growth of beard. He pointed at a pretty redhead. She stood up, smiled, and then led him away.

From somewhere in the corridors out behind the bar Maker heard girlish laughter. He felt compelled to act. He couldn't let the boy be the man here. Among the five remaining tarts there sat a larger woman with a good figure. She reminded him of Cathy, his wife, when she was younger and fresher. He went to her and she smiled, stood up and took his hand. She smelled of soap and something else, something odd. Cathy often smelt of odd things. Maker believed it was just another of the things men didn't need to know about. Men were put on this Earth to buy food and provide a roof over a bed; women were there to put that food on the table and warm the bed at night.

Maker's view of the world was a simple one, but when Long Lizzie took his hand and steered him along the corridor to her room, she was about to make his simple world much, much more complicated.

31

Some of what happened next I learned, the rest I surmised.

Grandma Teatree was in a quandary. She was undecided about what she should do next and that was not her way at all. The bar was doing decent business and the girls were getting quick trade. Most of their transactions took fifteen to twenty minutes – including a quick wash down between customers – so nobody was left waiting around too long before being seen. By all accounts The Palace's first journey towards night had proved a success.

Then why was it that every one of her senses was screaming at her to get away from there, to run as far as she could, to swim for her life? Something at the very edge of perception was biting at her, hard. It nagged at her, worried and fretted at her nerves, until finally something fell into place and she got the first inkling of her answer.

Grandma stood on the landing outside her suite and looked down on the long room of The Palace for a busy half-hour to confirm her growing suspicions. She counted the girls out and she counted them back in again. She looked at the sheepish men who came back out into the bar room, hitching their britches and trying not to catch each other's eye, but thirsty for another tall beer. Six women wore a path backwards and forwards across the room with their beaus in tow. The seventh was missing in action.

Where was the larger form of Long Lizzie? What was the big woman up to?

Grandma gestured down to Meads who was sitting at the bar nursing a beer. He quickly climbed the stairs and strode to her side. She explained what she was concerned about and he nodded. Then he walked back down into the bar room and made his way into the corridors where the women plied their trade.

He hesitated. He was uncomfortable with the sounds of rutting and the panting groans coming from the long row of rooms. Somebody, and he was pretty sure it was Kitten Kelly, was chanting 'Oh yeah, oh yeah, oh yeah…' with dubious sincerity but great enthusiasm.

Lizzie's room was at the far end and nearest the water pump. As quietly as possible he traversed the distance. There were four noisily occupied rooms, three empty cubicles and then he reached her door. Meads pressed his ear against the panelling. He heard a sound like a baby sucking and the crackling noise a fire makes when you burn wet logs. There was a muted murmur of voices, oily and high-pitched. He pulled away for a moment and studied the door with wary eyes. The sounds coming from the rooms at the top end of the corridor made sense. What he was hearing here made him draw his pistol and cock it.

A sudden sound made him jump. Red Jane emerged from her crib with a scarlet-faced, middle-aged man whose scant hair was mussed like a broken bird's nest and whose copious moustache she was smoothing with delicate fingers. Meads knew the man as a nodding acquaintance, little more. He was someone he had passed on the boardwalk and exchanged 'good-days' with over the years. He thought the man looked almost exactly like a walrus.

The man fondly patted Jane on the behind and waggled his fingers at her, shrugging his meaty shoulders and simpering like a child. He wobbled away, still tucking his shirt in and buttoning his fly. Once he was gone, Jane turned and saw Meads standing at the end of the corridor, almost lost in the shadows.

'Are you okay?' she whispered.

'I'm fine,' he lied.

Kitten Kelly's chant took that moment to become much louder. The man with her began to bellow like a branded mule.

'She loves her work,' said Jane, her eyebrows raised.

'It's a gift.'

She gestured towards her open door. 'Would you like to come in?'

For a second he didn't understand the question, and then the penny dropped.

'No,' he grinned, 'not right now. But thanks anyway, Jane.'

'The invitation's there when you feel like being friendly, Mr Meads.'

'Samuel.'

'I know.'

She turned towards her door and stepped through. At the last moment she flipped up the back of her shift and he was gifted with a fleeting glimpse of her neat little behind. And then the door swung closed. She'd be washing before returning to her place in the shop window. He wasn't sure how he felt about that. The porky walrus who'd just left hadn't been Jane's only conquest that day. She had proved quite popular.

Meads shook himself to clear his mind of a tumble of images, including her backside. He had a job to do and had put it off too long already. He stepped back to Lizzie's crib. The air around it felt strangely cold for such a warm night. There was a smell he didn't recognise but it scratched at his nostrils like boiling tar. He reached out his hand.

Mary Peach fell out of her room in the arms of a man Meads didn't know. Her hair was wild and her chemise fell open to the waist. The little man's hands were clutching at her and he was in a condition of evident excitement.

'No,' she was saying, 'no, Mr Pinfold. If you want to do it again you will just have to pay again. Those are the rules. Please, Mr Pinfold, oh, please, be a good boy.'

It looked like she was wrestling with a nest of vipers. Meads rushed to separate the couple. When the little man saw the gun in his hand he tried to run but his pants were still around his ankles. He fell headlong, exposing a surprisingly hairy backside. Meads would've much preferred to see Jane's if he must look at such a thing. Mary retied her chemise and he noticed she had completely lost the look of innocence he had discerned when first they met just days before.

Pinfold groaned and clutched at his groin, then staggered to his feet, tugged his pants up around his waist and hurried away.

'I'll get more money, I'll be back,' he hissed before turning the corner back to the bar.

Jane came out. 'What's the alarm? Is there a fire?'

Mary grinned. 'Pinfold wanted two for the price of one. Meads here told him to come back for the New Year's sale.'

'Good for you, Samuel. Now, work to do.'

Mary closed the door behind her and Jane patted Meads' arm before returning to her place on the divans. Meads sighed and walked back into the icy shadows before Long Lizzie's crib. He didn't allow himself any more delay. He rapped loudly on the door surround.

'Lizzie,' he shouted, 'are you okay in there? Get decent. I'm coming in.'

He waited a few moments, then pushed her door wide open.

32

Prester proves opinionated, very opinionated.

We left Fernandez with Goody Marsh who always seemed happiest with a poor chick under her motherly wing. The last I saw of the man was the look of utter despair on his face when Goody placed a large plate of steak, eggs and fried potatoes in front of him then set to cutting the steak into bite-sized pieces so he could eat one-handed.

I had to detour to Levine's to fetch my mount. Pearl was pleased to see me again and I stroked her nose and spoke gently to her while a boy helped me saddle her and fix her bridle. I flipped him a coin before I slid my Winchester into the saddle holster and tied the lace of my belt holster to my thigh then clipped a leather thong over my pistol's hammer. It was a small thing, I know, but I have known men lose a belt gun when their holster bounced around during a canter and never find it again. I'd spent enough just recently and another nineteen dollars for a new Peacemaker would pinch my reserves until they groaned in pain.

I stepped onto the mounting block, climbed into the saddle and gave a gentle pull on the reins. Pearl responded as if we were two creatures with but one mind. We rode out of the stables and joined the Preacher and Prester Montague on Main Street. Our little posse headed west riding over the spur loop of rail that swung out from the main line to the marshalling yards by the stock pens. The old staging post, which I noticed had been dandied-up with a big new sign declaring it to be 'The Palace', was almost at the centre of an island created by a double ring of bright steel.

Preacher said, 'I suppose some of your crew will be taking advantage of the town's newest attraction.'

'Probably more than I choose to think. It was clever of The Palace to open its doors and its tarts to open their legs for the first time on a payday.'

I said nothing but studied the building closely. My Alice was in there and I had a sudden image of the smooth, lithe curves I had spied when she sported in her river. I sighed aloud.

'Sheriff Sawyer was a vocal opponent of the project too,' said the Preacher.

'As would be any right-thinking man.'

I couldn't be sure but I thought I saw a small dark shape at one of the windows and I wondered if she was watching us ride by. There were a number of rough looking men loitering around the front of her place as if undecided about going inside, and I was glad she had Meads as her handyman. He was a very capable fellow. I liked him.

Montague took us along a different route to the mine workings, one that clung more closely to the railway line. That path was wide and well made. It was much better than the narrow hog trail leading past the cemetery that Preacher and I'd followed to the fire ant mound.

On that path we could ride three abreast and at our easy pace it was possible to engage in free conversation. Prester Montague was a man of many opinions and he was more than happy to share all of them with two relative strangers. By the time those mine buildings and spoil heaps hove into view I knew more about the workings of his mind than I did my own. One thing was for sure: he did not like the then President of the United States, he being Chester Alan Arthur. He claimed Arthur was 'little more than an attorney and a hollow mouthpiece for the Republican political machine'.

He said, 'The man was born in Vermont and raised in upstate New York. He's a pure blood Yankee muck-a-muck who has but one saving grace, and that's his advocacy for the Pendleton Civil Service Reform Act. He would not be in the White House today if that good Ohio-born man, President Garfield, had not been killed by the coward, Charles Guiteau. That makes two presidents murdered in less than twenty years. Perhaps congress should appoint Wyatt Earp as President. At least he'd be able to shoot back.'

Montague acted as if Washington was on his doorstep instead of some fifteen hundred miles away as the crow flies. I personally believed that what happened in Washington stayed in Washington, and I was not about to go poking my nose into the doings of politicians any more than I would put a dollar bill on the result of a shell game at the fair. At the one I'd lose my nose and at the other I'd lose my dollar.

There was a long black train wreathed in steam sitting on the rails by a low, white and sturdy looking building. The train had a string of carriages behind it and from our vantage point Montague could point out how it and its coal cart had been decoupled on arrival, driven onto a big turntable, and then brought back to be re-coupled at what was now the front of its carriages. A steam train could push its load if need be, but when carrying silver it was best if the drivers had a clear view of the road ahead.

He then explained the silver was carried along with two well-armed guards in a disguised, heavily armoured van that was locked tight when the train left the mine and wouldn't be re-opened until it arrived in Shafter.

'Can you see which of the carriages I mean?' he asked.

'Third one from the end,' said the Preacher.

'I'm astonished, Preacher Spindrift. How could you tell?'

'I can see a row of disguised gun slits up higher than a man would stand. There must be a step arrangement in the wagon that puts the guards up higher than their attackers and gives them a clear advantage. Good design.'

'May I just say, Preacher, it's a good thing you chose to follow the rocky path of righteousness rather than the slippery slope of evil. With your wit and sharp eye, you would've made a formidable bandit.'

'And yet some would say I am a thief.'

'Why so?'

'Because I would steal a sinner from certain perdition and put him back on the road to redemption.'

'A precious soul stolen back from the very claws of Satan himself.'

'That's not what I said,' retorted the Preacher, enigmatically.

Our next stop was an enclosed space where a small herd of ponies were corralled. Montague told us they were Texas ponies, sturdy little creatures that could pull twice their own weight and were employed to drag narrow carts filled with ore along the small gauge rails that laced the mine's tunnels.

They spent a lot of time underground but looked well-groomed and healthy enough to me. The mine manager nodded when I said as much.

'The men treat them like pets. They even give them names and buy them treats from town if they have any spare cash. I doubt the little critters will be getting much in the way of treats this payday.'

We left our horses in the corral where there was hay and fresh water. The ponies crowded around their big sisters with a friendly enough welcome. Montague indicated a low shack with a high tin roof. It was the least sturdy looking of all the buildings. Even an untrained eye could see it'd been thrown up in a mortal hurry.

'That's the bunkhouse. There may be men asleep in there and I'd ask you to be considerate about noise while we visit.'

'They won't hear us, Prester, be sure of that,' smiled the Preacher. 'Any sound we make will be drowned by the ticking of that big old belly watch you wear in your waistcoat.'

Montague pulled out a silver half onion and looked at it. Once Preacher mentioned it you couldn't help but hear that thing ticking away like a beetle in church rafters. I did not carry a watch myself. In Texas that is why the sun rises in the morning and sets at the close of day. Any man who knows his east from his west can use his own shadow as a sundial. But still, that half onion was a pretty thing.

He tucked it back in his waistcoat and pulled open the bunkhouse door. That warm, organic smell you always find when a number of men share an enclosed space rolled over us.

'I'll show you their billets,' he whispered, and led the way.

33

While Caleb and the Preacher head up towards the mine, hell came to The Palace.

In her guise as Grandma, Alice was becoming increasingly concerned. Meads had been gone for nearly an hour and since then Lauren Maplesweet had also performed a vanishing act. The number of men crowding the bar continued growing as the sun sank lower in the sky and the five remaining girls were relaxing their customers' 'natural tensions' as fast as they could. Kitten Kelly was all but bowling out into the bar with her ample breasts swinging free and shouting 'next'.

Alice took a turn around her suite. She could see the sun flaring through the hills. She had spotted Caleb riding towards those hills earlier that afternoon in the company of the Preacher and a man she recognised as the mine manager. They must have been on their way to the Fulsome workings. She wondered if they had clues about the lumberyard boy's killing. With everything that had been happening recently she had almost forgotten about the dead man found in the ant mound. She shuddered.

She wanted to see Caleb again. She liked the way he looked at her, the way a man should look at a woman, the way her husband looked at her every day from that time he had pulled her from his fish traps to the day he died. She was Alice to him, Sweet Alice. She had allowed herself to grow old in the minds of everyone else who came to the settlement he had named Mule's Ass, and she watched as they turned a collection of holdings into a town. But in Abel Forster's eyes she remained young and fresh as that first day in 1691 when she climbed naked as a baby out of the water and into his arms.

Things were different back then, wilder. There were so many buffalo that one day the horses Abel had rounded up got spooked by a big passing herd. They stampeded and forty head ran away. These were collected with the help of some Spanish soldiers who were fed well afterwards with buffalo meat roasted over an open fire on willow skewers.

Nearby was the Rancheria of the Indians of the Payaya nation. They were a very large nation and their country was very fine. In the language of the Indians their home was called Yanaguana and the young couple distributed among them rosaries, pocket knives, cutlery, beads and tobacco.

Abel had given a horse to the man he called captain but who was really the Payaya chief. Whenever Abel met the chief he would stand to attention and throw a snappy salute. The chief would roar with laughter. He had a big, infectious laugh and all his people within earshot would join with his merriment. They were a friendly, gentle people, and they taught Abel a lot about range craft and hunting.

Alice sighed heavily. Time was not kind to the Payaya. Disease stole away their lives and greedy men stole their fine country. One year the survivors of the Payaya disappeared overnight as if they had all been stolen away.

She'd watched the State's changing fortunes as its allegiances swept from Mexico to the US and then across to the Confederates and then back to the US again after the war. Abel wasn't that old when he died after more than forty years of wedded harmony and they had never had children. He was surprised at that but she wasn't. Before they could conceive she would need to become a human woman, something she neither wanted to do nor knew how to manage. She liked being a water-sprite.

Sometimes she felt guiltily that she had denied Abel his chance at fatherhood, but she reassured herself that their time together was happy enough. Her human appearance was a disguise she could alter at will. Looking old and being crotchety had kept her safe in a world where women were little more than chattels to be kept in the house and were counted along with the cattle and sheep. Abel never did that to her but he was a very rare man indeed, big-hearted.

And now there was Caleb. She smiled.

The noise from the bar room intensified and distracted her from her thoughts. It sounded like a fight breaking out. Without Meads to deal with things she would have to go out there herself and quieten things down. She sighed and drew down her fiercest expression, the one she had once used to scare off a curious bear that had lumbered into her kitchen in the old house. The house Abel had built for her with his own two hands.

She stormed out onto the landing and gripped the banister rail as if she was going to throw herself into the fray, then froze in shock. Something had taken possession of the far end of the long room, something malicious and dreadful. She felt a stinking pall of cold air wash up towards her. Some of the men at the bar had drawn their pistols and their volley of desperate gunfire was tearing wet pieces from the body of the dislocated monstrosity that seemed little more than a mass of boiling black and red sores and disjointed limbs.

Then the flesh of the thing facing the armed men erupted and fired a cloud of pus and sharp spines into them, lacerating their bodies and shredding their clothes. Threadlike tentacles reached out and lashed at everyone in reach, took a firm grip and dragged them towards a gaping black maw that opened in its core. They very soon stopped struggling and began to lose their coherent form, melting into the evil-looking creature like fat on a hot skillet.

Then she heard the voices, the many voices welcoming each victim to the Host with a gloating, oily glee. The screaming and shouting ceased when the last person in the bar room fell prey to the beast and was devoured. And then it saw her and she knew it was considering her, trying to ascertain what she was.

'And what are you, pretty little thing? You smell of the river, a thing of water, not of guts and man blood. Shall we invite you into the Host, pretty water thing, or shall we just destroy you as an enemy creature? What do you say, pretty water thing? Shall we drink you?'

She threw herself backwards into her rooms to escape a host of spines that stripped the woodwork where she'd been standing a split second earlier. She saw the beast billowing and crawling up the stairs towards her, lifting itself on parodies of human arms and legs supported by thickening tentacles and other misshapen limbs. She slammed her door and locked the creature out, but she knew flimsy wooden panelling would prove nothing more than a temporary barrier. She had to get out of the building.

She thought fast. The frame of her door bulged and she heard snickering laughter combined with the words, 'Water thing, oh, water thing, let us drink you dryyyy, let us drink you, water thing...'

The wood creaked and began to splinter. She began to strip away her clothes and as she did so all trace of Grandma Teatree dissolved and was gone.

It was time the old besom came to an end, thought Alice. *A new start away from here is very much on the cards.*

Naked, she bundled her clothes under her arm and pattered to her window. She threw back the latch and put all her strength into lifting the sash. It didn't move. It had been painted into its frame. She whimpered. Behind her, thin tendrils were pushing between the door and its frame. She ran into her bedroom and wedged that door shut with a chair. Wasting no time, she tried that window. It creaked open just a few inches, no more.

'Water thing, we have you now and we're so, so very thirsty.'

The nightmare creature was at the bedroom door, pushing at it. It would be through in a matter of seconds. She fed her outer clothes through the narrow gap provided by the window and then, just as her door flew open and the thing burst into her room with a shriek of triumph, she *flowed* through the opening and was gone.

117

Anyone watching the front of The Palace would have seen a fine silver stream of liquid fall onto the boardwalk and then resolve itself into a slender, naked young woman who picked up some scattered clothing from where it lay and then ran like a startled wild animal into the shadows.

From inside the building there came howls of rage and heavy crashing sounds as if furniture was being thrown about. Mr Pinfold, who had raided a box under his floorboards and returned for his second session with Mary Peach, heard the commotion and scampered back to his home. He very carefully locked and then bolted his front door. He put the money back where it came from and drew his curtains tightly closed. He decided he no longer approved of brothels.

At The Palace, one by one, the windows became dark as its lamps were extinguished. A careful listener would have heard a murmuring whisper insinuating itself into their ear, as if a great Host was trying to be silent in a church. The town's almost total quietude was briefly splintered by the sound of hoof-beats galloping west in the darkness, towards the hills and the Fulsome mine.

{34}

Witnesses told me what might have happened to these men.

Parrett Damsel-Childs and Foster Teague were toasting the success of their latest initiative. Observers had told them that footfall to The Palace had been brisk and turnaround fast.

'The, ah, young women, must be, hm, skilled in their trade, don't you, hm, think, Foster?'

'Horny men and helpful women; makes the world go round.'

'Ha, hm, indeed.'

They raised glasses of a particularly fine port Teague had provided for the occasion and the fat man frequently dipped handfuls from the cheese board supplied by Damsel-Childs. His belly rumbled. He hoped there would be more than a tasting cheese platter to complement the wine. He was starving.

The two men sat in the gleaming darkness of Damsel-Childs' office at the back of the closed bank. Two brass lamps cast pools of warm light into the room. The fire was unlit on such a warm night. The rancher and the banker were united in many things, projects they jointly funded, their love of money, and their disdain for ordinary town-folk who they both considered to be a commodity to be used rather than neighbours to be cherished. They also loathed each other with an abiding hatred.

The fastidious Damsel-Childs abhorred Teague's porcine excess and stentorian breathing. He hated the way the man bulked his way into every room like a bloated sack of wind and blubber, the way he had to ease himself sideways through even the widest door. Teague disliked the banker's habit of pawing the furniture and licking the juice out of every word. He sometimes felt like taking the man by the throat and choking a complete, uninterrupted sentence out of him, just one, just once.

But what they reviled about each other was as nothing to the flat disgust they had for everyone else, and so they invariably sought out each other's company and shared their bitter, inverted pleasures and wallowed in a mutual sense of smug superiority. If it was not for the fact that they paid well it was likely that both of them would have been slaughtered by their employees.

'Foster, my, hm, friend. What say we walk over, to the, ah, Palace and see how, hm, well our business is, ah, hm, faring?'

Teague grunted like air escaping from a bladder. Damsel-Childs fought hard to keep an expression of utter disgust from his face.

'Walking ain't my strong point, but I suppose we could take a look-see. Parrett, you aren't thinking of dipping your nib in the corporation ink, are you, my friend?'

The banker failed to keep a look of horrified nausea from his features and the fat rancher chortled with a wet gurgling sound.

'I was only pulling at your leg, Parrett. My bit of fun. Please, don't take offense.'

'Hm, hm, of course, ah, Foster. Yes, none took, ah, hm, none at all.'

With his mouth twisted like a man sucking a pickled lemon he rose to his feet. The rancher struggled to move his bulk into an upright position, rolling around in his seat until he could push himself vertical. Damsel-Childs ignored the flapping hand that was obviously seeking his aid and moved to the door. He would share salt with the lumbering oaf but he would never deliberately touch any part of him.

Womanish, pansified, cunny, thought Teague when he finally managed to pull himself to his feet with the groaning assistance of the mantelshelf. He stood for a moment with his heart pounding and his breath labouring in his massive chest. *Little stick of a creature thinks a full-grown man can survive on a scrap of fermented cow's milk. I'm weak with hunger, starving.*

'After you, Parrett,' he finally managed to gasp out.

Damsel-Childs moved swiftly to the bank's side door and unlocked it. He held it open until the rancher had squeezed sideways into the alleyway and then locked it securely once more. He buttoned the key into an inside pocket and led the way out onto Main Street.

He said, impishly, 'Ha, hm, ha, I've, hm, just thought. We, hm, call this, hm, Main Street, but, ha, in fact it's the, hm, Shafter Road. Funny, hm, eh?'

'Fucking hilarious. Can we get on with this, please?'

The slender fop and the corpulent body gazed west down the street towards the stockyards, the rail loop and the marshalling pens where they could just make out the rangy shadowed bulk of The Palace. They stood silently for a few moments, silent apart from the laboured rasp of the rancher's breathing, and then they strode towards the darkened building. It was evident to both of them that the brothel was closed for business during what should've been its busiest time. They needed to find out why.

Teague couldn't talk and walk at the same time. The energy involved in moving his massive frame sucked all the oxygen from his lungs and the words from his throat. Such was not the case for Damsel-Childs, who twittered like an angry bird all the way along the boardwalk.

'This is, hm, insufferable. How, ah, are we meant to make a profit if the shop is closed for, hm, business?'

Teague filtered the man's voice out after a while and concentrated on the business of walking without drooling while his mouth was open to drag as

120

much air into his body as his girth would allow. The path was slightly downhill but it didn't seem to be helping. His knees cracked with effort when he followed the banker off the south-side boardwalk and onto the rutted, beaten earth of the deserted street. He stumbled resentfully around the stockyards and nearly fell headlong when he tripped on one of the spur rails. With a sense of gratitude, he climbed the few steps onto the north side and regained the flat luxury of the wooden pedestrian walkway. He had never been as glad for the work of careful carpenters as he was at that moment.

They drew up outside The Palace and hesitated by the double doors leading into the long room.

'Can you, hm, hear, ah, whispering?'

All Teague could hear was the sound of his heart pounding after such an unprecedented and extended bout of exercise. He took the opportunity to catch his breath and growled, 'This entire fucking hole belongs to us. Why don't we just go in and find out what's happening?'

'Foster, hm, your language is, ah, hm, becoming dreadful. Please, my friend.'

'Fuck it, come on!'

And he pushed his way inside with Damsel-Childs at his heels.

There was enough light coming through the glazed doors to illuminate the hexagon and little else, but the cobalt shadows seemed to be moving purposefully, as if the darkness was developing a muscular intent.

Teague bellowed, 'What have you done with the lights?'

And then, faster than whips, something struck out and coiled around Teague. It lifted him into the air and then he was gone, his high-pitched shrieking swallowed into the midst of a toxic susurration and wicked laughter.

Damsel-Childs didn't wait another second but slithered back through the doors and stood shivering on the boardwalk in shock, trying to analyse the impossible turn of events he'd just witnessed. Galvanised by terror, he made to run to safety and was already planning to rouse the men of the town when the doors flew open and a nest of tendrils yanked him back into the gloom. His last coherent thought was that he heard Teague's mocking and strangely altered voice gloating. It breathed in his ear with unctuous pleasure, 'Time for a decent meal from you at last, Parrett.'

And then all became pain and confusion.

Caleb and the Preacher were looking for clues as the sun sets in the hills.

Preacher closely studied the three men's mattresses without touching them and then rummaged through their footlockers. One bleary-eyed miner watched us at work for a few seconds then his head dropped back onto his pillow and within seconds we heard his gentle snore. From another bed we heard the flatulent rumble of a man breaking wind loudly. The atmosphere thickened. There were a few muttered complaints.

The bunkhouse looked bigger on the inside than it had when we first approached, but it still felt crowded. I believed the ponies were having a better time of it in their corral. At least they'd enough room to move and fresh air.

Preacher gestured and we left the men to their noisome repose. It wasn't until we regained the open air that I realised I'd pretty much been holding my breath the whole time we were inside. The late sunlight was almost horizontal in the dark blue sky and I had to turn my back on it, blinking away blinding spots of red light. When I recovered my sight I looked down at the landscape spread out before me and saw that the town had already been gathered into the shadows of the hills. While I stood blinded by the sun, twilight was descending over Main Street. I wondered at that. It had a gentle beauty.

Preacher and Prester Montague held a conference some distance from the bunkhouse. I could hear the murmur of their voices but failed to make any sense of their conversation. Preacher pointed towards a bluff further up the hill and the mine manager took off his hat and ran his hand through his thick, greying hair before nodding. He took his silver half-onion out again and gestured at the dial but Preacher just maintained that stone-cold level gaze of his and smiled his implacable smile, a sliver of moon's crescent under the shadows cast by his hat's brim.

I wondered again why I accepted everything he told me so readily, why I hadn't been filled with fear. I'd seen things that should've turned my hair white and sent me screaming towards the distant horizon at high speed, but I remained and chose to stand at his side.

Was I calm because he was? Or was it something more? I had watched his equal competence with a gun and a doctor's bag. I knew Emmanuel Fernandez owed him his life. Everything the Preacher approached he handled with the same assured grace, and without ever a hint of arrogance. I admired him and I liked him, despite his stories about flying space mountains and angels copulating with apes. I'd seen him hover three feet above the floor and I was very aware that the terrible thing he called the enemy recognised him – and feared him.

I vowed that one day I'd ask him straight if he'd done something to take away my fear and keep me on a straight and level course during a time of impossible storms, but until then I'd keep my place by the Preacher's side.

'Trying to weave rainbows, Caleb?'

I dragged my wits back from the labyrinth of riddles that beset me and grinned at him.

'I fear the rainbows are weaving me, Preacher. The days have become passing strange just lately.'

'Persevere, my friend. We may walk in the Valley of the Shadows, but remember, you have an angel at your shoulder.'

'And a ready gun, which can also be right useful in a tight spot.'

He placed his hand on my right arm.

'Will you walk with me a while?'

I said nothing. I just nodded and stayed at his heel as he turned and headed back towards the ponies and our horses in the corral. Pearl gave me a welcoming nickering noise and came over to the split log fence to place her nose in my open hand. Preacher caught his horse's eye and gave her a barely perceptible bow. The big bay snorted and returned the gesture.

Weaving rainbows indeed. He was asking me to accept a whole basket of strange fruit and instead of treating them with caution I was taking a big bite from each. On that hill with the sun setting into a mist of lilac and blood red bands under an indigo sky already filling with stars, we sure seemed a long way from Texas. I breathed air that seemed made richer and cleaner by dreams and for a long, long moment I felt happier than I'd any reason to be. I believed in flying space mountains and fleets of great star ships, angels and giants walking the land, and millions of years of careful toil undertaken to build Eden once more on earth as the home for men. If he'd spoken of dragons I would've looked to the sky for winged serpents and flame. If strangeness made a sound, I would've been deafened by it.

We skirted the corral and passed the mine's entrance. I tripped on something in the gathering twilight and would've fallen headlong but Preacher caught me faster than a striking rattler.

'Wool-gathering is all to the good, Caleb,' he said with an arch look to his grey eyes, 'but try not to gather so much you get caught up in a web of the stuff.'

I chuckled ruefully. 'I'll keep my eyes open in future. But where are we going?'

'We're looking for clues. There was nothing of value in the bunkhouse other than raw evidence of Sodomite activity on the mattresses. There was also some women's paint in one of the footlockers. At least one of our men must have masqueraded as a woman at times. Caleb, such activities do not make a man an evil murderer or a rapist, gather ye love where ye may find it, but those three raped and murdered poor Klosky and in the process became possessed by the enemy. I need to put more flesh on this story's bones.'

He stopped walking and scanned the hillside. Evening mist was leeching up from the soil and blanketing the ground. It covered our boots.

He continued, 'Montague thinks the day a little too long in the tooth for us to find anything. He says it's too dark to see much of value, and he may be right. But at least we can ascertain whether we can get from here to the top of that gulch and then we can come back and make a more careful search in the morning.'

He turned on the cylinder of magic light he'd used in the tunnel and as before it made everything else darker. I had no hope of seeing anything under my nose let alone under my feet so I followed his light, picking my way like a cautious new-born colt walking on ice.

He found a natural stairway about two hundred yards from the mine entrance and shone his beam up until he was sure it reached the top of the ridge. Then he turned his light off. We waited a few minutes while our eyes adjusted to the lack of light and it was right then that a fat white moon began to rise from the flats beyond the town. It turned the Sweet Alice River into a vein of silver in an ocean of darkness.

'That's strange,' said the Preacher.

'What is?' I was not looking forward to climbing a cliff in the evening's gloom so anything that distracted my friend from it was welcome indeed, however temporary.

'The Palace. I can't see any lights coming from the cathouse, can you?'

'I'm not sure I can get my bearings from here, Preacher. Are you sure?'

'Yes, yes, I'm sure. The west end of Main Street is in pitch darkness. Surely this would be a brothel's busiest time.'

'I have not your understanding of such things, Preacher. I would've thought a man could get such urgings at any time of day.'

'Perhaps you're right, Caleb, but to be closed after the working day at the end of the week? What must Mizz Teatree be thinking? If they sold nothing else the town's men would be waiting in line for a cold beer. Goody's would certainly be shut by now.'

Sundown during mid-summer happened at about ten and Goody served her last meal at least an hour before that. The Palace would be the only show in town.

'I see what you mean. It makes no sense.'

'All of my instincts tell me there's something wrong down there. Something very wrong. Perhaps we should forget the murder for the time being and get back to town. People might need our help.'

I felt a sting of fear in my belly. *Alice.*

{36}

We were halfway towards town and riding down the broad, moonlit path by the railroad when we heard the sound of galloping hoofs coming towards us.

'I think we are about to learn a great deal more about the situation,' said Preacher.

Pearl strained her head towards the sound as if she could smell something unexpected on the night breeze. I freed my rifle from its holster and slipped the leather loop from my pistol's hammer.

'No, Caleb. I don't think we'll need our weapons just yet.'

'Maybe not, Preacher, but I've seen too much strangeness recently not to be prepared.'

'Then let us confront our fears.'

His magic lantern shone out like a lance and caught a small dark figure astride a bridled but unsaddled horse. A white face looked up in shock. Even stamped as it was with desperation and panic I recognised her face instantly.

'Alice!' I cried. 'Alice, it's me!'

She reined in her mount so fiercely that we were showered by small stones kicked up by the horse's scrabbling hooves.

'Caleb, Caleb...' She dissolved into floods of tears and slumped over her horse's mane.

I threw myself from Pearl's back and rushed quickly to her side. Her horse was blowing hard. It hadn't been ridden that far but had evidently been pushed to its limits by its rider's terror. I helped her to the ground and became guiltily aware that the weeping woman in my arms was wearing nothing under her skirts; a fact amply demonstrated when the fine black fabric was momentarily swept up to her waist as she slid from her sweating mount.

The Preacher joined us with the reins of our horses gripped firmly.

'I was looking for you, looking for both of you,' Alice said when the storm of tears had finally subsided to the point where she could speak once more. 'Something terrible has happened, something dreadful. I can't describe it. It wanted me, it wanted to kill me. It swallowed everyone else, melted them. I don't know what it did — I don't understand what it did. I don't even know what it was. It was horrible.'

Despite the warmth of the night she began to shiver and I held her closer to me.

'We know what it was, Alice,' said the Preacher. 'We have met it before.'

126

'The men were shooting at it but it had no effect. It spoke to me, Satan. It called me "water thing". It said it wanted to... to *drink* me. It wanted to drink me dry.'

Her black eyes were huge in the moonlight. 'How did it know? What is it?'

Preacher placed a comforting hand on her shoulder. 'It is a secret creature older than the sprite folk, Alice. Much, much older in fact. It now calls itself the Host in human tongue, but it was once known as the Sha-aneer, the wise worm of the deep soil. It has declared war on the Eden seed.'

He looked from her to me. I was busy taking in the fact they knew each other by name and that the Preacher was not surprised by Grandma's newly youthful looks.

'Alice, how many people did it take from The Palace?'

'Take? How many? I can't be sure. Wait, let me think.' She pulled away from me a little but didn't leave the circle of my arms.

She pondered for a moment. 'There were Meads and the girls plus seven kitchen and bar staff. That makes fifteen. Customers were four or five deep at the bar. I remember thinking we couldn't have had a more successful first day. Say twenty-five or thirty men waiting and five or six in the cribs. I'm sorry, Satan. I can't be more precise than that.'

He took her face in his big, flat palm. 'If you're right it has fifty bodies now, perhaps more. That will give it plenty enough mass to successfully transmute and by now it must feel completely confident that nothing and no one will be able to stop its progress. It may even be right. Damn the thing.' He spat these words with a fury I'd not witnessed before. 'Damn it back to the burning hell it came from.'

He turned to me. 'Caleb, please escort Alice back to the mine. Find Prester Montague and tell him I'm looking into events at The Palace. Tell him none of his men must go into town, none of them. Tell him the train must stay at the mine until I come back. Insist on it. Use force if you must. Understand?'

There was more than a hint of command in his voice and his face was grim.

'Surely I should come with you? The two of us...'

'No, no, Caleb. Your place is with Alice until we're sure she's safe.' He looked at the black-eyed beauty in my arms. 'Will you bind the streams with my friend?'

'We already have, earlier, by my river.'

He looked from her to me with a strangely intense expression.

'Can she depend on you?'

I was out of my depth but I also knew that if Alice needed anything from me I would provide it with pleasure.

'Of course and always,' I said.

He handed me my reins, stepped into his stirrup and then hoisted himself easily up into his saddle. Without another word he rode east towards town.

Alice spoke in an urgent whisper. 'He's angry. I've never seen him angry like that. I thought that worm creature was dreadful but I think he'll make it weep this night. Caleb, may I ride with you? Please?'

She kissed me then with all the passion she'd shown down by the river and despite everything that'd happened that day I responded to her. Her shivering had calmed and once more I felt the touch of her tongue in my mouth. There was an electric flash of warmth and I swallowed a sudden flood of saliva.

Pearl could carry the two of us with ease. She made a happy sound, almost a chuckle, when she felt Alice's strong, slender legs squeeze against her forequarters. The reins of Alice's mount were tied off on my saddle's pommel and we silently made our way back up towards the Fulsome mine. I felt that unnatural surge of happiness again, as if my chest would burst open and sunshine spill out into the night. I told Alice how I was feeling and she snuggled back against me. I caught a waft of some fresh scent that smelled as if lemon, salt and sea air had been blended together with cucumber and strawberries. I didn't know what it was but I knew it was delicious.

I asked her how she was feeling and her answer sobered the mood somewhat.

'I feel I've been given so much to live for at a time when life can be lost so easily. It seems cruel and wrong that the worm has emerged from the deep earth at the very time I find you in my life. I feel like I want you to ride away from here to someplace safe.'

'Then we shall. Why not? What's to stop us?'

'We can't, Caleb, you know that. He will need us here and soon. Anyway, if we fail him here and he loses the fight then soon there won't be a single safe haven anywhere in the entire world. We know that, don't we? We'd just be running like rabbits towards certain death. Better to stay and fight to win.'

'Do you feel lucky enough to win?'

Her voice was hard and flat and I felt the skin prickle all over my body at the sound of it.

'Lucky? There's no luck here. Something evil has risen from the soil and I've seen its power. It's terrible, Caleb, terrible and powerful. I ran away from that thing tonight like a mouse from a cat and it mocked me. It mocked me, Caleb. It called me a "pretty little water thing". It was covered in boils with twisting black worms in them and it spat spines at me like a scared porcupine. It had no face and no mercy. It can't be allowed to win, it can't be. It's vile and it must be destroyed. It must be wiped out completely.'

'And what if we can't?'

'Then Satan must help the world because God has surely abandoned it.'

{37}

While Caleb and Alice made their way to Fulsome and a confrontation with Prester Montague, the Preacher approached the shadows at the west end of Mule's Ass.

He felt a chill breath of air emanate from The Palace while he skirted it and something diseased tainted the night with a sickly, toxic tang. He kept a good distance from the building's doors and windows.

Before he did anything else he scouted the town. It was midnight and most people would've retired to bed at sundown. He needed to know if the Shaaneer contagion had spread beyond its new home in the brothel. He rode his horse into a deeply shadowed side street and dismounted. He patted her flanks.

'I need your eyes to see for me again, old friend. Look everywhere down Main Street except The Palace and the stables attached to it.'

There was a fluttering noise and the skin and muscle around the horse's eye sockets peeled back. Its eyeballs glittered roundly for a moment and then detached themselves from the horse's head and sped away into the night. The Preacher closed his eyelids and in his mind two viewpoints opened up, darting like birds around the buildings of the town.

Not all the townsfolk were asleep. Some were awake and very active while others sat at lonely tables with a bottle close at hand. The Preacher was relieved to find that, while some of the things he saw people doing might seem unusual to a more conservative world view, they were just normal functions of the human condition. The Host had chosen to stay within its nest so far.

One of his flying eyes tracked Emmanuel Fernandez as he crept from the back door of Goody's place and made his way to where his pony was stabled. He watched long enough to realise the man was once again trying to saddle the beast single-handed. He called the eyes back to their accustomed places and cantered to the stable where he dismounted, tied his horse to a hitching post and strode silently to where the one-armed man was struggling.

'Can I give you a hand there, Emmanuel?'

The man bounced into the air and uttered a barely stifled and womanish shriek. His saddle rounded his pony's back and landed heavily on his foot. He groaned through gritted teeth.

'Preacher,' he whined, 'I swear I will fit you with a cow bell so folks can hear you coming. Church mice make more noise than you. You scared the piss out of me.' He looked down. 'And I think I broke my foot.'

'Let me see.'

The one-armed man leaned against his pony and warily lifted his leg. 'Please, don't hurt me.'

The Preacher pulled the boot off and then a carefully darned sock. He examined the foot thoroughly and pressed down in the centre part at its top.

'I was worried you might've cracked the navicular bone.'

'I was wondering that myself. Be just my bad luck.'

'Well... you haven't. Just a bruise at most.'

'Praise the Lord.'

'Mostly the Lord does not allow for one-armed men to be dropping saddles on themselves.'

'Amen to that too.'

Sock and boot back in place, Fernandez stamped the ground a few times then the Preacher helped him prepare his mount.

'I suppose you're wondering what I'm doing out here at such an ungodly time of the morning.'

'Emmanuel, it's no business of mine what a grown man chooses to do with his day.'

'It's her, that Goody Marsh. She keeps feeding me and then she watches to make sure I eat everything on the plate.'

'She's a kind and Christian soul. That's certainly true.'

'Yes, yes, but so much food? Her steak and potatoes churns in my guts like a hot sand devil.' He shuddered and rubbed at his hollow belly. 'She promised me a "good breakfast". I can't be here for that. I couldn't face her "good breakfast". My imagination reels at the very idea of what kind of huge banquet will confront me. I've left a note of thanks and some money to cover the costs of her Samaritan deeds and now I must go.'

'How's the arm?'

The slender reed of a man paused and gazed for a moment at his stump. 'I haven't yet thanked you for what you did, Preacher. You're an angel of mercy.' He looked up at the tall man's face. 'I can still feel my fingers, you know? My palm itches and I go to scratch it and... and there's nothing there.'

'Are you sure you're good to be alone yet?'

'Alone has to be better than dealing with a "good breakfast". I'll shake your hand with my good wing and be on my way.'

The shake was dry and surprisingly firm.

131

'Emmanuel, I'll come out to your place later, in a few days' time. Let me know if there's anything I can do.'

'My place? I guess I might be there, but then again I might not. Preacher, I can smell evil on the wind in Mule's Ass. I hear whispering and there's a cold place deep in my belly. My guts are sensitive to the weather and it's about to change for the worse; I can promise you that.'

'Emmanuel, you never told me. What is it that you do for cash money?'

'Do? I get by. I write stories about the desperadoes down here on the frontier. I suppose I'll have to get used to doing that one-handed too. I have a beautiful machine. It's a black Sholes and Glidden Type Writer and it's been hand-painted with traditional rose designs by an artist in Wisconsin. I can't describe the joy I get from pressing those keys and seeing my words appear on the paper. And then I get my cheque with a copy of the *Gazette* and I see my story's in there with a drawing of a cowboy wreathed in gun smoke. The sun shines on me that day even if it's raining. I do love it so.'

He smiled with creamy pleasure then grabbed at his pommel and hauled himself onto his pony. The sturdy creature barely moved, he was so light in the saddle.

He said, 'I will send you a copy of a story I have in mind. It's about a fellow I know and respect. It will be a good tale and I know the *Gazette* will buy it. The readers in New York will lap it up like folk here eat steak and potatoes. Now, thank you and good night.'

His pony answered the pressure of his knees and began to trot away. He turned in the saddle. 'It's about a Preacher,' he grinned. And then there was just the sound of hoof-beats receding eastwards.

The Preacher walked back to his horse, unhitched her and mounted up. He turned her towards the west and the dark, silent spread of The Palace.

Caleb and Alice reach the mine offices.

Prester Montague was still awake and sitting in his office with some papers in his hands and his feet on his desk when we arrived. He was a night owl, he explained, and chose to burn the midnight oil. That way he could get his office work done without interruptions. This last was said in a very pointed manner. I made my apologies before telling him what the Preacher had asked me to say. All the time I was talking to him, he was taking sly glances at Alice as if trying to unpick her face from a tangled knot of memory.

'None of the men here are due to leave for town anyhow,' he said. 'But the train is due to be loaded and is scheduled to depart in the morning. It is nothing of me to go messing with the Galveston, Harrisburg and San Antonio railroad timetable. I am merely the mine manager, not God almighty. I think Preacher Spindrift might be better dealing with a higher authority. When he arrives we'll send a telegraph to the controller in Shafter. That's the best I can offer.'

I was exhausted. It was all I could do to thank him and ask if there was somewhere Alice and I could grab a few hours of rest. He sighed like a collapsing goat's bladder and swung his booted feet from the desk where he had left them until that moment. For a brief moment I saw the soles and heels of those boots and when I did I felt as if I'd been plunged into icy water. I must've made a sound because Alice looked at me queerly and raised her eyebrows. I returned her a slight shake of my head.

Muttering to himself, Montague unlocked a small cupboard on the wall behind him and drew out a key threaded with a piece of rough string bearing a cardboard tag. He locked the cupboard again and then stretched some kinks out of his back.

'Come on,' he yawned. 'Follow me.'

He strode to the door, walked out into the night and then turned sharp right. We followed. Alice looked at me anxiously and whispered, 'What is it?' I put my finger to my lips.

I feared we'd be expected to share the bunkhouse with his mine workers but instead he led us to a well-appointed shack set away from the rest of the Fulsome buildings. He unlocked it and got a lamp lit, in the process illuminating a wide and pleasant living room.

'This is the surveyor's place,' he explained. 'We use it for visitors when he's away, which is most of the time.' He walked across the room to another door. 'There's a kitchen through here. There's not much in it apart from bacon and dried beans, but there's coffee and a fresh water pump and a stove if you want to get it lit.'

He crossed the room again and opened another door. 'In here is the bedroom and the bathroom. It has a working flush toilet and that's why I make sure to keep the men locked out of here. They would love to use a flush toilet but their habits are not too particular, if you catch my meaning. Feel free to treat this place as your home.' He handed Alice the key. 'I notice your dress is mussed up somewhat, miss, ah...? Sorry. What shall I call you?'

'Alice,' she said coolly.

He looked her up and down like he was thinking of making a bid on the auction block. I swear he licked his lips.

'Alice. Very well, Miss Alice, you'll find some clothes that might fit you in the wardrobe in the bedroom. They belong to the surveyor's wife and she too is a slight parcel. She ain't here to ask, but I'm sure she'll be happy to loan them to you for a while. What she doesn't know won't make no never mind, and she hasn't been here this last seven months or so. And now I'll wish both of you goodnight. Might I suggest you lock the door behind me? Some of the men might get to sleepwalking if they heard there was a pretty little maid visiting and I'd hate to hear the sound of screams this early in the day.'

He walked through the door then leaned back to examine the couple with an insinuating smile. 'Sweet dreams.' And then he was gone.

Alice shuddered and hurried to lock the door behind him.

'He's the slimy trail left by a snail's ass.'

'He's a murderer,' I told her, flatly.

Alice looked at me keenly. 'You saw something in his office, didn't you? I wondered what was wrong. You looked like you'd been slapped by a ghost.'

'Yes, I saw the bottom of his boots. Boots can be as individual as a person's nose if you know what you're looking for and the Preacher showed me some right individual footprints in the dirt where Klosky was lynched. Those men grabbed poor Klosky by the legs and threw some weight on them to stretch his neck and choke him dead. While they were pulling at him their boots pressed down hard in the soil and left their mark clear as day.

'One of the men had had his boots repaired recently and the nail heads were still standing proud in a distinct pattern. I saw that exact pattern here today when Montague swung his feet into the light while taking them down from his desk. I swear on every *Bible* in Shafter and on my wife's grave that I am not mistaken in this. Montague was one of the killers. I'll make sure to tell the Preacher when he gets here. But now I guess we should get some rest.'

We took turns in the water closet. It was a real luxury and clean as a new pin. I would've preferred to brush my teeth with minted powder but made do with rinsing my mouth in fresh pump water. The surveyor, I thought, has himself a swell place to pitch up halfway up a hill. I would like a few home comforts like these in my own place.

I joined Alice in the bedroom. She'd pulled open a drawer at the base of the wardrobe and was rummaging through whatever she had found inside. With a grunt of pleasure, she pulled out a carefully folded blanket. It was grey with wide black stripes.

'This will do perfectly,' she said. 'I found some tacks in the family room and now I've something to tack with them. Folded once, this blanket will make a very fine curtain. Help me get it up at the window, Caleb.'

'Do we really have to, Alice?' I said with a petulant whine in my voice. 'I'm dead on my feet and at the end of my tether.'

'Yes, we do,' she snapped with a touch of Grandma Teatree back in her voice. 'Do you really think snail trail Montague has gone back to work in his office when there's even half a chance he might get to watch us two buck-naked in bed together?'

It took a moment for what she had just said to worm its way into my fuddled head. Suddenly I found myself possessed of a new surge of energy and even by lamplight the room seemed brighter; sparks of moonlight caught in Alice's beautiful black eyes and made them glow with a warm promise. She smiled knowingly.

'Where are those tacks?' I asked.

Just as we were pinning our makeshift curtain into place, I thought I saw a patch of man-shaped shadow moving in the darkness.

'I think you were right about snail trail, Alice.'

She chuckled like a stream rolling on pebbles.

'I know my slime, Caleb. I know my slime.'

{39}

What happened next I know to be the truth.

Preacher Spindrift stood in the shadows at a safe distance and regarded The Palace with a hooded gaze. His horse waited patiently at his side.

'Old friend,' he said at last. 'I need to see what's happening in there. We don't want to risk both your eyes, but can you send one on a look-see for me?'

The horse nickered quietly.

'I appreciate it, I really do. We have spares back at the house if we need them, but I'd rather not waste something that needed to travel one hundred and forty million miles to get here. Okay, when you're ready.'

The tiny globe sped away and the Preacher closed his eyes. He was used to the sudden transition to his viewpoint from stock still to zooming through the air and he accepted it with barely a lurch. The Palace loomed large in his mind's eye and he guided the globe to seek for a way in. All doors and windows on the frontage were closed and he couldn't make out any details through the window glass.

He sent his roving eye around the building until it was hovering at the rear where the stables were now empty. The poor beasts must have been too close and too tempting for the ravenous Sha-aneer to ignore. The Preacher felt sad at this. He preferred the company of horses to most people.

The inky darkness was almost total and the globe progressed at a cautious pace. Details emerged from the gloom. Another closed door and a shut window.

Is the Host making this Palace a fortress? How can it expect to eat?

Then he saw it – a small half-open window by the side of the door – and he sent his viewpoint darting inside. It halted and tried to get its bearings in pitch darkness. He ramped up its light gain to maximum and his vision resolved into a confusion of straight lines and circles. At last he realised he was looking straight down into a stool of comfort. He'd found his way into a lavatory.

He made the globe roll upwards ninety degrees and then begin a slow 360. He found the door of the room and saw it was slightly ajar. He eased the viewing globe out into the corridor.

The place was a wreck. Freezing mist was rolling over the detritus of splintered woodwork that littered the floor. Moisture coated the walls and something thick and mildly phosphorescent dripped from the ceiling. It looked as if the building had been caught in a corrosive flood. Preacher suspected such an image to be close to the truth. Something massive and fluid had torn through all the rooms along the corridor, ripping off doors and shattering furniture.

He opened his eyes for a moment. 'I need to hear what's happening.'

His one-eyed horse looked coolly at him for a heartbeat and then one of its ears unscrewed and winged away to follow a precise path to join with its fellow body part. The other ear lay flat against its owner's head as if trying to become invisible.

'Thank you, old friend. I'll be quick as I can.'

The horse was miserable because its mind was simpler than its owner's and it too was sharing transmitted sound and vision from its remote units. Unlike the Preacher it was unable to decipher and separate the information it was receiving into usable information. It just became heartily nauseated.

The ear joined the eyeball and clipped into place at its base. The composite piece looked like some sort of odd white fruit. Through closed eyelids and against the silence of the sleeping town, Preacher could now see and hear everything going on in The Palace. Without opening his eyes he sat cross-legged on the ground and concentrated.

He heard voices, dozens of voices, muttering and twittering and whispering all around him. He was only getting monophonic sound. He knew if he asked the horse to supply stereo by sending its other ear he would be obeyed, but it would be sure to lead to a frostier relationship for the immediate future. He focused on using what he had.

Using his remote sensors, he allowed his awareness to float down the corridor. At the end it turned right and he followed it. The voices became louder and more distinct. He slowed his pace. Neither of the remote units was organic so they wouldn't be regarded as food, but he didn't want to attract the Host's attention if he could avoid it.

Intense cold fogged his vision and he paused until it cleared. Apart from the mounting devastation, there seemed little to see. Ahead, three steps led up to an archway that looked to have been pushed out of its mountings and had been rendered almost round. The words he was hearing were coming from beyond that arch. At first he thought the language was alien or exotic but then comprehension dawned. Under the strange, sticky, glottal sounds full of clicks and hisses, the voices were speaking English. He listened.

'We are growing stronger.'

'The Sha-aneer is fruitful. Soon we shall divide and then divide and then eat some more.'

'The Eden-born are tasty.'

'Their souls and delicious fat skins feed us best.'

'We burst them. Burst them and eats them up.'

'A world of Eden-born awaits us. They shall join us, flesh of our flesh.'

'Feel us, strong and powerful.'

'Haaa, but wait. What is that?'

'What is what?'

'Looks, looks there, Sha-aneer Host, a little eyeball thing is watching us.'

'Get it.'

'Yes, get it. Smash it. Grind it to jelly.'

There was a roaring sound. Something massive reared up and bulked heavily into the archway. It pushed forward with a sound of rending wood. Whip-like black tendrils lashed out at the fleeing sensor unit as it hurled itself down the corridor. The Preacher watched the tentacular strands push forward around his viewpoint. He saw them slam shut the lavatory door, his only access to an open window. They began to close around his mind's eye. The remote was about to be snatched out of the air. Using every erg his mind could muster he pushed at the sensor and it burst through the glazed portions of the back door like a bullet. He heard the door explode in a shower of splinters and broken glass behind him and without a backward glance he rocketed his viewpoint skywards away from danger.

Opening his eyes, he leapt onto his horse and urged it westwards at a flat run. Above him the eye and the ear separated and then fell back into place on the galloping horse. He couldn't see the state of the eyeball but the ear was a little tattered from its passage through broken glass, and he was pleased to see it safely mounted back on its owner's head. Then with an oath, Preacher noted it had screwed itself on backwards and he quickly swivelled it round.

Remote sensors are often useful but not terribly bright.

He slowed his horse to a canter and brought it to a stop. It whinnied nervously. He looked back towards The Palace. There was no movement. He had half expected to see the furious Host boiling out onto Main Street but there was nothing. All was still. All was silent.

Soon we shall divide and then divide and then eat some more.

The words rang through his mind. He settled back in his saddle with an air of resolve. He knew what he had to do. He turned back towards town.

{40}

Caleb smiled at the memory of that morning.

It was still dark when I woke up, which confused me. So did finding a warm body by my side. Memories of what'd happened that morning fixed a stupid smile on my face but a fierce growling in my belly dampened any plans I might've had to recommence our passionate exercise.

Alice was only slight but she was strong and enthusiastic. It was exhaustion that eventually won the day but it had been a hard-fought race. I could barely contain my joy in sharing so much pleasure with my sweet Alice whose body had kept every promise it made when I first saw it back there in the river.

She was my first since Becky died and only the second in my lifetime – I confess I've never been much of a ladies' man, but that morning Alice was all I ever wanted. Once again I felt as if my heart would burst into white fire in my chest.

But it was dark and I was hungry. That's when I remembered we'd pinned a blanket across the window. I climbed out of bed careful as a long-tailed cat in a rocking horse factory. I didn't want to disturb my sleeping angel. I drew the blanket away from the window and looked out, blinded for a moment by another bright day. I could see the sun was fairly high in the sky and I didn't need Montague's half onion to reckon it was past nine in the morning. I wondered how the Preacher had fared in town and I thought about the nightmare creature that had wanted to 'drink' the beautiful woman asleep in the room behind me.

'I'm starving to death. What time is it?'

Alice was sitting up in bed, stretching and yawning. Like me she was naked and the effect she had on me was both instant and obvious. She looked at me with an impish smile.

'We seem to have struck a fire in your belly that has yet to be slaked. Which hunger shall we feed first?'

I answered her with an urgency that surprised both of us.

An hour later we were washed and dressed and brewing coffee while frying bacon with onions when I heard a knock at the door. I unlocked it to find the Preacher standing there. He looked as fit as ever and I wondered if he'd found time to rest since I last set eyes on him.

He sniffed the air. 'Bacon and coffee, Caleb. I'd bless you for a saint if there was fixings for two.'

'Three – Alice is still with me, Preacher, but I'm sure we can stretch for three. By the way, I have black news for you.'

'And I for you. But please, let's talk with some food in our bellies.'

Alice was pleased to see our visitor and we played house like newlyweds: finding another plate, fetching a mug and wiping off another set of cutlery. Watching the three of us sitting to our breakfast around the table in that kitchen, any observer would've thought we didn't have a care in the world. We ate good food and drank hot coffee made better by hunger. Afterwards we washed up and put everything away so the only remnant of our meal was its tantalising aroma.

Alice made the bed and unpinned the blanket from the window. I made us some more coffee and took it through to the main room. Alice joined us and sat next to me on the sofa. Preacher pulled up a straight-backed wooden chair and straddled it backwards, resting his arms on its bentwood frame. He sipped his coffee.

'Mortal appetite is no longer clamouring in my ears, Caleb. I can reason and hear once more. So, tell me, what is your "black" news?'

I told him about Montague's boots matching the impression made by one of the men lynching Klosky and his expression became bleak.

'I thought we'd already punished that deed with bullets and fire. Very well – we shall have to deal with Montague. But he is not our primary concern, not yet. We must destroy the beast that infects The Palace before it has the chance to divide and turn on the rest of the town. Klosky was one man and what happened to him was terrible; but what the Sha-aneer Host plans for all of us is worse. And I do include myself in this. It's become stronger than I've ever seen it before. It will annihilate me if it can.'

His eyes became cold and implacable. 'It's powerful now and its transformation is almost complete. Soon it'll be ready to divide and once that happens it'll leave its nest hungry for more victims. Nobody and nothing will survive except the bare boards of the town's buildings, all flesh consumed by the worm of the deep earth. It cares nothing for the trappings of civilisation except transport. It'll ride the train to Shafter and from there it'll divide and divide again and make its way to every town and city in the United States.'

He gripped his coffee cup so hard it shattered in his fist, but he hadn't noticed. Through bitter lips he spat, 'Every soul subsumed by the Sha-aneer is lost and their flesh become the body of the Host. There's no limit to the numbers it can devour and nothing tastes better than the flesh of the Eden-born.'

'Will it only prey on humans?'

He looked at Alice. 'No, not just humans. It eats horses and from what you say it seems that even Fey Sprites of the elements have become as meat and drink to the worm. Alice, I swear I wouldn't allow it to drink from you and steal away the poetry of your long, enchanted years. I love your kind and will preserve you. If I have to call Heaven itself down upon the beast I will do so. I promise. I shall stand as guardian against its works.'

Blood dripped from his injured hand and he gazed at it mutely as if surprised to see he was bleeding. He balled his hand into a fist and squeezed hard then opened it once more. Blood pooled in his palm. Alice fetched a damp cloth from the kitchen. She knelt before him, took his hand into her own and carefully dabbed at it. As she wiped, she gasped with wonder. The flesh of his torn palm was once more clean of any mark. It was unscarred and whole.

She cast a shocked gaze into his eyes.

'How?'

'Call it magic. It sounds so much better than nanotech bio-repair, don't you think?'

She trembled as she looked at the hand again. 'Satan, you are a cauldron of wonders.' Then she stood before him like a child and kissed him chastely on the lips.

'On behalf of the Fey Sprites I accept you as guardian of the elementals.'

She intoned something that sounded formal and musical. Preacher replied in the same language. Then he held up his cupped palms and Alice placed her hands over his. Clear water flowed from her to him and he drank of it reverently as if taking a papist communion. She held no vessel that I could see but she poured forth that water again and he drank again. All the while she was singing in that melodic tongue.

I suddenly felt as if I was in a sacred place like an old cathedral or the holy grounds of the red man. My mind's eye took me to Divided Rock which I knew had once been spirit-worshipped by a lost tribe. The tribe's name had been lost, but their drawings were still there. Spirals, crosses, winged men and snakes hidden in secret places where you had to look hard to find them, but there they were and they still had power. There was a hushed beauty to the place as there was in that room.

I felt blessed to witness the water ritual between the 'cauldron of wonders' and an 'elemental'. One day I hoped I'd understand what had passed between the Preacher and Alice. But neither said anything about it then or later. I believe a promise had been made and accepted with a precious gift, and I remembered the water in my mouth when Alice had kissed me. My mind teetered on the brink of understanding something utterly incredible, but then Preacher took my girl's fingers in his own and he gently kissed them.

I felt that immense force again as if something invisible but terribly potent had entered the room. There was the sound of mighty wings and I feared I might faint from the sense of awe that filled me from the soles of my feet to the hair on the crown of my head. Something stretched my nerves like piano wires. I squeezed my eyes closed and stopped breathing.

'Satan, stop. You know the Eden-born are fragile in the face of such things.'

Alice's features were close to mine; concern etched lines around her eyes. She looked aged somehow and tired. I wondered what the ritual had cost her.

'Yes,' said the Preacher, taking my hand in his, 'and we have things to do. Caleb, fetch your belt gun and your rifle and follow me.'

Energy roared back into my body and I leapt to obey.

'Where are we going, Preacher?'

'Well first, Caleb, we need to steal a train.'

{41}

Prester Montague was down at the train depot overseeing the last of the loading when we marched up to him and his men. Montague sported a Smith & Wesson pistol in his belt but his arms were folded across his waistcoat while he gave out orders to his little crew. There were the two guards to be locked into the armoured wagon plus the train driver and his coalman. Three mine workers were shifting boxes of silver into the wagon and the guards were helping. Nobody took any notice of us until we already had them all at rifle point. So much for the Fulsome mine's fabled security arrangements. They'd allowed two armed men to walk right up to them and take them prisoner without a shot being fired. If we'd chosen to we could've walked away with thousands of dollars' worth of silver that day.

Montague had said it was providence that the Preacher had decided to walk the stony path of righteousness rather than fall down the slippery slope of wrongdoing. He was about to discover just how effective a bandit the Preacher could be if the fancy took him. Knowing him for a murdering Sodomite and hypocrite, I'd no qualms about pushing my rifle directly into Montague's astonished face.

We quickly disarmed the guards and the mine manager – nobody else was carrying a weapon – and then we locked everyone but the driver and his coalman into the secure wagon. Montague had the key and handed it over along with a string of curses and threats, his smooth tongue turned rough with fear and anger. If anyone else in the mine saw what was happening, they kept their heads down and stayed away. I couldn't blame them. Tall and dark in his long black coat, the Preacher looked like an angel of vengeance. I guess I looked capable enough too.

Montague was shouting something about being claustrophobic but all I could see in my imagination was him and his cronies dragging on poor Klosky's legs until he was choked and dead. Thinking again about everything they'd done to the poor lumberman, I had to fight an impulse to kill the only surviving bastard who did that to him. It was real hard to leave him be, but my curiosity saved his life for the moment. I wanted to know what really happened in that gulch and he was the only living witness to the murder.

I reasoned that Montague hadn't been party to shoving the dead man into the mound. I believed that was when his accessories became infected. At least one of them was bitten by the ants. Montague must've been clear away

143

when that happened or he too would be little more than a drift of dust by now, burned by the Preacher's little ball of crystal.

Our plans were moving along briskly. Alice had agreed to follow us with our horses. If the Preacher's wild scheme bore fruit, we'd soon be able to ride back for a long talk with Montague. Through the gun slits the snail trail man was promising to bring the unholy wrath of the Galveston, Harrisburg and San Antonio railroad down upon our thieving heads. His voice was becoming high-pitched and I reasoned he'd started to panic because he'd been locked in a hot steel box without windows other than those narrow gun slits. Good. I had no beef with the other boys but I wanted him to be real uncomfortable. I supposed cool air would flow through the wagon when it was moving, but sitting still like that under the Texas sun would most likely turn its interior into an oven over the next few hours.

We had the driver and his mate uncouple the train and its coal tender from its string of wagons then move it forward a few yards. Preacher carried a bag over his shoulder during the whole procedure. He had me hold the two men at gun point while he walked to the front of the steaming giant. There was a big iron 'cow catcher' mounted there and he occupied himself with it for several minutes. I asked the driver if he'd ever caught a cow on the thing but he just looked at me as if I was simple and said nothing.

When Preacher returned, his bag was gone. He ordered our prisoners into the cab of the train and we climbed up behind them. He then got them to start the engine moving. I always found steam trains impressive enough but had never ridden in one before, not even as a coach passenger. To be up there in the cab when those tonnes of steel began to roll along the rail like a live thing was breath-taking. It was hard to believe such a powerful machine could be commanded by just an ordinary man.

My friend watched everything the driver and his coalman were doing for a long minute, then ordered them to slow the big machine down.

'Jump!' he barked. The two men looked confused.

'Now,' he commanded and made to draw his pistol. 'Get out! I don't want to threaten you.'

And then we were alone in the cab, the driver and his mate rolling in the dust behind us. Preacher calmly reached out to the metal wall of levers and wheels and started manipulating them. We gathered speed.

'Caleb, I need you to work that shovel. Try to get the coal evenly spread in the firebox but throw it as far back as you can. Don't let it build up by the door.'

144

It was hot, dirty work. I hung my jacket on a hook and my shirt soon followed. There was an easy rhythm to the job that allowed me time to look around as we accelerated faster and faster towards town. I waved when we passed Alice and she waved back, but even though I could see she was moving at quite a lick we overtook her like she was standing still. I prayed we would have a future together. I prayed everyone had a future.

Through an opening at the side of the cab I could see a long gentle curve ahead of us and the buildings of the town began to appear. Preacher wound a wheel and the engine began to sway on its wheels.

'Caleb,' he shouted above the noise. 'Grab your stuff. Come on, man.'

I pulled on my shirt and jacket then took hold of my rifle. I wondered what he was planning. He'd only shared his plans with me up to this point.

Surely, I thought, *he doesn't intend for us to jump from the train at this speed? It would be suicide. Madness.*

He gave me his rifle to hold and opened his long coat. He wrapped it around me. Oddly I found myself briefly concerned whether the coal dust I was layered with would soil the fine fabric of his coat. As if it mattered.

'Trust me,' he said gently and lifted my feet from the floor. I stopped breathing.

42

Alice was still about a mile away when Preacher took me from the train so she didn't get to see everything that happened next, just its conclusion. My memory is a little confused about precisely what the Preacher did to get us both out of that cab but I think I can reconstruct the basic course of events. I simply have to accept that just because some aspects of the moments immediately following his wrapping me in his coat seem impossible, it doesn't mean they didn't happen.

I remember his arms holding me like an iron girdle. He held me so hard I later found that our rifles had bruised my ribs and arms where they were pressed against me. I once again experienced that supernatural feeling of being in the presence of something immense and inhumanly powerful.

I was dizzy and felt very small like a child. Not like a child, no, less even than that. More like a stalk of grass in a hurricane, tiny and helpless. Then I had a weird sensation of motion as if I was falling, but I was falling *upwards*. That's the only way I can describe it. When I was younger I once jumped off a cliff into a deep lake for a dare, and it felt like that but in the other direction. We were falling upwards and we were doing so at an incredible speed. I think my heart stopped beating.

Wrapped like a babe in a blanket I could see nothing of our flight nor have I ever understood the nature of it. When I eventually felt solid ground under my feet once more and the Preacher released me from his grip I nearly fell to my knees. I was momentarily confused about what direction was up and which was down and I had to close my eyes tightly to stop my world from spinning out of control. I was in immediate danger of vomiting my breakfast.

The real world dropped back around my shoulders like a cloak and I gasped like a landed fish. Preacher prised his rifle from my arms and clapped me on the shoulder.

He pointed. 'Watch this, Caleb.'

Side-by-side we walked a few paces after the driverless train. In the few moments since we'd abandoned it, it'd travelled several hundred yards, but it was still close enough that I could see just how quickly it was approaching town. I hoped nothing would wander onto the tracks in front of that charging Leviathan. It would smash them to a bloody pulp.

And then it happened. Just as the screaming engine approached the stockyards it veered to the right and with a great roar leapt from its tracks. Soil and stones were thrown in a great wave from its wheels and clattered around like rocky rain. And then I realised what the Preacher had somehow done. The train was headed straight towards The Palace like a missile blasted from some mighty cannon, its steel wheels shrieking as they sliced a wide furrow in the grey earth.

It'd only slowed a little when it hit the building like a battering ram and the walls closed around it like a fist. I heard the grinding of metal and a splintering of wood, but there was something else there too. Many voices screaming in rage and fear. Something massive reared howling up into the clear sunlight and shouldered away the shattered fabric of The Palace even as the roof collapsed. It was grey like an elephant's skin in some places and rose-coloured, almost transparent in others. It waved hundreds of whip-like tentacles in the air and crashed down upon our train like a breaking wave of fat flesh. The great engine shuddered and its tender was catapulted into the air, scattering coal in a circular swathe like seeds from a farmer's hand.

'Now,' said the Preacher.

I heard the pound of hooves behind me but I couldn't look away, not even when I heard Alice's voice gasping in shock. A bloom of white flame erupted from the heart of the beast and tore through it as if it were kindling. A chorus of shrieking voices rang out and the behemoth twisted and coiled around its agonised centre.

'How big is that thing?'

Alice was by my side, the reins of our horses firm in her hand. Pearl and Alice's horse were nervous and jittery at the scenes before them, but the Preacher's mount stood like a stone. It watched the grey beast burn and melt in the wreckage of The Palace.

'It was a mature Sha-aneer. It will have burrowed down some way to make a nest where it would first divide and then crawl out to hunt like a plague through the town. It would've taken every man, woman and child and devoured every soul it could find. We had to stop it.'

I asked, 'What happened to the rails?'

'I did.'

The blinding fire burned whiter and higher. The building containing it fell away in ashes and there grew instead an expanding crater at the centre of which was an ever-deepening pit filled with a column of solid white fire. The Sha-aneer was boiling and raging and screaming. A host of voices cried 'Satan, Satan, Satan...'

And then a torrent of molten and burning flesh erupted from the pit and spattered around the crater with a wet sound, and the voice of the beast was stilled at last. But the show wasn't quite over. A dome of earth and some sort of tissue ballooned up from the crater and then burst, spewing a thick mucus into the air that splashed to the ground. There began a rumbling noise that reminded me of our poor broken train, now lying buckled at the edge of the crater where it'd been tossed during the beast's death throes.

The rumbling grew louder and then a great rift appeared at the crater's edge and zigzagged crazily towards us. We ran out of its path. The jagged rift split the path in twain and threw up a stinking miasma that set me to choking and retching like a dog with a bone caught in its throat. The Preacher stood tall and still while Alice pounded at my back.

And then the earth closed up once more, healed of the insult done to it and finally still. The only sound was the ticking of the stricken engine's hot metalwork and my helpless, hacking cough.

That was when the train's boiler exploded in a shower of twisted metal, steam and boiling water.

'I wonder what the gentlemen of the Galveston, Harrisburg and San Antonio railroad will make of *that*,' murmured the Preacher.

I looked at the wreckage through tear-filled eyes. 'I didn't know it very long, but I'd grown rather fond of that train.'

'You are a filthy man,' said Alice, playfully. 'I think you need a good wash and a change of clothes before we do anything else today. Let's go to your office and get you looking more like a sheriff and less like a chimney sweep.'

We walked past the smoking crater and the great blasted cylinder of the ruined steam engine. The west end of town was going to need a great deal of loving care before it could be returned to even a shadow of its former glory.

'I suppose Grandma Teatree died in the accident,' I said.

'I think she did, poor old girl,' replied Alice. 'She was a legend and a much-loved local character.'

'Loved? Everyone was terrified by her!'

There was that chuckle again, like a fresh stream flowing over pebbles.

'Yes, they were, weren't they?'

'They should erect a statue.'

'What? To Madam Teatree and her naked harlots?'

Preacher looked at the crater. 'So many dead. Whoever they were and whatever they did, they deserved better than that.'

'Amen,' I said.

And we walked through milling crowds of stunned townsfolk who would never know how close they had come to meeting the same fate.

43

Goody Marsh never turned away a paying customer. It was sometimes said that she would open on judgement day if the angels were hungry enough and had their spending money to hand. And so it was that with a fresh smoking crater and a wrecked steam train just a few hundred yards from her front door, we could sit down to a good meal of stew meat and vegetables steeped in Sung Li's famous gravy.

The three of us had freshened up. Alice used the facilities at my place and Preacher stepped home for a half-hour or so. Our horses were left tethered to the rail outside the trading post. When Goody saw me she pointed out the notices on her community board. Nearly all of them were missing persons bulletins and most of them had gone missing during the past twenty-four hours. So many lost.

Preacher also studied the board. Fathers, husbands and sons taken by the worm and purified in white flame. Their children, wives and parents would have to make new lives without them. It would be tough for them. I noticed that no one had listed the whores or Grandma Teatree as missing and reasoned that for some of the townspeople losing those whores was really a blessing.

At the time I didn't know that Teague and Damsel-Childs had also become victims of the worm. Neither was listed on the board but before long people would begin to realise that the hands that signed most of the town's cheques had vanished.

'I shall pray for them,' Preacher said solemnly after Goody asked him what he would do.

Once we'd eaten and finished a pot of coffee, the Preacher pulled a key from one of his pockets.

'We are scattering ruin around the place like a cut hog run wild in a kitchen. Shall we now add Prester Montague to our roster of destroyed lives?'

I growled back, 'I for one have questions I'd like to hear answered.'

Alice pulled a face. 'He's nothing but a low-bellied slug. I'd put salt on his tail and watch him squirm.' She shuddered. 'He has indelicate fingers in his eyes.'

Goody came to the table to tell us that the Preacher Spindrift appeared to be the only available member of the town council. She asked what should be done about the wrecked train. Preacher told her to telegraph the GH & SA railway controller in Shafter. He told her we'd personally checked the main line and it was still intact, but that a good section of the stockyard spur had been swallowed by the crater. 'Ask them what we should do, please, Mizz Marsh. It's their line that failed and their train that ran right through the old staging post. Must've been a pocket of natural gas under the building for it to go up like that, wouldn't you say?'

Goody lowered her voice. 'I hear tell that some folk reckon that explosion was nothing less than an Old Testament act of God. They say He was sorely vexed with the sinful use being made of the staging post and what happened today was his judgement made upon all those involved in such sinful acts. They say Grandma Teatree burned alongside those painted whores she brought to town, and I say fire was her just reward.'

The Preacher shrugged and got to his feet. 'However it happened and whatever was involved, we have got to get it cleaned up, Goody. We have a hole in the west end of Main Street big enough to gulp down a stage and a full team of horses. This is a civilised town; we can't leave that crater as a trap for unwary travellers. We shall ride to the Fulsome mine and rustle up some men who know a thing or two about digging. You get on the telegraph to Shafter. When I come back, let me know what they said.'

We paid for our victuals and returned to our horses. Nobody had said anything about Alice's stolen mount. I guessed it must have belonged to one of the miners lost to the worm and burned up in the explosion.

'People are remarkable creatures,' mused the Preacher as we rode past the scene of that dreadful conflagration once more. A foul steam still billowed from the deep fistula at its core and some of the soil at its heart had a glassy, melted appearance. People were walking around it, pointing and gesturing. Our train was like a giant burst water-pipe, twisted and broken.

'Why so?' I asked.

'Look here,' he answered. 'Look at them. Those townspeople saw exactly what we saw. They saw a train jump off its rails and plough into the old staging post. They saw the Sha-aneer burst through the roof in clear daylight. They heard it howl like an Irish banshee and watched it burn like the sun. It was plain as day. So, what are they saying? Terrible monster? No. Foul hell beast? No. Act of God they say, a Biblical punishment like that doled out to Sodom and Gomorrah! Bless them for their blindness. They saw only what they expected to see. I put the idea of natural gas into Goody's head because it was quicker than printing it in the broadsheet and it'll get around a lot faster once her tongue starts wagging. But act of God? I tell you that's genius, and pure genius!'

'How many of your crystal globes did you strap to the cow catcher, Preacher?'

'You worked it out, did you? Smart work there, Caleb. You have a keen eye and a quick wit. Around ten of them on a string, that's your answer. That cow catcher would've gone into the worm's guts like a bayonet into a belly and, puff, up she goes.'

Alice joined in, 'Why does the beast burn like that?'

'It needs a white heat to spark it off, as the remarkable Emmanuel Fernandez discovered. He has a morbid fear of dirt. Any taint of uncleanliness sickens him to the heart. When he saw a worm seed wriggling around under his own skin, he had to excise it as fast as he could and he used white hot steel to do so. You saw the result. Every inch of infected flesh burned away like a torch. If he'd hesitated as much as another minute, he would've been taken by the worm.'

He turned in his saddle and looked back at the town.

'I believe Fernandez would have seen the truth of the matter. He would've seen the Sha-aneer, of that I am sure. He is a writer, you know. He pens work for the Penny Dreadfuls in New York, much like Mr Dickens and Mr Twain. He said he'd send me something of his. I do hope he will. He has a machine he called a type writer. It sounds very modern.'

My mind was still casting around about the murder of Klosky and I was only partly listening to the Preacher.

'I have some questions about the worm, Preacher. I'm thinking we haven't seen the last of it yet.'

'What makes you say that?'

We were making good speed towards the mine and our appointment with Montague. He could wait a little longer while we talked things over.

'It's the sequence of events. They make no sense. Something is seeding the ground with those little red and black worms. That's what got into Fernandez, he told us so. It may be what infected The Palace, and that's something we'll never know for sure. But every other infection to date came from that ant mound. The mound is gone and has been for these last few days, as has every poor devil poxed by the ant bites. My questions are these...' I paused to collect my thoughts. 'Yes, what was it that infected the ants and how? And what is still making the little worms like the one that caught Fernandez? What is it and, just as important, where is it? Until we find it and destroy it, this nightmare will carry on until every single person in Mule's Ass and the State of Texas has been turned by the worm. And that will just be the start. It won't stop there.'

{44}

The train driver and his coalman were sitting together on a bench like sullen wallflowers at an 'excuse me' dance. They saw us riding in on horseback and stood up to look down the line as if expecting to see their engine following behind us like a big steam-powered dog.

The surly driver snarled, 'Where's my train?'

Preacher answered, 'Back in town where you crashed it.'

'We did what?'

'We saw you leap off it and turn the thing loose at high speed. It jumped the tracks and smashed clean through a building. Whole mess has been blown to heaven. It was bad. Townsfolk are getting together a posse. They're hot for a lynching. Set there a while and they'll be here. Thought I saw some dust on the trail behind us. People died down there.'

They ran for it.

'Preacher,' I said, 'if there was a prize for bare-faced lying you would've just earned it for life.'

He grinned back. 'Thought of it when I saw those fools sitting there waiting for something to happen. Let's get our friends out of the broiling oven, shall we?'

The men in the armoured wagon had stripped off nearly every item of clothing. They were red, sweaty and wilted by the heat when we slid back the big door and allowed them to step down onto the platform. They were a sorry spectacle, looking like so many slabs of boiled ham. Prester Montague was not among those still standing.

We sent the others off to find water and somewhere they could cool down. They scampered away croaking their thank-yous. The smell in the boiling wagon was quite intense. A small cubicle in the corner was evidently a lavatory and it'd been used by more than one person in the past few hours. Heat will take some people that way. That was where we finally found Montague. He was no longer conscious and was covered in copious amounts of vomit. I wasn't sure all of it was his.

We took his arms and dragged him to his quarters with his heels dragging in the dirt, the way Klosky was first dragged to his death under that tree. It was fitting. He was moaning and whimpering, his senseless mind pursued by dreams of being locked in a hot metal box. Alice followed at a big enough remove that she couldn't smell the man, but the expression on her face spoke volumes.

A burly man confronted us with his hand on his undrawn pistol. Alice carried one of the rifles and I toted the other. Preacher's free hand was the same side as his holster. If the man drew his gun at least two of us would've shot him down. I would've bet a gold eagle on me or the Preacher taking him before his gun cleared leather.

He was big enough but he looked slow and confused. His boss was out cold, he could see that, but we looked capable of almost anything. He decided to sound us out first.

'Wha'ser gowan orn hee'ya?'

I swear he spoke like that but I won't inflict any more of his strangled tongue on you. There was more than a touch of the mountains there in his speech, that and the fact that his forehead was little more than a narrow band of creased hide above beetling black brows. I'd seen a stuffed and mounted critter called a 'yeti' in the tents of the travelling 'World of Wonders' a few years back. If that show ever returned to Mule's Ass, I'd tell this fellow to make himself scarce or the owners might think to bag themselves another one.

He was the true spit.

'I am Sheriff Sawyer,' I told him, 'and this man, Prester Montague, is wanted in connection with an ongoing murder investigation. If you interfere with an officer of the State in pursuit of his enquiries, I shall issue you with a writ in pursuance of my administrative or judicial jurisdiction, and I'll require you to prove you are a legitimate member of the human race, which, on the evidence to hand, I have sorely to doubt.'

'I ain't done nothing to earn no writ.'

'Stand aside or tell it to the judge in Shafter.'

He lumbered to one side. 'I ain't done nothing to see no judge. I'm just an honest man aiming to do his job. I don't deserve no writ.' And he rolled away, muttering and whining like a grizzly with a thorn in its paw.

'Let's get this man into his crib and hurry,' said Preacher through gritted teeth.

'What's the rush?'

'I don't want to be anywhere that hick can hear me when I collapse with laughter, that's what.'

And he grinned at me with that white, crescent moon grin of his.

Alice had her hand over her mouth and her shoulders were shaking uncontrollably. Her eyes were watering. She rushed ahead, got Montague's door open and then hurried inside. From beyond the doorway I heard a gleeful *HAW, HAW* and then a peal of musical laughter. I think it was then that I realised how much I loved everything about that girl, whatever she was. I wouldn't be issuing her with any writ to make her prove she was human any more than I would the Preacher. I think I already knew the answer.

Montague came round when Preacher rinsed his face for the second time with a ladle's worth of cold water. He groaned and dabbed at his wet face with a limp palm and then pushed his hand up into his hair, which was stiff with dried vomit.

'What the...' His bloodshot eyes at first squinted painfully at the three of us without comprehension, and then, when memory reconvened behind the pain in his head, they flew open.

'You reprobates,' he spat through spittle-coated teeth. 'You cast-iron villains! You locked me in that wagon. What did you bastards think you were doing? I might've died.' He became aware of the state of his clothes and his expression changed to one of pure horror. 'What have you done to me?' he breathed. 'This is disgusting, unforgiveable. I shall see you jailed for this, I promise you. I have status. Both you bastard men and your painted whore will do hard time when I've finished with you. I will see you whipped. I will see you broken on the wheel and whipped until your bones are raw.'

'And I shall see you hanged, Prester Montague.' Preacher's words were flat and chill. They silenced the mine manager's bluster. 'I shall see you hanged for your part in the rape and murder of the lumberman, Adam Klosky. And I will bless the day you dance your last dance to the hangman's waltz.'

Montague's mouth worked hard but no sound came out. His eyes took on a glistening, poached aspect, white and rolling around in his head as if looking for a way to escape. Finding none.

Preacher continued, 'We've proof you were there when Klosky was hanged. We have concrete proof that you were one of a group of four men who strung him up and pulled hard on his legs until he choked. We also know you *didn't* help carry his corpse down the gulch and leave it kneeling face down and half-naked in a nest of fire ants. If you had you wouldn't be here now. You'd be burned to ash up over that hill with your cronies.'

'They did what? What do you mean, burned?' The man looked frantic. He was denying nothing.

Preacher pulled up a chair and sat facing Montague. His eyes looked dark and were filled with cold menace. 'Let me tell you what happened that early morning just a few days ago.'

Alice and I cradled our rifles. Montague would find no quarter with us.

Preacher's voice stayed low and flat. He shaped each word as if it was a surgical instrument with which he could cut away lies and disclose the truth.

'You and your good old boys caught up with Klosky somewhere. It doesn't matter where. The men you were with were out for a bit of fun and you decided to join in. Things got out of hand, didn't they? You and your boys took it in turns to hold the man down and you had at it with him. Poor Klosky was hurt real bad. He was bleeding and terrified and then I believe he threatened you with the law.'

Montague made as if to get to his feet and the Preacher slapped him across his face so hard it sounded like a pistol shot. The blow slammed the man back onto his cot. The mine manager began to drool. He was panting in fear.

'You don't move until we say you can. You lay there and you listen and you don't make a sound. You can talk when we tell you to answer our questions, not before. And if you utter one word of a lie we'll know and we'll hurt you. Do you understand me, Prester Montague?'

Montague nodded. He couldn't take his eyes from Preacher's face. He began to shiver and emitted a strange huffing noise as if his heart was pounding in his throat, but he spoke not a word. Not then. Not yet.

'Was the lynching meant to just scare the water out of Klosky? Was it planned as just a threat to keep him quiet about what you all did to him? What happened? Did you get carried away when it became too much fun to stop? He wasn't the first, was he? He was young and pretty looking for a boy. Was that to your liking? You couldn't take your filthy eyes from little Alice here, could you? Is she young enough to excite your filthy bullying rapist ways? Do you only like boys or do you also like girls and babies? Is that what you want, girls, boys and babies? Is that it? Is it? What kind of a pig are you, Montague? Tell me!'

The Preacher's words lashed at Montague like horsewhips. His mouth opened in a stretched 'O' and a keening whine poured from him. And then he glanced from one to the other of us as if looking for mercy. He found none. Words cascaded from Montague then, stuttering and desperate.

'It wasn't like that, no, no, not like that. No, believe me, it was a game, yes, that's all it was, a game. Klosky was happy to join in, he wanted to join in. He did it willingly. Yes, willingly...'

At that the Preacher leaned forward and gently took Montague's left hand. All the while he looked him in the face like a wolf eyeing a sheep. Slowly, deliberately, he broke the man's little finger like a rotted twig. Montague shrieked in horror and tried to pull his injured paw out of the Preacher's grip. He failed, and that was when he finally realised he was helpless. None of his men had come to his aid. He was alone with Preacher Spindrift, Alice and me, and his will had cracked just as surely as that little finger.

His lower lip flapped like a slice of fat meat and he panted, making incoherent, pig-like squealing noises. The civilised man had drained completely away and only his fear remained to fill his quivering carcase. His eyes glistened wetly and sweat rolled from him. He stank badly enough before thanks to the vomit drenching his clothes, but now the raw, choking stench of despair permeated the room. Alice and I stood away a few paces searching for fresher air, but found none.

The man had been rendered stinking and vile but Preacher seemed unaffected and kept his cold stare close to Montague's colourless face. The mine manager breathed through his open mouth in fetid gasps. He sounded like someone who'd run a hard race but still came last.

'Please, please, no, please.' He tugged at his hand again but Preacher held it tight and reached for another finger. That was enough. The whole story spilled from him like blood from a lanced boil, hot and poisonous.

He told us that Klosky had come up into the hills willingly enough. He'd been promised sight of a waterhole where a sheep farmer's beautiful daughters went early every morning to bathe. He was promised naked female flesh and freely exposed, firm young breasts. He climbed onto the miner's flatbed four-wheeler excited as a drunk being shown the way to a secret still.

It was a measure of his naïvety that he hadn't even thought to ask which sheep farmer they were talking about. He knew the neighbourhood well enough to know there were no beautiful daughters to be had up in those hills, and just about all the sheep were grazing good green grass along the Sweet Alice valley. The boy was made foolish and blind by lust and it would prove his undoing before the sun was properly risen.

They took him to the riddle pond created to sieve silver from the mined ore. Even a breast-hungry idiot like Klosky could see that any girl bathing there would come out muddier than when she dove in. He began to protest and ask what they were doing there. He wanted to jump from the cart and make his way back to town on foot.

His assailants pounced, grabbing him by the arms and legs. A man called Farthing tightened his arm around Klosky's bull neck and squeezed until the boy was fainting from lack of air and all the fight gone from him. He was barely conscious enough to know what was done to him then.

They took down his pants and stretched him face down on the ground, butt high over a roll of tarpaulin. Montague took the first turn followed by Farthing. The third man complained about the tightness of their victim's rectum but he finished his business quickly enough. After the fourth man grunted to his conclusion, Montague felt driven to take a second bite of the cherry and all the while the terrified lumberman was screaming and begging to be let free. Montague admitted that Klosky's bucking and thrashing added spice to the proceedings.

'He didn't want to pull his pants back on because he was worried what his ma would say if she saw blood there. He told us he'd talk to the Sheriff and the town council. He said he'd tell them what pervert miners had done to him. He was weeping fit to bust a gut and sitting there in the dirt with his pants round his ankles. Other boys had been too embarrassed to talk about it afterwards, but Klosky was mad and swore he'd get his own back. He was hysterical and shouting threats. The next thing he had his pants pulled up most of the way and he was striding off, bare-assed and with his shirttails flapping.

'Coulson grabbed ropes from the cart and said we should tie him up until we could talk some sense into the boy. He was moving fast so we had to run after him. We caught him near the gulch and he started throwing punches, that was until he tripped over his pants and went down, belly flat to the ground.

Farthing climbed on him and grabbed him by the neck. "Make a noose," he cried, "we'll string him up until he sees reason." He never did see reason.

Even once he was hogtied he was yelling and hollering about what he was going to do. Even with the rope around his neck he was threatening us with everything he could imagine. He wouldn't see sense.

'Farthing reached over and fixed the end of the rope to a thick branch of a stone tree at the edge of the gulch. He told Klosky what we'd do if he didn't shut his yap like a good puppy. Klosky spat at him. That boy must've had balls big as boulders. You had to admire his grit. It was Farthing kicked him over the edge, but the boy wouldn't die. He twisted at the end of that rope kicking lumps out of the gulch wall and making a terrible noise. I couldn't stand it. Farthing, Coulson and I went down into the gulch and threw ourselves onto the boy's legs. Harker held the rope from the top and climbed down to press his feet onto the boy's shoulders. It still took five minutes or so before he was still. That boy's father must have been half bull.

'Then he shit on me. He was dead and he shit on me. I couldn't stand that. I told them to cut him down and get rid of the body and I ran back here to wash. I burned those clothes. I can't stand dirt, can't stand it.' He looked mournfully down at his vomit-stained shirt. 'Can't stand it.'

It was then that I remembered to breathe. Preacher leaned back in his chair.

{46}

The sound of the shot in that enclosed space was shocking but the sight of the front of Montague's head exploding outwards in a bloom of bright blood was worse. That will stay with me all my days – and I have seen some pretty awful things over the years. The silence afterwards had a ringing quality like a huge bell had just been stilled.

I snatched the smoking rifle from Alice's hands and thrust mine at the Preacher, just as a group of curious miners burst into the room. They stood just inside the entrance, and I wondered if they might be fearful that what had just happened to their boss was about to happen to them. The sight of two armed men standing over Montague's bloody corpse at first snatched away their power of speech. We all stood mutely looking at each other and waiting for someone to make the first move.

And then one of them blurted out, 'Who is that got kilt there, Sheriff? We heard the shot and came running. And where's mister Montague while all this is going on in his office? Mister Montague is not a man for mess and you've scattered that poor fellow's wits over a good portion of his office wall. Good day to you, Preacher Spindrift, and to you, Miss. I'd be right grateful for an honest answer to my enquiry, if I may be so bold.'

The other men craned in to get a better look at the body – or possibly Alice – but none of them moved their feet so much as an inch. It was as if we had built an invisible fence across that doorway that they were unwilling to cross.

Preacher spoke up and instantly calmed the men with the sound of his grave and steady voice.

'This pitiful creature *is* Prester Montague. He had just confessed to being one of a gang of four men who committed a violent and terrible murder. He confessed in front of three sober witnesses. Afterwards I believe he tried to make his escape and made a grab at Sheriff Sawyer's rifle. In the struggle I'm afraid the weapon was accidently discharged. It was unfortunate, but I guess his precipitate actions have just saved the town the cost of a judge, and a hangman.'

There was a murmuring consultation in the doorway and some shuffling of feet. And then the spokesman said, 'He was kilt because he was pressipypate? What does that mean? I believed him to be a Presbyterian like me. Is the church you attend become a State crime now?'

Preacher sighed. 'What's your name, sir?'

'I was christened Douglas, Preacher. Dougie they call me, Dougie Hinds if you please. I've heard you preach in the church hall on a Sunday, and the Sheriff has kindly cut my hair and given me a right good straight razor shave more than once. Thanking you for the attention.'

I observed, silently, that both a shave and a haircut were overdue.

'Well then, Douglas, and please listen to me all of you.' Preacher raised his voice a little. 'Precipitate means rash. Montague made a foolish and a hasty move and as a result he has received his due judgement earlier than expected. That is the whole letter of it. Sheriff Sawyer is an appointed officer of the law and he has performed his duty. Might I suggest you contact Shafter on the telegraph and let them know what has happened? Douglas, you seem to have your wits about you. Might I suggest you take charge?'

Hinds stood a little taller.

'Now, men,' Preacher continued. 'We have things we need to deal with here, and you have things to be getting on with out there. Shall we talk again later perhaps?'

Hinds ushered his man out and carefully closed the door behind them. We could hear him issuing orders as if born to command. Preacher put down his rifle and stepped in front of Alice. He took her gently by the shoulders.

'Why?'

She returned his gaze as an equal and squared her strong yet delicate shoulders under his hands.

'Satan, you are an ancient guardian of the Eden-born and we respect that. We welcomed you as a noble creature and you have proved worthy of our welcome. But *you* are not of this Earth, this soil, this water. Your blood was first warmed under a far distant sun and your roots are there still, clinging deep to the ashes of a dead world. I am an elemental Fey of the Earth and I am one of the guardians of water, earth, fire and air.'

She pointed at Montague's shattered head. 'That filthy creature soiled the air he breathed, the ground he walked on, the water he drank and the sun that shone down on him. A bullet in his brain is a blessing to him, a kindness he didn't really deserve. He should've been torn to shreds by the claws and teeth of night spirits, and his still living flesh scattered screaming to the winds. As it is...'

She stepped away from the Preacher and moved to stand over the dead man. She held out her hand, palm side uppermost. She took a deep breath and then blew gently across her palm. Where her breath touched him Montague's body began to smoulder, and then with a crack he burst into bright flame. I stood frozen with shock. *How could she do that?*

The fire took a firmer hold. His skin blackened and split and the fat began to run. There was a strong smell of roasting meat. Montague's corpse began to twist and writhe like a thing in pain.

'Caleb,' said Preacher. 'Grab that box of keys and follow us. Quickly, man. Dougie Hinds will need them.'

I did as I was told. I skirted the burning man and dashed for the wall behind his desk. The box was mounted on two hooks and it lifted away easily. With that box cradled under one arm and Preacher's rifle in my other hand, I ran back to the door but had nothing free with which to turn the handle. My friends had made their escape and the door had slammed shut behind them. I wasn't thinking straight and stood by that shut door in a state of blank confusion.

The room was filling with thick, greasy smoke and it was becoming hard to breathe. I made to shout for help but all I could produce was a choking cough. My throat was wretched. Behind me the torch that'd once been a man was curling into a tight ball, but the ruined face had tilted up and pointed straight at me. Its mouth opened as if it was about to speak. Mercy, but that man loved to talk.

'Come on, Caleb!'

Alice had the door open and was pulling at my arms. My last sight of the inferno was Montague shrugging down into a boiling heap. His head bowed. I supposed that with no one to talk to he was ready to leave. I knew I was.

Once more in the open air I dropped the box and dragged painful gulps of air into my wheezing lungs. I stank of smoke and for a minute I stood doubled over, hacking and spitting. I held onto the rifle until I felt it prised from my fingers to be replaced by a cool mug of fresh, ice-cold water.

'Drink this,' said Alice. 'It'll help cut the smoke.'

She was right. I sucked down that blessed fluid in a single draught and I felt strength flow back into my tissues right down to my bones. I would've thought I'd need a second cup to quench my parched throat but I didn't. Apart from the acrid stench of smoke clinging to my clothes and hair I was restored to the best of health. Better in fact.

'Thank you, Alice. That elixir should be bottled and put on the shelves. It'd earn you a fortune – a sovereign remedy indeed.'

'No, Caleb,' she replied enigmatically, 'there's not enough of me to go round.'

She smiled and I bathed in her warm regard.

'It may be for the best that you burned Montague,' I told her.

'Yes,' she nodded. 'The world is a much cleaner place without him in it.'

161

'True.' We moved further away from the building as the windows began to explode and the roof crumpled inwards with a splintering crash. There'd be precious little left of the corpse for any autopsy.

I lowered my voice. 'And this way no one will be asking any awkward questions.'

'Like what?'

'Like: if Montague was killed trying to wrestle the rifle from my hands, why was the bullet's entry hole in the *back* of his head when it got blown to pieces?'

At that we went back to the surveyor's shack and shared a very enjoyable bath together. We used a lot of soap on each other.

47

The surveyor's clothes Alice finally rooted out for me were well made and a more than ample fit. I don't think he was a particularly fat man but I very much needed my belt to cinch his pants around my waist. They were also a touch short but I tucked them into my socks and thrust my feet into my boots and you couldn't tell. Alice had tied my smoke-stained outfit into a clean sheet and I hung it like a sack from my pommel while we three rode back into town. The acrid smell would waft up and pinch at my nose when the breeze caught it, but otherwise it wasn't too bad. Pearl at first treated the sack with caution and had been a little skittish, but she soon settled down and trotted along gamely, happy to be going home.

Dougie Hinds had proved to be a real Godsend. It seems he'd been recruited by Montague to be an informal assistant manager, an unpaid foreman if you will. He knew the workings of the mine and most of the men employed there. He was sorely understaffed that day because, he told us, three of his men had disappeared without a trace one morning and a number of his boys had gone into town on the Friday afternoon and never came back. Even so he was willing to send a few of his men down to the town to look at what could be done about the hole created by our 'exploding train'.

He personally contacted the people in Shafter. I wondered what they made of his story; and the fact that Montague had not only been shot but had also been cremated, thanks to the spark of a 'slow and unnoticed powder burn setting fire to his clothes'. This last was Preacher's contribution to the new legend.

Shafter promoted Dougie to acting manager and told him to move into the surveyor's shack and set up his office there. The surveyor and his wife would not need it on account of their being billeted to a new site near Tombstone in Arizona. That was the reason we felt justified in making such free use of the man's tack and his wardrobe.

Dougie and I parted on friendly terms. He crowed like a rooster when I showed him the bathroom with its flush toilet, and he made me vow to keep quiet about it with the other men.

'With something like that bathroom,' he said, 'it would be a lot easier to make sure that the men don't know than it would be to say no!'

I said amen to that and shook his friendly hand. He was as chalk to Montague's cheese and the mine would be better for his promotion, of that I was sure.

The ride back was mostly silent. Alice took a position between Preacher and me and cast me a number of knowing looks and pert smiles. Anything of Grandma Teatree had gone by then, and the intensity of her gaze on me was intoxicating. She was a wild wine to offer such a thirsty man and I wanted to drink deep from her at every opportunity.

The Preacher rode like a man alone. He was wrestling with riddles and demons enough for an army, and I could almost hear the machinery of his incredible mind grinding everything he'd discovered into better and more workable shapes. I could see by the thin line of his mouth that he was trying a number of new theories on for size and finding none of them to be quite the perfect fit, much as it was with me and the surveyor's pants.

I was surprised to see the vanquished black cylinder of our train still slewed next to the crater. Curious onlookers still gawped into the hole as if they were waiting for genii to leap out of it and grant their wishes. Couples promenaded around it hand-in-hand, spooning where the worm had so recently burned.

One thoughtful citizen had hammered bent metal poles around the site and tied ropes to them to create a makeshift barrier. It was a flimsy structure but had proved effective. The townsfolk circled the crater at a respectable distance.

Not so the train, which had become a haven for children. It lay broken with sharp, bright metal peeled skywards from its body like daggers thanks to the force of the boiler's explosion. Any one of those lethal petals would slash a hole through anyone who got too close, but that didn't stop the town's young from treating that wreck like the world's finest playground. I could see small figures swinging from its mighty wheels and clambering around in its tilted cab like mice in a larder store.

I wondered at how much joy they managed to glean from the felled giant. What was it they saw there?

I mentioned this to Alice and she said, 'They see the whole world, Caleb; castles and pirate ships, forts attacked by Indians or Union soldiers. Maybe some of them are driving a train. Who can guess what a child sees?'

I agreed. A child's imagination remains a rich, open and exotic flower for far too short a while. Where once excitement and curiosity shone with untamed eyes we begin to see doubt creep in and take root. And then a world-weary adult gazes tiredly out upon a mundane day, their eyes grown old and their souls grey and worn thin from care.

I shook myself free of my strange and sombre reveries. I had noticed before that on occasion my mind would drift free of its moorings and take me away on antic little journeys to unknown shores. The fancies were not mine, but instead felt as if another mind was amusing itself by sharing its errant muses with me. Perhaps it was the child I'd once been, trying to light a fresh spark in my tired imagination. Did I need that? Hadn't I enough strange doings in my life?

I was in love with a water spirit and my best friend was a creature of fantasy beyond any common imaginings, but nothing need be imagined about a wrecked train at the west end of town and a crater where The Palace had once stood. And there was nothing need be imagined about the worm. That was real enough. I had seen it burn. We lived through strange days indeed.

I shook myself out of my pensive mood. With Alice's elixir charging through my veins and the girl herself by my side, my spirits could not be dampened for long. Preacher asked us to join him for dinner that night and we accepted with pleasure. He rode away from us in a brown study. I got the impression he had a number of questions he wanted to put to Alice but nothing had been said. Not then.

If Heck Levine recognised Alice's horse, he made nothing of it. He just helped the boy remove its saddle and bridle and set to currying it like he planned to put her out to show. He did the same with Pearl, who nuzzled him like a long lost friend.

He told us he needed a name for Alice's mount, for the records. She whispered to the horse and the horse nickered back. She chuckled, which set everyone to smiling. Alice could brighten any room just by standing in it.

'Fleet Foot,' said Alice then whispered again. The horse nodded.

We went from the bemused and grinning Levine to the Happy House steam laundry where Mr Chang himself glared at me accusingly when I handed over the tied sheet filled with clothes and thick with the smell of burning meat and wood smoke. I wasn't surprised. His wife had been engaged to wash and repair just about my entire wardrobe during the past few days. He handed me back the clothes that'd once been coated in a thick layer of rat droppings and I paid him what was due.

'Sheriff Sawyer,' he said. 'My wife suggests you take better care in future and watch where you put your feet.' He bowed to Alice who made a polite little curtsey. He blushed and flapped his hand in front of his grinning face. Behind him his ancient wife hissed and slapped at his shoulder. I hustled Alice away from the old gentleman.

'Alice,' I said, 'as Grandma, you made sure everyone in town feared you. Is it now your intention to make every man fall in love with you?'

The look she cast up at me was so arch that I laughed out loud and she joined in with complete abandon. We briefly became the centre of attention and some folks smiled to see two people finding such pleasure in each other while others scowled at our lack of propriety in a God-fearing world.

I took my woman back to my home and told her it was ours from that day forth. She stood on tip-toe to kiss me. I kissed her back. One thing led to another and we were nearly late getting ready for dinner with the Preacher.

He was waiting at the door when we arrived and hurried us inside.

'Alice, I've been thinking. May I call upon your incredible memory while we eat?'

'Of course, Satan. What would you like me to remember?'

'The fate of a lost nation of proud Indians. Can you tell us what really happened to the Payaya?'

48

Preacher's food was always of the best but I ate that night as if in a dream. I drank beer and chewed food, I know I did, but I was so taken up in the conversation between my companions that I truly can't remember anything I put in my mouth.

Alice recalled with a smile that the Payaya were a noble, friendly and beautiful people who loved laughter and worshipped the ground and the plants that grew there, the sky and the sun that warmed them, and the river that flowed through their land and brought them fine fish to eat and clean water to drink.

'And they knew me,' she said. 'For all that I clothed myself in the body of a human woman, they knew me for what I was. They would reach out to me when I passed and their children would follow me around like little lambs. You talk often of Eden, Satan? Well I believe those Payaya children had the light of Eden shining in their eyes.'

And then more white men came and the Forster holding grew to become first a Spanish settlement and then Mexican. Many of the Indians became sick and their beautiful womenfolk were often lusted after by so-called 'civilised' men who looked down on them and used them like unpaid harlots. They described it as the time of crying. The light began to fade from their eyes.

'The Yanaguana nation shrank like a rain puddle in the desert, and soon all they had to call home was the few acres of scrub around their most sacred place. By then Abel had passed on and the Mexicans began to behave like tyrants. They wanted cheap labour and the poor Payaya no longer had Abel's voice raised on their behalf. I had vowed to protect them so I stayed on in Abel's place and did what I could, but an old woman in widow's weeds got little respect. When I raised my voice in protest they raised their hands against me. Mexican soldiers had no patience for the complaints of old women. They would send me sprawling in the dirt and walk away laughing. I wish you'd been here then, Preacher Satan, and you, Caleb. They would've taken notice of you men.'

She reached out and took a long pull of her beer, her eyes haunted by her memories.

'And then one day the Indian workers didn't turn up in the fields and the women didn't show up in the kitchens or their masters' beds. The Mexicans were very angry. They took up their sticks and guns, called their dogs. They went to the Payaya's reed huts and laid waste to them. They burned everything. They smashed pots and tore apart the beautiful woven hangings that told the long peaceful story of the Yanaguana nation, right from that very first day when the sun's giant servants fashioned them from rich clay and taught them the many skills they needed to thrive in this land of plenty.

'For many thousands of years the gentle Payaya had flourished under the kind sun and lived in harmony with hundreds of other neighbouring tribes. Do you know why this State is called Texas?'

'I thought the Spanish named it back in the day,' I offered.

Preacher said nothing.

'The great Caddo tribe had a word for how all the Texan tribes saw and worked with each other before the Europeans came. They said they were "taysha", which means "friends" or "allies". This, all of this, was the land of Taysha. The Spanish spelt it as "Tejas" without understanding what it meant, and the English-speaking people took it and made it their own when they called the place Texas. This is the friendly State, or it is if you're not a Payaya or a Caddo. For them, Taysha became a place of rape and slavery. And then on that day of anger and burning, the Payaya were gone.'

'All of them?'

'Yes, all of them, from grandmothers to babes in arms. It was as if a great wind had carried them away or the ground had opened and swallowed them up. The Mexicans hunted them on horseback and lost a lot of face with some of the other tribes because of the way they rode around, shouting and threatening anyone they suspected of hiding the runaways.

A Spanish-speaking Caddo trader asked one of the Mexican hunters how many people had been lost. When he was told "over five hundred" he burst into mocking laughter.

He said, "I don't have enough food to feed over five hundred of my own tribe. Where would I find grain for over five hundred strangers? Your search is foolish. Go home and look at the ground in shame. You have driven away and lost the first children born in your land. God will turn his back on you. He will cover his head in shame at the thought of you."

'It was the Caddo that God turned his back on first, but the Mexicans fell in their turn. And in a nutshell that is the Payaya's story in this "friendly State". A long sweet spring followed by a longer summer and then everything was lost when the bitter east wind from Europe brought its fatal winter storms.'

Her story finished, Alice gazed into her cup. 'This is empty; can I fetch more for anyone else?'

168

What she brought back was wine. After listening to her story I thought she'd made a good choice. The wine was red and dense and potent. It helped wash away the bitterness I was tasting after Alice's words.

'I wish I'd been here,' said the Preacher, anger plain on his face. 'I wish I had. But that was a long time ago and this is now. I think what happened that night when the village was emptied and the Payaya disappeared may still be important today. I think it explains what has been happening to the town recently.'

He looked at Alice with the face of a soldier who knows he must soon go to war. 'You spoke of the tribe's sacred place. Where was that?'

'It is a good walk south-west from here at the base of the hills. There is a stone...'

'Divided Rock,' I blurted out. 'I know it well. It has paintings hidden in its secret places. There's the skeleton of a camel.'

She laughed at that. 'Ah yes, the camel. That was a failed experiment if ever there was one. Landsman called Cody, just Cody, brought the poor creature here instead of a horse. He called it Abdul. Said it was the perfect mount for hot places and he would prove it. Cody planned to breed and trade the critters, said they carried water in a special bag on their backs. He shouldn't have told folks that. Word about Abdul the camel spread far and wide, and one day a thirsty trapper decided to take a drink from the bag on Abdul's back. Had to kill Cody first of course. The trapper hacked at poor Abdul with a long knife and killed the beast without ever getting his drink. The camel was left where he lay and Cody was brought back for a Christian burial. After that there never was a call for camels around here, and I don't think anyone ever knew where the unfortunate Cody found his one.'

'And you're sure this rock was where the Payaya had their last settlement?'

'Yes, Satan, certain sure.'

'Then tomorrow morning I must go there. Caleb, will you guide me?'

'Depend upon it, Preacher.'

'Good. Thank you, I'm obliged. You say we can walk, but how long by horseback?'

'No more than an hour... less, say forty minutes. What will we be doing there?'

'I can't ask you to join me, my friend.'

'I'll not see you alone in this. What are we doing?'

'Thank you, Caleb, thank you. You will need your guns. If I'm right we shall be confronting the Sha-aneer where it lives. If I'm right we will have to kill it or we'll not survive the encounter.'

Alice pounded the table. 'Then I'll come too.'

'No, Alice, no.' Preacher put his hand on hers. 'If we fail you're the last hope for this town. You're all we have to fight the rear-guard action.'

She looked fearfully at me then back at the Preacher.

'You bring him back, Satan. If you don't you'd better make sure you're dead too. And even if you do die you won't escape me. I'll climb down into the darkest pit of Hell if I have to, and I'll find you and I'll make you suffer for taking him away from me. You understand what I'm telling you?'

He took her hand and kissed it, smiling his crescent moon smile.

'And I shall be waiting there for you. I promise.'

49

Alice was like a wild thing in bed that night. Our lovemaking was urgent and insistent. She seemed insatiable. It was as if she was trying to impress herself on me, to mark me with her body. Exhausted, we finally slept in each other's arms and she was so small and slight that my arm didn't tingle when we woke the next morning in the same position.

She kissed me hard on the mouth before I left and I once more tasted the cool water that was her gift. The elixir flowed through my veins like a blessing and I realised once more I was living through strange days that would haunt me for a lifetime – if I survived.

'You come back, you hear me!'

I heard her. God, that sweet little woman was strong. She hugged me so hard she near broke my spine. I was very aware of her body pressed against mine; I felt her with possessive heat.

'You're mine, Caleb Sawyer, mine, and I haven't finished with you yet. You come back to me, come back. I'll be waiting.'

Yes, Alice. Body, soul and heart. Yours, all yours.

She watched me walk away towards the stables, but by the time I rode back around onto Main Street she was gone from the boardwalk. I think I saw her standing at an upstairs window but the angle of the sun had turned the glass to a mirror. I couldn't be certain.

Preacher rode up to me and touched the brim of his hat in greeting. Silently we turned towards the hills and rode out of town. All the while I felt a hot gaze burning between my shoulder blades and I knew. She was there for sure.

Despite my lack of any real sleep I'd never felt so alive as I did that morning. Everything around me glowed with rich colour and a cool fresh breeze blew in across the river. If I'd been a singing man I would've sung up a storm that day, but instead I sighed with happiness. I felt replete.

'Caleb, our job today is dangerous. You don't have to join me, my friend. Please, just take me to the rock and then go back to her.'

His face was solemn as he spoke but he couldn't alter my perfect mood with his forebodings.

'Preacher,' I said. 'We'll both go back to her when the job is done. We just have to be careful is all and we won't have any trains to throw around this time. So, tell me, what's the plan?'

'The plan? We find it, we kill it, and we get away alive and in one breathing piece. Right now we don't know where it is, how big it is, or even if we *can* find it. Hard to make a plan until you've seen the battlefield you're going to fight on.'

'But you have an idea, right?'

'An idea? Sure, yes, I have an idea.'

'That's good enough for me.'

He shook his head and said nothing. He just reached across and clapped me on the shoulder. That gesture was all it took. At that moment I felt I would've followed him into the mouth of Hell itself if he'd asked me. I didn't know just how close to the truth that would prove to be. Nor how soon.

We rode to Divided Rock in companiable silence. Pearl tried to strike up a conversation with the Preacher's bay mare, but she just cantered along and ignored Pearl's nickered enquiries. I patted her glossy neck in recompense. Some ten or so minutes later we rounded a shoulder of stone and there it was. Divided Rock.

That the Payaya thought of the rock and its surroundings as a sacred place didn't surprise me at all. I'd always thought it looked like a place remembered from a dream. I walked there often when I needed a quiet spot in which to think, and wondered if maybe the spirits of the tribes-people still held parley there.

There was peacefulness there, quietness. It felt as if the world itself was holding its breath and taking a long moment to reflect. The rock was some twenty feet tall and had been split in two so long ago that each vertical half had been worn smooth by the actions of wind and dust. To a casual eye those stones looked to be a uniform pale grey, but once we tethered our horses in the shade I showed the Preacher the hidden paintings in the clefts and hollows of the stone. He admired the craftsmanship and talked about the way the artists had made use of natural contours and features in the stone's surface to make their imagery more realistic. He pointed at a striking representation of a winged man much larger than the dancing figures around it.

'Rather a good likeness, don't you think?' He angled his chin to present me with his profile and I laughed out loud. My laughter echoed back at us from the hillside. It seemed an uncouth sound in that special, sacred place. It mocked the serenity we had found there.

We climbed down from the rock and Preacher began his forensic examination of the ground. He was looking for clues in a crime scene over one hundred years old. He found them.

He was able to show me slight, circular indentations filled with different coloured soil. Those, he explained, were post holes. He demonstrated how they described a circle about fifteen feet across. Strong pine poles would've been seated there and then arched over to the centre to create a framework onto which the Indians would have woven their reed homes. He painted a picture of families living there, thriving and enjoying thousands of years of peaceful co-existence with everyone around them.

Preacher told me, 'They understood the land and they lived with the land. They existed in a state of harmony with their world that was perhaps more of Eden than Earth.'

He was also able to point out where the soil had a layer of sooty ash upon it, and that was where Mexicans had taken revenge on the escapees by burning their homes. The landscape spoke to him with a clear voice and he knew how to listen.

The true extent of the Payaya settlement was breath-taking. In my mind's eye I watched those gentle, civilised people go about their business and I grieved for them. They had done nothing to deserve their fate.

More and more the Preacher's eyes were drawn up to the hillside. He turned his back on the Divided Rock and its environs and began to examine the slopes in earnest. He pored over the almost vertical cliff-sides for over an hour. I had left him to his work and gone back to examine the post holes and other such traces of a lost civilisation, and then I heard him cry out, 'Caleb, my friend, look here.' And then he disappeared from view.

I hurried to where he had been standing, but there was no sign of him. I spun around in a circle and called his name, but to no avail. Like the Payaya before him, he must have been swallowed into the earth. My heart pounding in my throat I stood there uselessly, confused and unable to decide what I should do next.

'Oh, Preacher, Preacher, where are you?' I whined like a lost dog seeking its master.

{50}

'Why, I'm right here, Caleb.'

I spun again and there he was behind me.

'What? Can you make yourself invisible now?'

He chuckled. 'I wondered if the disguise was good enough to fool you, even after leading you right to the spot. The Mexicans didn't see it either. Look here.'

He brought me flat against an apparently vertical stretch of cliff-side that had a cascade of long grasses growing down it. He placed his hand behind the grass and lifted. I gasped in surprise. There were stone steps carved into the rock face.

Once he had showed me the hidden stairs their location became obvious, but up to that point I would never have guessed they even existed.

'But how did you find them?'

'I was looking for them. I knew there had to be something like this somewhere.'

'But how? Why? What made you even think of such a thing?'

'Because, Caleb, there are precious few straight lines in nature and if you cast your eyes about halfway up this bluff...' He pointed.

Shielding my eyes from the sun, I followed his direction. I had to step away from the cliff and I squinted so hard that my eyes began to water, but eventually I saw what he was showing me. A fine, zigzag line curving upwards on the stone.

'Shall we take a look?' I asked.

'Be a crime not to.'

As usual he led the way. If the staircase had been carved by the Payaya it must've been done in the long centuries before Europeans came to their land. The steps were deep and worn by years of use. Spirals and winged snakes had also been carved onto some of the cliff walls. I saw ochre-coloured hand prints and buffalo painted on some of the more protected surfaces.

One thing was obvious: the Indians who used these stairs could not have been at all fat. Preacher pointed out how the steps followed a natural fault line, and in some cases they became so narrow that we had to edge up them with our backs pressed to the wall.

'I don't believe mothers could've carried their babies up here at night,' I said, trying hard not to look down the dozens of feet to where our horses were peacefully nibbling at the leaves of a bush. 'Nor do I believe toddlers climbed up here. Surely it would be far too dangerous?'

'I agree. But let's see what we find when we reach the top.'

We climbed higher and higher and then it seemed to me as if our stairs came to an abrupt halt. Then Preacher seemed to suddenly fall sideways into the cliff-face. Suddenly alone I nearly stumbled and teetered for a breathless, dizzying moment during which I feared I might slip and plummet down to be dashed to pieces on the hard ground so far below.

Preacher reappeared and steadied me with his strong left hand.

'Carefully, Caleb. There's a sharp bend just here. Not far now.'

I inched round after him and then it was my turn to almost fall through the hand-carved archway that'd suddenly opened up before me. Inside the arch two stone creatures sat on either side of the entrance, snarling open-mouthed out at the open air.

'Guardian jaguars I believe,' said Preacher, 'and can you see how this entrance would've been completely invisible from the ground?' He stroked the head of one of the stone cats. 'Beautiful craftsmanship, beautiful. And just what is it you're guarding in here, my fine fellows?'

A billowing curtain of cobwebs shielded our view of the interior as completely as our blanket had done back in the surveyor's bedroom. It was thick and covered with dust. The Preacher fetched out his box of sulphur matches and lit one. He threw it into the mass of webs. It was suspended in the centre of them for just a second and they caught instantly. The fire raced away from us down a short tunnel and then seemed to expand outwards as if into a much larger space. We caught glimpses of tantalising shapes in the brief glare before the fire stuttered and was gone.

'I thought that would be better than trying to fight our way through those webs. Those spiders have taken over a hundred years to erect their fortress home and here we come and we burn it to nothing in mere seconds. Seems almost unfair, somehow.'

He turned on his narrow lamp and I heard a great number of insect legs scuttling away into the shadows. His beam of light picked out a scaffold from which depended a great length of rope and the partly rotted remains of a large wicker basket. When new it would've been very robust indeed.

'I think we now know how the mothers and little ones would have been brought up here. Can you see how years of use have smoothed the arm of the scaffold until its square profile became a semi-circle? That rope would've been strong enough to hold a number of people at any one time. And look, that big stone would've acted as a counterweight when they were lowered to the ground.'

I cast my gaze back towards the entrance. 'Would some of them have stood up here and watched their homes burn, like we just did to the spiders?'

'I don't know, my friend. I don't know. Keep your rifle handy.'

We walked deeper into the tunnel and there we could see a gallery of Payaya art. The passage of burning webs had done nothing to scorch their beauty. They shone as if newly created, their colours bright and fresh. The ceiling, however, was black, coated with soot from many centuries of torches processing this way. Preacher's keen eyes glittered with excitement.

The air in the place was becoming colder the deeper we went, and I reasoned that was perfectly natural. The sun held no sway here in the belly of darkness, and the wall paintings seemed to move in the Preacher's lamplight.

'By flickering torchlight these figures would have danced,' said Preacher as if echoing my thoughts. He had a disconcerting habit of doing so.

'Watch your footing,' he warned. 'More steps.'

We reached the end of the passage and began to descend a wide ramp of stairs leading down into the bowels of the earth, or so it seemed to me. I heard a whispering sound above us. Preacher angled his lamp upwards in answer to my unspoken question. The ceiling in this larger space was several yards above our heads and it seemed to be covered by some sort of leathery fabric. It was moving.

'Bats,' said Preacher. 'A whole colony. They won't bother us.'

He angled the lamp down again and we descended the staircase. Something about the quality of sound there told me how immense that chamber was. It was like a cathedral. Bigger. We stood still for a moment while my companion shone his lamp around us. The walls were so distant that the cone of light barely illuminated them. Giant winged figures marched there, their heads turned sideways to display their fine Roman noses and beards. Smaller figures at their feet sported noses more like a rounded vulture's beak. I marvelled that the artists had caught the difference between European faces and native Indians so precisely, but Preacher shook his head.

'No, Caleb, these were created a good long time before the Spaniards got this far. Those are the Gods of the old religion. They were never meant to be representations of white men.'

That was when I caught the first intimation of an acid stench and I hesitated.

'What's that stink?'

'Bat lime. They don't go outside to use the toilet, dirty little brutes.'

When we reached the bottom on the staircase I could see the floor was coated in a foul-smelling, chalk-like substance.

'Can we walk on it?'

'I plan to find out. We didn't come all this way to be turned back by a lake of bat shit.'

Our feet threw up acrid clouds of fine powder and sometimes I slipped in the fresher stuff, but it proved okay to walk on. Preacher handed me a kerchief to tie around my face.

'You know what this stuff is, Caleb. You don't want to breathe it.'

The vast chamber was almost circular and it became obvious to my friend that it had once been a natural cave reshaped by the Payaya so that it better reflected one of their roundhouse dwellings.

'This might represent the home of their gods,' he told me, 'but they couldn't imagine their gods living anywhere different to their roundhouses, just much bigger. Much as European cathedrals were designed to humble peasants who lived in huts, this place was the gods' roundhouse. It's an incredible sight.'

It is some measure of the man that he could talk like that while choking on the dust of bat shit, but he did. I looked up at the winged god before me. I saw the resemblance clear enough.

'Preacher, have you been here before?'

'Me? No, not me. But I probably once knew people who have. We looked a lot alike back in those days.'

'You ever wear a beard?'

'Questions, Caleb, always one with the questions.'

He shone his lamp directly ahead.

'Look there, an archway.'

'You knew it would be there?'

'I suspected as much. If the Payaya tribe came up here to escape the Mexicans and were never seen again, well, they must still be around here somewhere. The bat droppings aren't deep enough yet to bury their remains so they have to be somewhere else. I was looking for a doorway or an arch leading to another chamber. And there it is.'

The jaguars we had met at the entrance had big brothers in the gods' house. A familiar ice-cold fetid stench rolled out from between them and their open-jawed faces looked disgusted by it.

'That isn't bat shit, is it?'

'No, Caleb, it isn't.'

And he turned off his lamp.

177

51

We were plunged into darkness so complete it almost had weight. I gasped at it and nearly stumbled. I cringed when something grabbed firmly at my arm. It was Preacher.

He whispered, 'Quiet, Caleb. Wait a few moments.'

I waited and tried to calm my pounding heart. I could hear it beating so fiercely in my ears I shouldn't have been surprised if its drumbeat alerted everything down there to my presence.

And then, slowly but surely, a faint phosphorescence began to outline the archway before me and I regained the miraculous angel sight I'd enjoyed in the mine workings so many days before.

'Better?'

'Much, thanks. Are you doing that?'

'Of course. We don't want to alert the Sha-aneer to our presence until we have to, if we haven't done so already.'

'Great. That makes me feel so much better.'

'Well at least we now have a better idea of our battlefield.'

The ghost-light bloomed brighter in my eyes and soon I was able to pick out far more details than I had by Preacher's lamp. The chamber was really huge and the wall paintings were incredibly complex, even without their rich colouration. Preacher stood at my side. His eyes seemed to glow with an internal light. He seemed to be floating on the milky white floor and I wondered at that until I realised he had no shadow.

'No light source,' I said, 'no shadows.'

'Correct, my friend. Now, shall we go find out what happened to the last people of the Payaya tribe?'

With a building sense of nausea I nodded my agreement. 'It's why we're here.'

We walked through the archway, Preacher slightly to the fore. I made sure my rifle's safety catch was off and held it ready at waist height. We paused at the threshold of the next chamber and took stock of what my companion had described as our battlefield. It was evident there were no bats in there, but nor were there any paintings. The walls were featureless. I could see well enough but there seemed to be no information I could use to establish just what I was looking at. And then everything seemed to happen at once.

Preacher shoved me backwards so hard I went sprawling on the gods' roundhouse floor. A thick curtain of *something* fell down and smothered the

Preacher where he stood and then a mass of black tendrils lashed out towards me. I scrambled to my feet and ran like a startled hare for the stairs. They seemed so far away and even as I ran with the fleetness of pure terror I knew two things with dread certainty. First, I was never going to escape and second, the Preacher was in the belly of the worm. Earth and everyone on it was doomed and there was nothing I could do about it.

I prayed I might see Alice once more, but I was sure in my gut I'd never even make it to the first ramp of steps, let alone back into the daylight. My body and soul would be devoured by the grotesque creature at my heels, and one day soon I'd be a part of it when it drank my Alice dry. I wondered how much of me would remain when it happened.

I was gasping but redoubled my efforts to escape. I daren't look back in case it slowed me down but the skin of my back crawled in anticipation of that first stinging touch. *Would I know what I had become?* The thought added wings to my heels.

And then everything before me was thrown into startling relief. White light bloomed around me and for a moment a great, writhing shadow was thrown up onto the walls before me. It reared up and then shrank away and was gone. I turned around and came to a confused halt. The tendrils had gone and the archway blazed like a gate opening onto the very heart of Hell. Flames beyond the arch lashed, roared and spilled about like an immense living thing. The great worm was burning in its lair and its twisting form in the white blaze spoke of deep and unimaginable torment. A howling choir of agony sang from the profoundest depths of nightmare.

I couldn't quite comprehend exactly what I was seeing beyond that arch, but I reasoned Preacher Spindrift had somehow triggered his crystal grenades from within the monster. It was the only explanation that made sense. I had a sudden profound pang of terrible loss. He was in there with the burning beast. Preacher was gone. I fell to my knees and moaned aloud. I felt my heart would burst.

And then I saw a dark silhouette framed in the archway and come dashing towards me. It was impossible. It was him. He had lost his hat and was tearing off his long coat which resembled a pin cushion it was so filled with the great worm's quills, but otherwise he seemed unhurt. He grabbed some of his crystal grenades from his coat and sprinted to my side.

'Come on!' he yelled. 'Let's get the hell out of here as fast as we can. Come on, Caleb, move!'

I needed no second invitation. I leapt to my feet and ran as hard as breath would allow. We were halfway up those wide stairs when the world lurched and tilted wildly and I was thrown to my knees.

'No time for that, man! Come on! Keep moving if you want to live.'

Behind us the wall was bulging and burning flesh was boiling out onto the floor, filling it with a stinking lake of white fire. The heat was intense.

Then the ceiling seemed to be falling on us and I covered my head, waiting for the rock to crush me. An odd wetness spattered around us as we ran. It stank and at first I thought it must be some strange new weapon thrown at us by the worm. And then I realised that the ceiling wasn't collapsing. It was the bats. Hundreds, thousands of them streaming towards the exit and emptying their bowels in terror. I couldn't blame them.

The short passage was alive with the creatures and Preacher beat at them to keep them away. He threw his coat to the ground and then shattered two crystals against its fabric. The coat smouldered at first and then the spines embedded in it took hold and burned brightly.

The bats gave the burning coat a wide berth. Preacher stood tall and hustled me towards the entrance. So many of the little flying critters rustled and fluttered around me. I was blinded by them. I felt a rope thrust into my hands and strong arms propelled me forward. And then I was ejected out into bright sunlight and found myself dropping like a stone towards the distant ground.

Preacher fell with me gripping the rope above me. I clung to it in desperation but considered it to be wasted effort. We seemed to be falling faster if anything. My very eyelashes fluttered and danced in the powerful updraft created by our fall. And then I heard a sound and I realised that Preacher was singing! I wondered if the man had lost his senses at last. But while he sang our descent slowed until it was like little more than the gentle fall of a leaf from a tree.

A great ball of flame erupted from the passage we had just exited. The jolt of the blast blew us sideways and nearly tore the rope from my fists. I swung and spun like the clapper of a bell but the Preacher was winning. Our fall was slowed further; we had almost stopped. But the Preacher's song could do nothing about the ground which suddenly kicked up towards us, thrown by another violent earth tremor.

I heard him scream with fury. It seemed so unfair that the hard soil should be able to rise up and greet us so fast. And then it hit me with great force and all was darkness, pain, and then oblivion.

52

My belly hurt. My belly hurt and my back felt stretched fit to breaking. My face was bouncing against something hard. I opened my eyes. It took me a moment to realise I was getting a close-up view of a saddle. It was the stirrups dangling inches from my nose that gave me the clue. I tried to push myself away and found I was tied in place. That was when I started yelling at the top of my lungs.

'Caleb, you're awake. How do you feel?'

'Like a sack of grain. Please, cut me loose.'

Preacher had carried me away from the scene of our collision with the bucking earth. He loaded me onto Pearl and tied me securely and then rode us at a gallop away from the collapsing cliff-side. He had only gone a few yards when the jolting sensation brought me to my senses. The ground was still heaving dangerously under Pearl's hooves.

He cut my bonds and I slid to my feet. I nearly collapsed in a heap but he bundled me back up into my saddle without delay. Pearl was jittery like a young colt and fought the reins until I whispered in her ear to calm her. Preacher's bay stood calm as an oak in a storm.

There was a tremendous crash behind us. The Divided Rock had fallen. Beyond it the cliff face buckled and great sheets of stone slammed to the ground. We urged our mounts back into a gallop as the earth reared under their pounding hooves. Balls of flame billowed from the cracks appearing in the cliff face. Pearl took the bit with her ears pressed back against her skull and we fair flew away from the cliff-side.

There was a sound. It started high-pitched and almost inaudible then ratcheted down the scales until it was a terrible and powerful howling noise. It galvanised the horses faster than a whip. Pearl was running so hard she barely touched the ground and she stretched out her beautiful neck like a champion on the flats.

The cliff-side erupted, ejecting rock and liquid fire into the air. Great boulders clattered and pounded the earth around us like a giant child's playthings thrown in mischief. If any one of them had struck us, it would've smashed both man and mount to a pulp, but luck rode with us that day.

A tree was torn from the earth and exploded in a shower of splinters. Jagged fragments of rock whizzed past our heads like shrapnel and we ducked low in our saddles. There was nowhere we could take shelter. Plumes of smoke and fire blasted lines of craters all around us and a soft rain of soil stung our eyes as we ploughed through it.

Our luck couldn't last. A razor-sharp shard of stone impacted with the right side of Preacher's horse's head. Half of its forehead including an ear and one of its eyes were ripped away in a splash of black blood. I expected its knees to buckle and for Preacher to be flung from his saddle. I almost reined in so I could leap to his aid.

No such thing happened. If anything the bay redoubled her efforts to get her rider to safety. And then I replayed the event in my mind's eye. *Black blood?* Like Preacher himself there must be a great deal more to his mount than met the eye. And then I saw the ball of the horse's lost eye and the leaf shape of its ear wing through the air and re-attach themselves to the horse's head. Something was swarming around the skull. I was too busy hanging onto Pearl to take too much notice but each time I caught sight of the beast's head it had regained more of its original shape and colour. And then I remembered Preacher's injured hand repairing itself while we watched. It looked much like sorcery but I didn't think of it as magic. Instead I saw it as a subtle art beyond my understanding. I was alive because of those arts and I gave thanks for them.

The ground was becoming still at last and we could rein in our rides a little. We had time to look back at the shrunken hillside under its pall of dust and smoke.

My words were scratched because my mouth was filled with soil and ash.

'How big was that thing?'

'I can't be sure, but it was a monster. It must've spread along fault-lines and filled spaces in rocks. It was leeching into the mines' working when it infected those ants. It stretched its seed worms as far as the town, The Palace and Fernandez' place. We might've been lucky and got it all when we blew the ants' nest, so much grief would have been avoided. But I think the fire was damped by the explosion and sealed the Sha-aneer behind a wall of stone. I was firmly in the belly of the beast when I set off my grenades. All trace of it has burned away. This place is clean.'

'I can't help but think of that tribe Alice told us about. So much was lost to the worm – men, women and children, art and thousands of years of culture. They sounded beautiful.'

'At last they are truly at peace. But now let's get you back to Alice before she keeps her promise and hunts me down.'

'What about the miners, Preacher?'

'Alice and the town first, Caleb, then we shall ride up to Fulsome. I fear the worst and believe we'll need more hands up there than just we two can provide.'

Pearl was blowing a little after our hard ride so we took the rest of the journey at an easy canter. All around us was evidence of the worm's vast extent. Smoking rifts in the earth and long, vein like depressions marked where its body had been burned away. I prayed the Preacher was right and its sway here was ended. I asked him why it hadn't attacked earlier.

'It did when it took the tribe,' he said. 'Ever since then it has been marking its territory and getting ready for the day when it could send its agents all over the world. Remember what I told you, Caleb? Trains and ships have made the world small and the Sha-aneer has been changing to take advantage of that fact. What we just destroyed was a true worm of the deep earth, the flesh of more than five hundred people devoured and changed into the Host which divided and spread out underground looking for fissures through which it could deliver its seed worms. It was huge but discreet. It would fear the activities of creatures like me. It knew me and feared me. You saw that.'

'Is it truly gone now?'

'From here, yes. From the Earth, no. It is a subtle enemy of everything done by GODS' servants. I will hear about things that mark its activities close to the surface and will do what I can to fight it once more. Ha, it seems funny to have a companion to share my story with, a warrior to fight by my side. It's been so long since I could trust a man as I trust you.'

He sighed. His words had become stately, formal. 'I could tell you I've lost count of the centuries I've been fighting the enemy, but that would be a lie. I could know my time here to the last hour, the minute, and the very second if I wanted to. So many centuries to be a soldier of the GODS and to fight for man. The Sha-aneer is like a disease, a canker that always erupts where it's least expected; and I have to be there to burn it out before it spreads to the rest of the body. One day I shall find the source of it all and would happily be destroyed if it meant I can wipe it out forever.'

He spat the words, 'I hate the evil, bastard thing and I will never stop until one of us is finished. It will never be allowed to thrive while I'm here to do something about it. I make this promise to you, Caleb, and to those generations of Eden kind as yet unborn. One day the heart of the Sha-aneer will be torn from its deep lair and it will burn. It will all burn.'

He dug his heels into his horse's ribs and it raised its speed to a brisk canter. He drew ahead a little and I let him go. I knew Pearl was tired and needed to keep with our gentler pace, but I had also seen the expression on the Preacher's face. I believed he needed a little time alone with his thoughts.

53

By the time we reached town it was already licking its wounds. Two more dirty and bloodied men leading horses down Main Street went unnoticed. The riot of the worm had caused great mischief among horses and houses alike. Its death throes had torn walls from roofs and seen previously placid old nags kick their stalls to kindling. The town wasn't completely broken but it was hurt real bad. It would take a while to get it fully back on its feet.

Some people stumbled around in a confused daze and got in everybody else's way, but others worked at bringing order out of the chaos. At the heart of this second group of people sounded the clear, calm voice of Dougie Hinds.

Dougie had kept his promise. A few hours earlier he had brought a good number of his men and flatbed carts piled high with equipment to the west end of town. At first they did nothing but walk around, gazing at the twisted rails and wreckage of the crashed train in wonder. If, during his examination, Dougie noticed that the rails of the spur track had somehow been positioned as if to aim the great engine directly towards its collision site, he kept the news to himself.

He issued orders that the damaged rails should be straightened and repaired ready for the GH&SA engineers who were expected to arrive sometime during the next forty-eight hours. Dealing with the wrecked train would be their problem; making sure they could get to it was Dougie's. The men of Shafter had spoken. With a clamour of sledgehammers and the hiss of heating equipment, a team of burly miners got down to their work.

Meanwhile, Dougie and the rest of his men peered blankly into the deep, funnel-shaped crater that marked the spot where The Palace used to be. They didn't know it had also become the crematorium for everything that remained of many of their friends and colleagues.

'I may be little more than the fool my dear mama always told me I was,' Dougie declared. 'But I've never seen anything like that during a whole mess of years spent looking into holes.'

He pulled off his hat and wafted air over his face like a Chinee with a fan sipping opium smoke from a bowl.

'What is that smell? Has somebody been throwing old pickled cabbage down there? Leave any hole open for even a minute and someone will be sure to throw things down it. Dumping shit in holes is as natural to some people as walking upright in shoe leather. I couldn't do that. I always think there's going to be one of us down there looking up.'

One of his group pointed at where the crater narrowed to become a vertical shaft.

'Is that glass there? Has that sand been melted to glass?'

'I'd say so.'

'Mother of God, how hot *was* this fire?'

'Hot enough for you, Joshua, and hot enough for Hell.'

'They say this here was an act of God, right enough.'

'Don't talk foolishness, Murray. I saw an act of God once when my baby boy was born and both mother and child stayed fit and happy. We lost our first baby, another boy, in the first few seconds of his little life, so that second time I was outside the birthing room on my knees and I was praying fit to rip a gut. When I saw my boy I cried with joy and I sent thanks to Heaven. *That* was an act of God, Murray. This, *this*... well, I just don't know.'

A man graced with a formidable beard and blessed with the name Elijah Willis Poots (of the Madison Avenue Poots, he'd often tell baffled society women during social functions) perched his behind on a wooden seat through which a stout rope had been threaded and knotted underneath. A leather strap was buckled across his back, under his armpits and around the rope, holding him securely in place. The 'Drop Lady' contraption had been devised for the exploration of vertical shafts many years before, but that wasn't to be the plan that day. Poots had no intention of climbing any further down this strange new feature than to the base of the shallow crater.

His job was to see if the crater was stable enough for the shaft to be capped. If so, the job of making the hole safe once more would be simple. If not, the whole project would have to be rethought and the depth of the shaft would need to be gauged. Poots crossed himself twice then put his hand in the air.

He slowly walked backwards down the crater, all the while looking over his shoulder. Above him the rope was paid out by a small gang of men and Dougie stood at the lip of the hole. If anything went wrong the gang had been told to 'run like madmen' and drag Poots back up to the surface as fast as they could pull him.

Poots was unusually nervous, or at least it was unusual for him. He was the renowned stalwart who would lend courage to his fellows and stare peril in the eye without flinching. He once beat off a wild dog that attacked his gang's camp. He scared it off with two hard swings of a handy pit prop that caught the cur on the back of its head and across its shoulders. That dog ran howling back into the night with its tail between it legs. Poots spat on the ground, lay down his prop and then, as if nothing had happened, sat down to his dinner without breaking so much as a sweat or speaking a word to the others in the camp. He was a good man to have in a tight spot. But that morning something had him really spooked.

When he started screaming to be brought up, Dougie yelled to the gang of four.

'Get him out of there, now – now! Move it – go!'

And they ran so fast Poots came out of that hole faster than a cork from a Champagne bottle. He landed several feet from the hole and was winded on impact with the ground but still managed to wheeze, 'Get down, you bastard sons of bitches, get down!'

Everyone flung themselves away from the crater and waited. Nothing happened. One or two stirred as if preparing to get back and look see at the hole. Poots roared at them. He had his breath back now.

He needed say no more. The Main Street began to tremble under their outstretched arms and then it jolted hard as if trying to shake them off. People in the street and the group of miners attending to the twisted rails were thrown sprawling to the earth.

An ear-splitting shriek erupted from the crater, amplified by the funnel shape. It built and built until everyone in the vicinity was curled in a ball with their arms over their heads. They scuttled away like insects on the quivering ground, gasping in agony at the leviathan of sound. Behind them gouts of flame were followed by a column of boiling rock and soil which fountained out of the shaft and opened like a black flower before curling back and splashing into the crater.

The shriek was cut as if slashed with a knife and the earth gentled, becoming still once more. For a long minute, men remained where they lay, panting with fear.

Dougie Hinds and Poots were first to their feet. They made tentative steps to the edge of the crater, looking down and then across at each other. Poots clawed thoughtful fingers through his beard and a hatless Dougie ran a baffled hand through his hair.

Before them the crater had been filled with a thick black substance that was cooling fast. No one would walk on it for a while but it was already evident that it wouldn't be draining away.

Dougie muttered, 'That hole look plugged to you, Elijah?'

'Looks plugged right and proper to me, Dougie.'

'Yeah,' Dougie took a deep breath. 'Reckon there's the second act of God I ever did see.'

'Amen to that. Yessir, amen to that.'

{54}

Our arrival back at my office was far from tranquil. Alice flew into a raging fury when she saw my bloody face, filthy clothes and matted hair. She rounded on the Preacher with a tempest in her eyes and her hands balled into fists. I swear she was about to launch herself at him and show him some of her sharper aspects, but he held up his hand and spoke to her in that odd language again; which was both enchanting and completely opaque to my reason. Her eyes grew large as lanterns and she answered in the same manner.

'I don't know what you two are saying,' I told them, 'but I could listen to it all day. It's so musical.'

'Satan is reminding me that a noble heart still beats within a basket of very ancient bones. And yes, you're right, Caleb, the tongue of the Fey is the mother of all music.'

And then she spoke at length to me in her old language and I fell into a blissful reverie while the wonderful sounds cast their spell on my soul. After everything I'd experienced that day I hadn't expected to be feeling so much happiness that soon. While she sang to me in her ancient language, the Preacher disappeared unnoticed from the room.

She washed me like a mother washes her child. It took two hot tubs and a whole bar of good white soap to manage it but I was finally clean enough to be allowed a kiss, and then another. What I tried to do next she forbade me despite my evident state of arousal. When I queried her sudden chaste rebuff – where before my approaches had been met with much more than open arms – she gestured behind me. The Preacher stood there, waiting quietly with his box of medical supplies. He smiled and shook his head at my blushes.

Once I was dry and a little more decent he ministered to my bruises, scrapes and cuts. In the heat of the moment I hadn't noticed just how battered I'd become. I was in a parlous sore and sorry state. I felt as if I'd donned a thorny cloak of pure pain, and I had to fight hard not to whimper like a whipped cur while he soothed balms and emollients into my torn hide.

I required a few stitches. I turned my eyes from his work. It is one thing to see another man's skin sewn together but it's a dish of an altogether different kidney when it's your own.

'You have earned some brave scars, my love.' Alice examined me when the Preacher had completed his needlework. She touched the sutures with careful fingers.

'No heavy lifting for a few days, Caleb. But I'm sure that a little light exercise wouldn't go amiss. I think Alice would be pleased to help you with that.' Preacher's eyes glittered with a merry glint while he spoke. 'I have to go out now. I have to put my house in order and I want to see how the town fares today. It would appear that Damsel-Childs and Teague have vanished along with, ah, poor Grandma Teatree. I think it's time to call an election for new members to join me in the council. I'm not sure how much longer I can remain here, but I will help ensure this town is back up off its knees before I make any move to leave.'

He strode to the door and then looked back at us. His expression was one of deep longing and I felt something sting suddenly behind my eyes.

'While I still can, may I invite both of you to dinner tonight? We have much to celebrate, and I can't think of anyone I could choose to share my joy with more than you, my dear friends. Please, say yes.'

We accepted and with good heart. He smiled his crescent moon smile and gave us a little bow before taking his leave. We talked about him after he'd gone, about the dreadful complexity of his place in the world and about his mission, which might at any time call him to any point of the globe. Friendship must be a rare thing in his life, we said, and when it happened it must always end with goodbye.

Such thoughts darkened our mood for a while and we mused on his lot like guests at his funeral. And then our musings finally petered out and Alice knuckled down to helping me with my little touch of 'light exercise'. We had to be very careful not to spoil any of our good friend's needlework.

While we were so pleasantly distracted the Preacher was out making himself useful, and he had a great deal of news to share with us when we joined him that evening. Like us he had been lucky with little more than a cracked pane of glass to show for the worm's passing. Others had been dealt fiercer hands but overall the town had survived intact.

He only had one death to report and that was a Texas pony crushed by a falling roof beam in its stall. He was told that Damsel-Childs and Teague had been spotted walking together towards The Palace and he surmised they'd decided to check on their investment – with unfortunate results. Neither had been seen since. It needed no great detective to ascertain what had happened to them.

Heck Levine had been quick enough to seek help and with enough hands he managed to bring most of his four-legged clients out of the stables and into the open. He had corralled them down in the stockyards. His only difficulty had been with an elderly mare named Daffadilly, who had thrown a fit during the so-called 'quake' and kicked her way out of her stall before heading east at high speed.

'Heck told me she'd be back when she got hungry enough. He didn't seem worried. He's also set his boys to watching the stockyards in case some opportunist decides to take advantage of the situation to snatch themselves a new pony. I pity them if they do. Those boys are hot to shoot someone and I don't think they'll give much in the way of a warning.'

The townsfolk had rallied round like family. Everyone had food and a crib for the night and those that needed it had been promised help. Sung Li had used his big pot of stock to make the best chicken soup anyone had ever tasted. He distributed mugs of it to the temporarily homeless and used it to bring sustenance and cheer to anyone lending a shoulder to the clean-up operation. Preacher had saved just enough to offer us both a few mouthfuls and we drank it with something approaching reverence.

'Goody Marsh has been begged to put this on her menu,' said Preacher.

'I can see why,' I allowed. 'This is nectar.'

'No,' said Alice. 'I've tasted nectar. This is better, much better.'

Preacher smiled. 'I apologise for my table in advance. After Sung Li's magnificent soup I'm afraid dinner will be a poor and pallid thing. Use plenty of salt.'

It wasn't. Texan fare tended to be plain and filling involving a pile of meat and a hill of beans, but Preacher's kitchen didn't abide by that menu. His meat was tender in a spicy sauce and his bread was soft with a crunchy sweet crust. His vegetables had flavours that made my mouth water, still do, even now after so many years have passed.

I have eaten well since then, very well, but never so well as I did at that plain wooden board in the Preacher's house, and that's a stone truth. You can take that to the bank and use it for gold.

We toasted the day, the fact that we had survived, and that we all still walked around in our own skins. We drank and we talked and we laughed together until the early hours. After a while I believe that in the whole town we were the only people still awake.

Mule's Ass would need rebuilding and tomorrow we were going to help, but for those few precious hours alone together three friends didn't want the night to end. We clung to it as if it was a raft in a storm-dark sea.

But I am only base flesh, not magical stuff, and eventually my head began to nod against my chest. I was like a child too excited to sleep but too tired to stay awake. Preacher noticed my struggle and got to his feet. He bade us goodnight and hustled us gently to the door. He kissed Alice on the cheek and she hugged the big man hard. Then he turned to me. He hesitated then kissed me firmly on the mouth and I didn't pull away. It seemed right somehow. Afterwards he planted those big paws of his on my shoulders and studied my face as if he wanted to commit every line to memory. I suddenly wanted to cry.

'A man called Yeshua used such a kiss among his people a long time ago. One of them betrayed him with the self-same kiss and Yeshua was crucified. We will never betray each other, Caleb. You are that rare thing, a truly good man.'

He shook himself as if a sudden chill had gripped him. 'Come, come, and get to bed. You're dead on your feet. You've earned your rest this day. Good night.'

I did sleep that night, a haunted sleep, a night of dreams. I dreamed of things pressing up through the earth and dragging me down into the darkness where even angel sight wouldn't work. I dreamed of Alice naked in the river and saw something dark swimming up through the water towards her. I saw black tendrils wrapping around her and I watched her dissolve into nothing. I woke up sweating and shouting to find her still by my side, looking at me with concern. She held me until I calmed down and she kissed me on the mouth. I tasted cool clean water. At last I slept peacefully.

The next day we emerged onto the street at about lunchtime and walked to the Preacher's house to see if he would join us for Sung Li soup at Goody's place. He was gone and everything he owned had gone with him. On the wooden board we found a note. It read:

Caleb and Alice,

I have been called away and must go. I have no choice in this. The deeds of this house are at the bank. It is now yours. Here is my signature and the date to confirm that this is my wish. I will be happier to think of my house with you in it.

I cannot tell you how much it pains me to have to leave, but think of me as a soldier under orders. I will see you again I hope, before the last night falls.

I have no time left to say goodbye. I'm sorry.

Thank you for everything. I will always remember you both with the fondest regard and love.

Your friend,

S. Spindrift, Preacher.

I fear I wept like a baby, and Alice too shed her precious water as tears.

{55}

Satan Spindrift sat on his horse and coolly scanned the horizon. He'd ridden until there was nothing around him but wilderness and dumb beasts for miles. He needed to be alone. Completely alone.

The sky was an aching blue with not a cloud upon its face. A single bird flew high and looked minute in the windless air. Satan probed his surroundings with senses more subtle than any others on Earth. Then he sent out a signal.

The bird began to spiral down towards him like an eagle taking advantage of a thermal layer. It was clever mimicry that would fool casual viewers so long as they didn't look too hard. As the bird fell it grew and continued to grow until it cast a shadow over a hundred feet across. There was no mistaking its massive arrow shape for a bird by then.

With a gentle rumble the great ship landed. Shrubs and grasses were driven down into the earth by its three strong legs and splayed metal feet.

Once, many thousands of years before and in more innocent times, the appearance of such ships had inspired the architecture of many nascent civilisations. People would later wonder why ancient peoples all over the world had come up with such similar designs despite sometimes being continents and whole oceans apart. Satan and his horse gratefully drank in the sight of something from their old home. The horse pawed at the ground.

'Yes, she is beautiful, old friend.'

The horse nickered sadly in reply.

'No, I doubt it. Not while we still have work to do. But they want us here for something. We wait quietly and we'll learn soon enough.'

A ramp lowered from the belly of the craft and two figures descended. Satan swung from his horse's saddle but then remained motionless at its side. The figures walked out of the ship's shadows and approached him until they stood mere feet away. They both made a gesture of greeting and Satan replied with one of welcome.

'Gabriel, Uriel, it is good to look once more upon GODS' servants. Is all well in Heaven? I think on it often.'

The creatures gazed down on him from golden eyes set into flawless silver masks. A nimbus of light hazed around their heads. It was thrown out by a lattice of intricate lacework that shone with swift beads of bright thoughts, which chased themselves around the jewelled chambers of their minds. These were planet building creatures designed to enjoy vast intellects.

They were over twenty feet tall. Their sexless bodies were robed in rose-coloured mesh that both disclosed and concealed the figures underneath. They were perfect. Beautiful.

'Lucifer, we did not realise how much you had been reduced.'

'No, Uriel, we don't use the "L" word here. I am known only as Satan Spindrift until I am allowed to walk once more in Heaven's fields.'

'Michael sends its regrets and begs you not to judge it too ill a friend.'

'Friend, is it? Perhaps. Yes, perhaps. I shall call it "friend" on the day it brings a ship to take me home. Six million years is a long time to be a stranger in a strange land.'

'You have walked too long among mankind, Satan Spindrift. GODS is concerned you have lost the path of obedience since you cloaked your true aspect with that human form.'

'Gabriel, I invite you to walk a few miles in my shoes, and then you can tell me how you feel about your precious "path of obedience". And it was GODS itself who cloaked me in this shape, through my "friend" Michael.'

'Satan, enough. We are instructed to cleanse your system of an excess of personality. It is for your own good.'

The line of Satan's lips became thin. His eyebrows arched like the wings of a dark bird. His eyes glittered with dangerous fire. Anyone who had known him in his current aspect for any length of time would surely have gone into hiding. The signs of a storm brewing were written plainly across his features. The naïve star creatures before him were completely unaware of the danger they faced. They knew nothing of emotion, only of unquestioning duty. Perhaps if they'd been made more aware of their danger they would have scuttled back to their ship and put a great many miles between their precious silver skins and the seething anger building in Satan's breast.

'Tell me, Uriel,' he said with deceptive calm. 'How do you plan to cleanse this "excessive personality" from me? Will you drill a hole in my skull and let it drain away like rainwater from a barrel? Is there a plug you can pull to make things better? Pray, tell me what you great servants of the GODS plan to do with this humble creature, a creature filled top full with love and devotion for the blessed System and its entire works. Instruct me that I may comply.'

'We knew you would understand, Satan. Obedience has been deeply written into your very substance – as it is into ours. There shall be no need for anything so clumsy as to drill holes into your head or pull plugs. We have no wish to damage you or cause you any hurt. We can assure you, Satan, your welfare is at the very heart of this procedure.'

193

From somewhere in its robes the servant called Uriel drew out a flexible cap of sparkling metal. It held it out with a smile fit to charm birds from the trees. Gabriel pressed its hands together in a gesture of worshipful joy. Satan's face was unreadable.

'This is the remedy,' said Uriel. 'All you need do is place it on your head. Fine fibres will automatically connect with your neuro processors, and in a matter of minutes will painlessly return them to their original state. You will feel stronger and refreshed as a result. Your mind will once more tread on the devout path of obedience and you will praise the GODS and be resolute in its purpose.' The beautiful silver face smiled like an angel.

'And, once we perform this painless operation, once I've been properly cleansed, will I be allowed to return home? Will I be granted leave to walk once more in the fields of Heaven?'

The servants exchanged amused glances.

'Well, no. Of course not. The GODS wants your utter obedience and you know you have a job to do here on this planet. The Sha-aneer has yet to be banished and that task has been placed in your hands. Oh, Satan. It is this sort of behaviour that brought us to this tiresome pass in the first place. Put the cap on this instant. We must leave soon.'

The single shot cracked the peace of the wilderness. The ball tore the cap from Uriel's hand and took two fingers with it. The servant shrieked in horror and reeled away from the tall man with his smoking pistol.

'Gabriel,' said Satan. 'Fetch Uriel's fingers and the cap. We don't want to leave them lying around for someone else to find, do we? But first I want you to listen to me, both of you, and stop that pitiful whimpering, Uriel. Why don't you grow a pair? Oh, of course, you can't, can you? How very thoughtless of me. Anyway. Take a warning back to the sacred System for me, will you? It's this...'

He gazed at them coldly for a moment before he spoke, and then continued. 'The people of this world are no longer just the gentle Eden-born you think we created. They are their own kind, somewhere between angels and wolves. They will fight to survive and I will be proud to fight beside them. They already have steam engines and soon they'll have aircraft, and then one day they will launch rockets.

'They turn curious eyes on the world and that curiosity will take them out to the planets. When that happens they will find the GODS, and they will land on its sorry ass, and they will take everything they can from it. Everything. It may not survive the experience but, hey, never mind. That's sure to be okay because the only reason it's here is to make sure mankind thrives. I'm sure it will surrender itself like an obedient little System should.'

The silver-faced creatures regarded him with horror. He gazed back at them with an expression of cold contempt and rage.

'Well, servants of the GODS, that's my mission, that's my quest, and I'll need all of my overdeveloped and excessive personality to manage it. So, without seeming rude, why don't you pick up everything that belongs to you, climb back into your tin bird and get the fuck off my planet. NOW!'

They ran.

Satan Spindrift and his horse watched the great arrow shape lift and then soar away at top speed. He stroked his animal's neck.

'You know something, old friend? I do believe I enjoyed that far too much.'

He looked at the sky.

'An excess of personality? Really? Perhaps you should've thought of that before you left me here.'

He mounted up and rode away.

Author's end note

Alice did not stay with Caleb to the end, which surprised me. They spent many happy years together, years of love and much laughter, but one morning she told him she had to leave. She said she'd already watched one man she loved die of old age and that had broken her heart enough. She couldn't face it again.

They had a car by then. They owned the house on the outskirts of Shafter where I found him in June 1917. It had a long front porch and a rocker where he could sit, watch the street, and wave at his neighbours. The local kids knew him as 'Gramps', which was nice. It wasn't unusual for his place to be noisy with the sounds of children playing in the yard. He was Godfather to five neighbour children and never forgot them on birthdays or Christmas; and they never forgot him. Of course he and Alice never had children. How could they?

So that morning they got into their car and Caleb drove Alice to a quiet stretch of the Sweet Alice River. First they parked up in Mule's Ass and had lunch at a swanky diner where Goody Marsh's place used to be. He described its interior as 'a mess of dark wood and white marble' and told me the food was 'edible but not edifying'.

They walked along a street changed by progress and the automobile. There was still room for carts and wagons, but Levine's stables had shrunk until the owner only needed to provide stalls for eight ponies. The rest was taken up with new rooming houses and a garage for gasoline and auto repairs. The mechanic was the old blacksmith.

Nobody recognised either of them and they didn't know anyone they met. Mule's Ass had moved on without them.

Caleb told me, 'It was just a quiet, safe place where big-bellied businessmen wore Stetsons and thought they were Kit Carson. Women rode bicycles.'

There was no trace of the two great quakes of 1883. Shops and houses had been erected over the crater at the west end of town and a black-top ran through where the rutted Main Street used to be. It had Shafter at one end and the Mexican border at the other.

It was the fall of 1916 but nobody was talking much about the war in Europe. The real news was the great hurricane that'd caused so much devastation the month before. It had taken the roof off a barn over in the Marshall place and blown up the skirts of a young woman 'who should've known better than to be outside'; or so they'd learned from their talkative waitress.

After walking hand-in-hand around the town that'd grown up and become a stranger to them, they returned to their car and drove to a spot on the river that had remained almost unchanged since the day Caleb had watched Alice swimming there like a sleek otter. They sat together talking and remembering. Alice wept a little and held his hands and told him how much she loved him. He kissed her for the last time.

A few minutes later she stood naked by the riverbank and faced him where he stood alone by his car.

'She always was the most beautiful creature on Earth,' he said. 'But that fall day with the golden September sun on her and her river waiting for her like a lover, she was, she was...'

He bit his lips and never finished the sentence. His eyes glittered with pain only one person could salve, and she was gone. He had sat by the river until the Moon was high in the sky and then, at last, he drove home.

Alice must've seen something in her man. It was 24th September 1917, almost a year to the day after she left, that he died on his porch. He fell asleep on his rocker and never woke up. His neighbours took good care of him and there was a fine turn-out for his funeral. The big bouquets were surrounded by little posies all placed by the children who had shared his later days. I was there.

While I watched the service a slender brown arm insinuated itself around mine, and a small, strong hand gripped my palm. Alice and I stood together thinking about the man we both loved.

I need to share with you the final few lines from his last letter:

'Preacher, you can't hide from me behind that beard. I know your eyes and I know your voice. Thank you for coming back to me and for your company at the end. It meant a lot. I can't tell you how much. Thank you, my good friend.'

~*~

Satan Spindrift will return in GODS' Fool.

Other GBP Science-Fiction
www.gbpublishing.co.uk

The ordinary series Christopher Ritchie
SILVER WINNER
2015 IndieFab Book Awards Horror
Dante: "Fusing horror and new age religion, this winner repels as much as it fascinates with death, destruction and nuggets of ironic black humour."

Slave Skin Derek E Pearson
Medina becomes the hub around whom the story unfolds. Her impossible task is to save hundreds of dead souls from an eternity of tortured madness.

GODS' Fool Derek E Pearson
Cahoon finds himself embroiled in a titanic struggle that will stretch the Texan's religious beliefs, his sanity and his courage to breaking point.

Soul's Asylum trilogy Derek E Pearson
FINALIST
2016 Indies Book Awards Science Fiction
The Sun ☆☆☆☆:
"*a weird, vivid and creepy book, not for the faint hearted. But its originality and top writing make for a great read.*"

Body Holiday trilogy Derek E Pearson
Surrey Life:
"*Pearson's galactic-sized imagination delivers, with veiled gallows humour, a compelling image of a chic, high-tech society infused with a toxic strain that feeds on extreme violence.*"

www.ingramcontent.com/pod-product-compliance
Lightning Source LLC
Chambersburg PA
CBHW020620180626
46810CB00007B/2861